VANISH
LIKE A
DREAM

STEVE SCHROEDER

It is my hope that while reading, someone thought
of you and passed on this copy of *Vanish Like a Dream*
hoping you would enjoy it.

I hope when reading, if it brings someone to mind,
you share it as well.

To the five women who read the first version of Vanish.
I thank and love each of you for giving me the courage to tell
a story, the incentive to finish, the strength to start again.
I can call myself an author because of you.

To Regina:
You read the first drafts of Vanish and encouraged me to dive
deeper. You gave me the courage to believe in myself.

To Mary:
Your enthusiasm kept the fire burning in me
to keep rewriting until I got it right.

To Laural:
My shelter from the storm.
Your wisdom and grace are astounding.

To Melissa:
You have made many hard days beautiful.

Lastly, and most importantly,

To Carol:
For your love, support, and hours of reading so that
this book is what it is. Because of you I could start
over and build a life worth living.

"Thank you" is too small an expression for my gratitude to
all of you. Love is too small a word for how I feel about you,
but they are the only words I have.
I love and thank you all.

Finally, thank you to all of the professionals that I have had
the pleasure of working with along the way.

I notice her resting on the tension
between water and sky.

She moves only to stay unmoved by the water endlessly
hurrying beneath her feet.

She is master of both worlds
but lives in neither.

Living on the water
her wings folded like origami.

How can I learn to be as comfortable in my space
the atoms' width where time and the universe intersect?

The water skipper lives effortlessly
in the changing rhythms of her duality.

She lives on the water and never gets wet.

I cannot find rest in either one of mine.

I am lost.
Being tossed by time.
Always looking for the next signpost to point the way.

She sits on the pond
as if waiting for me.

She shows every person who visits
how to sit comfortably on the tension of time.

In a single moment, she exposes my nature,
By juxtaposing how she embraces hers.

Sharing stillness,
her nature,
she points me toward who I am
and how to be still in the perfection of that.

CHAPTER ONE

I AM LOST IN THE THOUGHT that it is a random week-day, and all of the people around me ought to be at work. I was scheduled to start my shift hours ago. I have not missed a day of work in sixteen years. I love my job, but instead, I am sitting in my local park on a beautiful fall day with my guitar, a world-class glass of wine and a plate of incredible food.

My dog is lying at my feet, eyeing me. She is trying to decide between asking for a bite or running with a pack of dogs. A pack that has been growing in numbers for the last few days. She looks at me with eyes more wild than tame. I see the same energy in the man across from me, from my neighbors, and I can feel wildness increasingly coming from my own.

The sounds and smells are those of any block party, but my

neighbors are unraveling. I am unraveling. I can feel each of us trying hard to keep our well-worn masks in place. Masks formed to serve another time and another way of life.

I am watching a couple that a week ago were poised professionals, now crying inconsolably, holding their daughter. Another man is laughing hysterically. A third has been essentially comatose for days. These are the exceptions; most of the group is dancing and singing along to songs I am playing.

I feel a nudge on my foot from a gentleman I have recently met. I missed my cue to start singing for the second time. I smile at him, and he winks back. We are all having trouble concentrating. We are sounding good, better than I could have expected. We are a larger group than I could have imagined. To my surprise, a number of my neighbors play instruments. We have joined each other in the park for a hootenanny for the ages.

As my attention turns to the song, I think the recurring thought that I would give anything to hold either of my children again. I know that is never going to happen. He taps me again, and I focus. I nod at him and pick up the song they are playing and begin to sing.

I have interacted more with my neighbors in the last few days than in the ten years that went before. I look at each face, into each set of eyes. I know only a few of their names. Names seem unimportant, as we all face the same fate. Each of our paths destined to intersect at an exact moment, a moment that I know is not too far away.

If this were a normal block party, this would be a

burger-and-beer affair with surface chatter and me sneaking home as quickly as I can, but not today. Today everyone has brought their very best food, the most exceptional wine, and their most curious selves. The people surrounding me have lived on my block for years.

Now there is a chance that I may have to rely upon them to live. My survival may depend on this group of people.

We have been through a recent event that has radically changed our lives. A week ago, everything was normal. Today it is not. We are all waiting to see what will happen next. I have stopped worrying about tomorrow. I hear my neighbors talk, and we waver between being sure and unsure of our fate.

I listen more closely, and Switzerland is no longer the only subject everyone is talking about. The topic has changed to "What do we do if tomorrow comes? Will we be ready for it?" We have all been brought face to face with the prospect of living a new lifestyle, one we have no choice but to embrace.

Each of the people around me is finding their way of making sense of our impossible circumstances. Some are blaming, others are making excuses, a few have adopted a stoic resolve, and a dwindling group is holding out hope that the cavalry will arrive.

My way of coping with this new reality is to learn to emulate the lives of the birds. I am becoming wild, as remaining domesticated will not serve me. My world is moving from safe to feral.

Like the birds, I am teaching myself to be adaptive to whatever comes next. To listen for subtle changes. I am losing my need for the expectations of a tomorrow. I am becoming aware of my environment like my life depends on it, as it very well could.

A few days ago, most of the systems my society relies upon failed. At first, I panicked, but now I am rejoicing in my freedom. I have one more day, one more day than I expected. I am reveling in it because—for the first time in my life—I am free. Nothing is binding me. I have no boss, no to-do list, no responsibilities, and mostly because I have no thoughts about sacrificing my happiness today for a better tomorrow.

Today, this day, is all I have.

I take a long drink of my wine. I look at the bottle and remember that I saved it for a day that was special enough. Now is the definition of the right occasion. It is Tuesday, and all I have to do is enjoy wine, eat food prepared by my neighbors, and play the music I love.

Tuesday…the sound of it is odd in my ears. Tuesday? It has no relevance in my life anymore. I know my end is coming. I have focused my attention, in the time I've had, to contend with my grief. I have done what I can to set aside my anxiety.

My emotions come at me in waves, and I surf each as best I can. Surfing my feelings has become easier and more heart-wrenching. Each wave is a surrender. This state of mind happened once I became sure that I have nowhere to run, I can't hide, and there is nothing I can fight.

Days ago, the park was envisioned as a place to gather and share information. It has become the last refuge where I can hold on to the fading remnants of my old life. A place I can almost live my life as I have always known it to be. I am enjoying the last small comforts of the abundance I had taken for granted, a way of living in the world that is quickly vanishing.

I am thankful I get to do one of the things I love most in life. I am playing music for an appreciative crowd. In college, I played at local bars during happy hour. I was thrilled that the bar would give me drinks, food, and a few dollars a couple of nights a week to do something I have done for free for years . I learned a catalog of crowd favorites that are still my go-to list. They are a collection that satisfies most song requests. I am playing "Here Comes the Sun." I like songs people know by heart.

I am leading a drop-in band of my neighbors; the whole crowd is singing along. I survey the faces, some I have never seen, and some I have known forever. The most familiar people are moving closer to join me as I sing some of the most recognizable words ever put to music. I look around and wonder if it will be all right. I smile and sing with my new clan.

The people I love are taking their final step toward me, and I reach to touch them when I vanish. Vanish, gone like when someone in my dream goes *poof* the instant I awake. Today, I am the one that stops existing, the one on the other side of the dream. I'm disappearing into a new reality that started for me in my kitchen.

While having breakfast, what seems a lifetime ago, my existence was changed with a single question from my husband.

DAY ONE:

The plant doesn't bloom for the wolf to admire.

The wolf doesn't believe the deer was put on Earth to feed him.

The deer doesn't believe that the grass
is happiest when being grazed.

The grass doesn't believe it alone should possess the prairie.

The prairie doesn't believe
the next season will be more ecstatic.

A season doesn't believe it will hold forever to center stage.

Everything is fleeting.

Performance art.

Astoundingly beautiful,
not to be possessed,
but to be celebrated.

CHAPTER TWO

HOW DID I GET HERE? Here in a moment I could not have imagined the course of my life ever bringing me to.

My life with my husband has been an adventure, but I never conceived that his work would bring me to this place. I have been married for decades to a man who thinks in the level of detail only a PhD theoretical physicist can. I could easily be okay with this, but he processes his thoughts out loud. I tease him that I know more about his day than I do my own.

For more evenings than not, he will use me as a *sounding board*. No detail is too small for him to share. He regularly tells me these talks keep him sane. I tell him they drive me crazy. It's been like this so long we don't know how to live with each other any other way. Ours is a matured relationship. We make each other happy and drive each other crazy in equal measure.

I listen to him, understanding his technical jargon just enough to nod at the right moments. I think being a couple means doing things that I would do for one person on Earth. Helping him understand his day—every day—is one of the things I would do only for him.

My husband approaches his work as a ritual, either in his office at home or the university; he does the same things in the same ways every day. His job consists mostly of parsing large amounts of data and looking for the secrets hiding in plain sight. He says his career is to let go of what he thinks he knows until he can see what the data is actually saying.

Today he's listening to Van Morrison's "Brown- Eyed Girl." He plays this song over and over when he prepares to travel. It's both charming and a little annoying. He calls it "your song." I sang it the afternoon we met. From that day on, he requested it every time he came out to see me play.

It happened so often that it became a running joke with the bar's staff where I played. They nicknamed him *La Te Da*. For a couple of years, I'm sure I played it more often than Van did.

I look at him and see him as that young man. Then both of us just turned twenty-two. I was living a great life. I was going to school, working, and playing guitar for food money.

I first noticed him sitting at a table by the stage. I was playing a Friday Afternoon Club at a tavern that booked me for a regu- lar gig. I had been performing for almost a year and had built a consistent following around town. I had seen him occasionally, but he was no more notable to me than any of the other college boys that drank beer and talked too loudly.

He, like everyone else in the place, was nursing a dollar pitcher of Pabst Blue Ribbon at a table full of friends. The difference was that, on that day, he wasn't talking to anyone. He was sitting still and intently watching me play.

In between sets, I chatted with the doorman, asking him to keep an eye on him. I had learned long ago not to take chances with patrons I didn't know, especially those that seemed overly interested in me. I was a good performer by the standards of a college bar singer, but I was uncomfortable and unaccustomed to anyone giving me their undivided attention.

I finished my final set, and I knew he was going to come over and ask me out. I was almost done packing my guitar when I realized I couldn't see him anywhere. This meant one of two things. The best for me was that I was home free. The other was that he was hovering behind me.

I stopped looking around. I had to decide between hurrying to get packed or acting like I was a diva. I caught a glimpse of shoes behind me and slowed down my packing. I was hoping he would tire or feel awkward and return to his friends. To my chagrin, he was persistent. I tried to make eye contact with the doorman, but couldn't spot him and couldn't stall any longer.

Before standing, I rifled through my mind for the perfect excuse. I was ready. I had been in this situation often, and as predictable as the sun rising, he followed the typical script. He stood with a goofy "I'm a fan" look and said what they all say: "You're great."

I said nothing and tried to walk around him when he stepped back, allowing me space. He asked me if I wanted to go next door for coffee. As a single woman singing college dives, I got hit on a lot, and had worked out several let-them-down-easy stories; little white lies that allowed it not to be too awkward for the person asking me out, and gentle enough to make it okay for me if I saw them again. I had a set of standard stories I told. They were simple and easy to remember if they came up in any future conversation.

I was about to start letting him down when I heard myself say, "Sure." I think I was more startled than he was. I never said yes. I had no space in my life for a date, much less a relationship. As an introvert, I looked for a way to backpedal out of it. Seeing no easy way backward, I went forward.

"One cup of coffee, I have to go home and study for an anatomy test." He smiled and did a little hop before he excused himself. I pondered running to my car, but for some reason, I stood and waited. I never wait; I have things to do.

He told me later he had to ask his friends for money for coffee. I teasingly told him he was lucky he did because if I had had to pay for that coffee, it would have been our last interaction.

The doorman stopped me on the way out the front door and asked, "Do you want me to get rid of him?" I said, "It's okay, we're going next door for coffee. Can you pop over in thirty minutes in case I need rescuing?" The doorman nodded. I could feel him watching me as we went next door.

The doorman's still a close friend to this day. I haven't talked to him in a while; I need to call him so we can reminisce about the grand escapades we had in those days, and the next adventures we are both planning. He was in my nursing class, and for those four years, we were inseparable. Sometimes I wonder if I should have married that man.

I didn't expect much from the quiet man in the Birkenstocks, but as we talked, he made me laugh. I waved the doorman off when I saw him enter the shop precisely thirty minutes later. He and I locked eyes, and I can still see the look on his face. He a soulmate, but fate would never allow for more.

I am snapped back into the present when my husband texts me, and as I answer, I smile thinking about the thought I might need protection from the man currently filling a briefcase like it is a game of Tetris.

I recall how one cup of coffee turned into dinner, and then another cup of coffee. My future husband and I chatted late into the night. He was—and still is—funny. I didn't realize until later he was not trying to be; he sees the world from a perspective I had never heard, and it still intrigues me. At twenty-two, he was intelligent with a quick wit and had something I liked that I couldn't exactly put my finger on.

Chapter Three

WE HAD THAT COFFEE OVER THIRTY years ago, and I still describe him as quirky to my friends. I wonder how it is we ever came to live in the same house. We are not very much alike. Charitably speaking, we can drive each other nuts. The bottom line is that I love him, and he loves me. After all these years, a few things haven't changed; his love for me, physics, beer, and acoustic guitar. I do occasionally wonder where I rank on this list. I like to think I am still first.

I know and his co-workers have told me he always has music playing in his office. When I asked him why, he told me it soothes him while he does the more mundane data work his research demands. He once tried to pass this work to assistants but felt he lost his communication with the story the experiment told.

He said the numbers stopped speaking to him if he didn't wrestle with them.

This work can be a significant portion of his days. His roles have expanded to include spokesman, salesman, authority, fundraiser, and manager, but his passion has always been crunching through the details. He loved the numbers from the very beginning. He likens it to a miner panning for gold.

Yesterday at dinner, he told me that at work that day, he was playing Michael Hedges' "Aerial Boundaries" and working through the latest download of a friend's experiment when he noticed a small blip of energy lasting nanoseconds longer than expected. With his phone, he took a picture of his computer screen and texted it to himself. He told me how he made a note asking, "Why and what is causing this?"

He said he thought about calling his friend, who's running the experiment when another colleague appeared at his door. He wrote himself a note to call, grabbed his coat, and they left for lunch.

For years, he has used sticky notes to support his memory. At any one time, he will have fifteen Post-it notes on his monitor. This note said, "Review the blip, phone CERN." He had a note that hasn't moved in years, and all it says is "milk." He texted me if we needed to get some more every night.

He tells how he patiently waited through their walk to the restaurant, to be seated, and after they ordered before mentioning that he saw something odd in the CERN data. He says how he slid his phone across the table to show her the same screen he is trying to display for me now. "Work and lunch," I said. He nodded.

Early on in their careers, they had ruined more than a few lunches discussing different interpretations of data, mathematic impasses, and physics' chairs, all making their lives difficult. Years ago, she sent him an email with the subject "not again at lunch." It contained a video lecture about how native Polynesians would remove all the food from the table when the discussion around their meal became heated. She insisted they adopt this practice to honor the food and the other people around them as they ate. His friend touted other additional benefits, including proper digestion and maintaining their friendship.

He tells me his friend glanced at his phone, then up at him. "We have talked about this before," she said. "I have no context for this data. Besides, I have adult eyes. I can't read that tiny print. Put that away." They have shared lunchtime almost daily for fifteen years, and she has forced lunch to become a sacred *no-work* exploration of other life topics. He tells how he sighed still wanting her opinion. He valued it as they have worked together for years building mathematical models of the first millionth-of-a-second after the big bang.

She slid his phone back across the table and continued, "After lunch, we can play scientist. For now, I want to talk about where we are going to dine while we are in Geneva. You know I am going for the food and nightlife."

They laughed, both knowing *nightlife* is bed at a reasonable hour, after dinner at one of the three walkable restaurants and a nightcap of choice in the front room of the house made available to visiting scientists. Workdays always started at 5:30 a.m.

They have stayed in the house before; this time, it would be home for the next few months. He told me how she rolled her eyes when thinking about having roommates and wanted to know if she needed to pack a Sharpie so she could label her food. She said half-jokingly, "I've had male roommates before. So, I can say from experience that all men are pigs."

I nodded in agreement and pointed to a sink full of coffee cups that he finally remembered to bring home from work. We laughed.

Chapter Four

I THINK ABOUT MY LUNCH AT WORK and how they
are nothing like my husband's. Mine rarely has friendly conversation and mindful digestion. I spend my half-hour in the hospital cafeteria wolfing down whatever semi-palatable offering the
food staff has prepared for that day. I usually only get twenty
minutes to eat.

This is the best-case scenario, and me sitting for lunch
happens rarely. I relish any respite during the day and always
try to steal a few minutes for myself. Today, I finished my soup
and tea and close my eyes for a short meditation before I begin
to make my way back to the elevators. As I put my tray on the
conveyer belt, I hear James Brown's "I Feel Good" coming out
of the passageway between the cafeteria and the recesses of the

kitchen. I start to half-hum/half-sing along with it as I begin shuffling across the tile floor in full smile.

As I walk to the elevator, I daydream about being a backup singer. "Ladies and Gentleman, Mister James Brown..." The lights come up, and I am on stage with two other women. We are dressed identically in burgundy satin evening gowns and elbow-length gloves. I picture us swaying in unison and singing. Our harmony is golden. My smile and humming fade as the doors open, and I step onto the elevator.

My mind shifts as my responsibilities as a nurse fade my singing fantasy to black. It is replaced by thinking about the infants that need my help. I spend my workdays going from one room to another, each filled with a tiny little patient, sometimes two, and any number of worried adults.

Of them all, one has me especially worried. I visit him often during the day. I have never been able to understand why one newborn tugs at my heart a little harder than all the others. This little one is special to me; I am not sure why him.

Who am I kidding—I have always been a sucker for anything in need. I was the kid that brought the stray kitten or puppy home. The one who fought the bullies in school. The one who organized the food drives at work. I loved and still love giving care to anything in need. This little one needs all the love he can get. His entrance into the world was brutal. I am on the planet to help spirits like him as much as I can.

In retrospect, my career choice seems to be perfectly logical. My parents were surprised when I pursued nursing at university. I remember them saying my picking a stable and mainstream occupation was a shock.

My mom told me she assumed I would be a street busker for a while, traveling with my guitar; then, who knew what I would do. I couldn't argue with her since throughout my entire youth, with a few exceptions, I had not wondered what I was going to do with my life; I was going to be a musician.

All that changed when I was a junior in high school, walking through the student union at the university. I was looking for a drop-in guitar jam I had heard about. Playing music, especially folk music, was a passion at the time.

The union was packed with students being students. I recall watching two young men tossing a Nerf football to each other and pretending they were scoring the dramatic game-winning touchdowns by diving onto a communal couch, then re-enacting the celebration they had seen players do in real games. They caused bystanders to duck and dodge them. They were oblivious to the havoc they were creating.

It was because they made me roll left to avoid them that I ended up face-to-face with a college student recruiting for the nursing school. I stopped at the booth and decided this was as good a place as any to ask directions to the music college. I didn't want to be rude, so I asked the woman staffing the booth about nursing. She told a story about the history, the rewards, and the modern realities of the profession. She talked about a tight-knit nursing community and the joy of training to be of service to people in need.

I instantly knew it was for me.

Later, I tried to run from it. Not wanting to let go of the dream of making music, but everywhere I turned, I saw something else that convinced me nursing was for me. I surrendered to it as something to investigate, then study, then pursue as a central aspect of my life's path.

I applied for and was accepted to the music school, but on my first day, I registered for the pre-nursing classes. I called home and told my parents I had heard the call to be a nurse. They had lived through my callings wavering, and expected me to return, as I always had, to music. I never looked back. Occasionally, I wished the call would have remained to be a singer, but over the years, I know I made the right decision.

Most people I work with and have worked with did not pursue or even hear their calling. They followed a career path, one job leading to another. They all suffer, knowing they are not happy but feel too trapped to find their way to an occupation that would more align with their hearts. Why fate has blessed me to have lived my whole life on a path that is a calling is a mystery. I am grateful to the fates. So is my husband, who found a career that aligns with his heart, too.

My son followed his father and sister instead of his nature. He says it is like his shoes are always on the wrong feet. I have for years told him life is way too long not to stop and put them on correctly. He smiles and shakes his head, saying he would love to, but he has kids and a mortgage. "It is too late to change direction now."

As parents, my husband and I have offered to help him, but he needs the security of a steady eight-to-five job. His pride will never allow our help. He is a caregiver. I'm afraid he won't ever live as he longs to live. Feeling trapped is brutal.

The elevator doors open, and I step into the circus that is a neonatal unit of a major hospital. It's a place where the greatest joys and most heart-wrenching lows can occur in an hour, on any day at work. The burnout rate is astronomical. The emotional roller-coaster takes a heavy toll.

I have learned to leave concepts like "fair and unfair" and "good and bad" behind. Occasionally, I get caught in my idea of what should be. These times are stressful, and I have to be vigilant to nurture myself, so that I can thrive in my hectic and heartbreaking profession.

CHAPTER FIVE

MY HUSBAND'S JOB AND MY JOB are so different. As I rush into a fire drill, he returns from a leisurely lunch to pick up where he left off. It's a single blip. I think he is the only person on the planet that would notice it. One piece of anomalous data that is bothering him. It is an energy surge recorded by one of the millions of sensors that are part of one of the most massive human-made devices on the planet, CERN.

CERN is the acronym for the European Organization for Nuclear Research in Geneva, Switzerland. It is one of the largest complexes dedicated to scientific research in the world. It is where the Large Hadron Collider resides.

My husband was sought out for his input on the current series of trials taking place in the collider. His friend and colleague, a

Nobel laureate in physics, had asked him to work on the design and monitoring of six months of experiments concerning the overlay of Newtonian and quantum physics. The razor's edge where the two interact.

My husband had been receiving real-time data since the beginning of this work five months ago. He is baffled as to why this current research is producing an unexplainable energy reading. The current data is from a set of experiments designed and being performed to prove a hypothesis his friend had tossed around for years. It is a set of experiments his friend hoped to have the opportunity to conduct. This work is tangential to the initial proposal and was added as an addendum to the research application.

Fortune had smiled upon him and allowed his work to go smoothly so that this additional series of tests are being carried out. Although this exploration is secondary to his main goals, if the results were positive, these experiments will be ground-breaking in science's understanding of the nature of existence on Earth.

The hypothesis is controversial. I have heard him speak about it, but my eyes quickly glaze over. As a Nobel laureate, he is given a wide berth, and he made very compelling arguments as to the relevance of these tests. The concern of CERN's board quieted, and they approved the proposal.

If successful, these experiments will prove the existence of a set of theoretical particles in the thirteenth dimension that mathematics had been pointing to for years. It will be a pioneering discovery toward explaining how matter is formed. It will confirm that matter is a state of light like ice is a state of water. He hoped to prove that light continually shifts from a wave to matter and back again. It is because of the fluid natures of these particles that he hopes to prove that what appears solid to an observer, is not at all solid. Confirming their existence will change science's understanding of time, material, and consciousness. It will be a significant step forward in understanding the nature of the fabric and origin of the universe.

These are the experiments that are now taking place on a device of mind-boggling complexity. CERN is the only super-collider in the world where this kind of discovery is possible. Each run of this experiment generates millions of data points. My husband, while culling through this data, notices that one reading is out of place. A blip. An energy surge that has made the man I married curious. He adds his observation to his ever-growing question list. He closes his laptop, then places the readouts aside. For now, his work on his friend's data will have to wait. Tomorrow he and his team will be on a plane to Geneva.

The transition from the test currently running to the first experiment my husband proposed is likely to take the better part of a month. This will give him plenty of opportunities to investigate the long list of questions he has compiled to discuss with his friend and their combined teams.

My husband saves these notes on his laptop and returns to preparing for his trip. He continues checking off items completed on his to-do list. I read a series of texts from him where he tells me he is bracing himself because if his research proves his mathematics correct, the findings will revolutionize the generally accepted theories on the beginnings of the universe. The validity of the "big bang" would be brought into question.

He knows all too well the firestorm this hypothesis generated when his mathematics proposed it. He writes to me that he hopes that the experiments validating his theory might end the debate once and for all.

I text back that his current workload seems to be enough for one person's plate. "Forget your friend's work and focus on your own for now," I type. He responds that the data blip won't leave him alone. He has explained to me his idea that it is in the small details that the most important discoveries in the history of science have occurred.

The single unexplained anomaly regularly reveals a secret that challenges the accepted wisdom and requires a new set of ideas to explain what the latest data shows. His whole career is a testament to paying attention to detail. He says he feels this blip is something big. He is frustrated because he is unable to put it into words quite yet, but he is hopeful it will be worked out during his stay in Switzerland.

I send a "thumbs-up" emoji and move on with my day.

For a physicist, the Large Hadron Collider is the stuff of dreams: A $10-billion underground complex that is larger than the island of Manhattan. Simply stated, it is designed to use magnetics to accelerate sub-atomic particles to nearly light speed and then to cause a collision that— for a millionth of a second— allows scientists a glimpse at the building blocks of the universe.

Four years ago, the managing directors of CERN had chosen the research proposal submitted by my husband's team. After much discussion, his dates were set. He received five months of access to the collider. He has jumped through hoops ever since, refining his work and the parameters of his research. He wants to assure no time is wasted while his team's theories are tested. CERN signed off on his final guidelines, and the date set for the experiments to begin has finally arrived.

Tomorrow he and his team are going to Switzerland, hoping to expand science's understanding of the universe.

He's hoping the data extracted from thousands of investigational trials lasting a millionth of a second will prove twenty-five years of quantum mathematics. Positive results would likely mean a Nobel Prize, and along with that honor are several large monetary prizes and hefty research grants for his team. This honor would free him from seeking endowments and the funding restrictions that accompany getting financial support from large corporations and governments.

He would then be free to pursue further study doing more or less what he chose for the rest of his working life.

The thought of him fulfilling his life's dream makes me smile. He says he doesn't like to think about what could be, but I have lived with him for decades, and I know at his core he is an idealist. Recent pillow talk has him telling me he feels sure this is his chance. If all goes well, this will be the fulfillment of his dream, and his name would then join the list of history's great theoretical physicists. He hesitates, then says to me, "I have spent years standing on the shoulders of giants, and now I want to be the next set of shoulders on which future physicists will stand." I hug him tight and am as proud as I can be.

His life's work questions some of the core assumptions of quantum physics. In a month, he will be running experiments designed to prove his work to be valid or not. The waiting is over, and he is finished preparing. What lays ahead of him has had him pacing the floors in the middle of the night for years. He tells me he is as ready as he can be.

I tell him I love him.

I return to finishing my charting and am running through what I have to finish before I can go home. He messages me that he has closed his laptop and says that in a few days, his ideas will take center stage in the world of quantum physics. I feel overwhelmed for him. He is ready. I know he is ready. In his computer is the analysis of data generated by the collider for over ten years.

His work is the product of thousands of hours of diligently monitoring experiment after experiment; none as closely as the research that is currently running. These experiments are being conducted by a man that my husband's path first intersected with decades ago. Like-minded, he is one of my spouse's closest friends.

They have been drinking beer, playing chess, and discussing physics since they were freshmen in college. He will be joining his comrade and confidante in Geneva. My husband will support his friend in the final trials of his research, and likewise, his friend will aid in the transition to my husband's work. They had started school together, and now the last and most notable experiments of both men's careers happen to overlap.

I begin to cry, realizing how far he has come. His office wall is filled with awards he has earned; a Wolf Prize in Physics, a Breakthrough Prize, a Crafoord Prize, and an Albert Einstein Medal, all hung in neatly arranged frames.

As a joke, I conspired with one of his students to hang the first prize he was awarded on his wall, knowing he saw the displaying of awards as self-importance gone to seed. "I'm not a peacock," he used to say to me.

I waited for his reaction. It took him three weeks to mention the framed certificate of recognition for his work, and when he did, he bristled. He told me he was going to remove it, but—as expected—he soon became lost in his work and never took it down. The addition of each subsequent award was a running joke his staff and I enjoyed. With every move to a new research facility or university, his team would take them down and rehang them in his new office.

I remember a night I was picking him up for dinner when a janitor friend took the opportunity of my being there to tease him. Emptying the trash, he winked at me and said, "That is a lot of awards, Doc. I am a member of a profession that, unlike acting, the arts, and science, is not obsessed with the awarding of very public prizes for going to work and doing my job." We all laughed. My husband loved to tease and be teased by the people around him. The janitor was one of the finest men I've ever met. Three of his children had taken advanced physics from my husband. The last is preparing to go to CERN tomorrow.

I am proud of my man. He has come a long way from the days when he was an adjunct professor who taught basic Newtonian physics to overwhelmed students. He is now a lettered, gray-haired man working to change the understanding of the moment before and moment after the creation of the Universe.

A small smile finds his lips as the janitor asks him about the single misplaced item on his cluttered walls.

CHAPTER SIX

MY HUSBAND POINTED AT ME and started to tell the story. Its presence on his wall still makes him shake his head. He calls it outlandish. He says that it hangs there because of me and a wager that I cheated on to win. The subject of this discussion is a professionally framed poster of Michelangelo's "The Creation of Adam," with "46 to 44" printed on the matting. The janitor asks about the numbers and takes a seat beside me to revel in my husband's growing discomfort. I tell him to settle in; it is a long story.

I start telling my side of the story by saying that when I hung it, I made sure it was the most prominent display in his office. It's my not-so-subtle reminder that I interpret his work to be a modern examination of the same subject, the creation of the universe. I nod toward my husband and say how he recoiled at my idea of his work being the connecting point between in his words "tangible science and a medieval myth."

I said to him back then that he sounded like a cross between Richard Dawkins and Christopher Hitchens. He quipped that he thinks of this as a compliment. I tell him it was meant as an observation. I said that the peoples of the world have generated at least 10,000 creation myths, most of which have been lost to history, and that his work was just the latest in the series— number 10,001.

I tell our friend how the debate started the night I first made this point over dinner. That night, he interrupted my rhetoric and cleared his throat before he said, "You cannot even begin to understand how ridiculous your arguments are. You are not a scientist. You are only a nurse."

Our friend of twenty years turns to my husband and says, "Doc, you didn't?"

"I've learned a lot since then," my husband says as he shuffles through some paper on his desk.

I told how my eyes flashed and darkened in color as I stared at him. He instantly regretted saying it and tried to backpedal, but it was too late. I loved and still love him deeply enough to forgive him, but I also made sure he never demeaned me or my profession again. The janitor nods with a knowing smile.

I continue by saying that I made it clear that if we are going to have a continuing relationship, he has to understand that he has his genius, and I have mine. Brilliance exists in many forms and has a million pursuits.

I grasp my friend's hand and point at my husband.

"He and his classmates have been heralded for their gifts their whole lives, but we have seen him and many of his colleagues in action over the years. My friend and I laugh in unison as I say that while it's true that as a group, they were exceptional at theoretical mathematics and quantum physics, this is also a group of people whose members can't keep a checkbook in balance or remember where they had parked their car. I grab my husband's hand and say that he is the epitome of the absent-minded professor— the cartoon cliché with his hair a mess and a desk full of clutter. A man that is unquestionably brilliant, but cannot keep track of his keys, make the simplest house repair, or boil an egg.

I continue with the story and tell that at the time, we were having an ongoing myth vs. science debate. My point was that myths are the central stories of a culture, and that modern scientists are simply the myth-keepers of this society; he and his colleagues I deem to be the Priests of Progress. The janitor asks me if I came up with that. I say no, John Anthony West did. We both laugh.

I tell how my husband would interrupt me to say that science is simply a discipline that proves truth through a rigid method, period. It has no room for myth.

The janitor is sitting with a bemused look on his face. "I hear the same from my kids. What do you say to that?"

I had four questions for him—my husband groans.

"The first was, does science require money? The doctor nodded *yes*."

I next ask, "Do scientists have money?"

The janitor smiled.

"My husband mumbled no."

I then asked, "Do the funders of research often have non-scientific reasons for the scientific work they sponsor?" We both laugh, and my husband grunted, saying, "See what I live with every day?"

"Damn, you are better than Perry Mason," my thoroughly amused cohort interjected.

The janitor howled. "What did you say next?"

I smile and say, "Do scientists do what funders ask, or vice versa?"

I then sat, a Mona Lisa grin on my face, until he formulated his rebuttal. It sounded like a compliment on the meal being particularly tasty that evening. Not another word was said.

"Never argue with your wife, Doc," the janitor snickered.

I tell him how I purchased the poster the next day and pinned it to the bulletin board in our garage. "I soon found it rolled up in the corner of our mudroom where it stayed for over a year."

"Let's get to the numbers on the bottom," he said.

I answer, "While lying in bed one Sunday morning, I found a Science Friday quiz on the National Public Radio website. We decided to make a wager. We each would answer the fifty questions as we lay side by side.

"The bet: if I answered more questions correctly, the poster would hang in a place of my choosing. He asked, "And if I win?" I said, "If you win, you will prove that a man who is a tenured professor of physics at a world-class research university knows more about science than a humble nurse." All three of us laughed as I continued.

"Soon after, I had the poster framed and hung it in his office. He called me a cheater, but he knows I beat him. He asked me how I did it, and I said, *Slumdog Millionaire.*"

My friend laughs, and while standing, says, "I'll miss you, Doc." He gives my husband and I a hug. "Thank you for the story. It's time for me to get back to work."

He looked my husband in the eye and wished him all of the good fortunes he deserves with his time at CERN. He said his daughter is thrilled that she is part of this adventure. "She is brilliant, and I am lucky to have her as a member of this team," my husband says.

I get one more hug, then grabbed my husband's hand as all three of us head for the door. I have known him for a long time, and I am glad he confirms my plans to join him and his wife next week. I will be lonely by then and in need of their company.

I am startled out of my musing by the *ping* of my husband's text. He says he is tired of circling his desk like a carousel horse, and that he is done fidgeting, he is done packing and repacking. He has what he wants to bring to Switzerland.

He assures me he would have been done sooner except for the interruption of people stopping by to wish him good luck, not to mention electronically from all over the world. I know him and the outflow of support touches him.

It is now close to 6:00 p.m., and he tells me he finally has given up. He knows if he needs something, I can bring it to him when I come to Geneva in a couple of weeks.

With that realization, he says he empties his bag onto his desk, put his laptop, and a couple of other items back and zips it closed. He changes his work voice mail and emails to inform callers that he will be away for months. He checks his pockets for his keys, then shuffles through the papers on his desk until he finds them.

He has his routine leaving his office. He stops to make a move with his rook on the chessboard, and then he texts the move and the word *check* to his friend in CERN.

He then turns off the lights and heads for the elevator. He messages me to tell me he is nervous and excited about this next adventure. He says he is getting on the elevator and heading home.

I count to ten, knowing what is coming next. As if on cue, he asks me to grab milk on my way home.

CHAPTER SEVEN

I SET DOWN MY PHONE with a chuckle. He is predictable, and I have become comfortable with that. He will soon ask if I want to watch Netflix tonight and will suggest Chinese food.

My life with him is a running stream of consciousness. It used to be just when we were together; the invention of the iPhone has made it a constant in my life. He tells me that he is almost ready for tomorrow's flight, and assures me he needs, at most, thirty minutes to put together what he is bringing. I wish I had a dime for every time I've heard a statement like this from him. I know him, and I know he will be at it for hours.

My workday has flown by quickly. My charting is nearly finished. I plan to make one more pass through my unit before I head for home. I finish my last note, pack my bag, and stop to look in on my little warrior. His parents are quietly watching him fight to breathe on his own.

He is so tiny, but he has the will of a giant. His was one of the hardest births of my career. We thought we lost him twice, but he fought his way back. He knows he wants to be here and decided to come two months early. I have much to learn from this little one. I stop and listen to the rhythms of the machines keeping him alive.

Hold on tight little one. Please be here tomorrow.

I turn to his parents. His mom and dad sit motionless, watching me. "Try to get some rest. Your boy is getting stronger by the hour. If you need to get personal things done, around dinner—or better yet, later—is ideal. The night shift will be making rounds; you are in good hands."

He stands and hugs me, too exhausted to speak. He nods that he understands. I know he isn't ready to let his family out of his sight, even for a minute. I have planted the seed, as I know he is growing restless. He will soon need to move. The movement will help him to begin to feel like his life is returning to normal, a new normal. I touch his arm, then the incubator as I say goodnight. I breathe deep as I leave the room and head for the elevator.

Riding down, I read my husband's text, suggesting Netflix and Chinese. I text back, *Bleh, no Chinese*, but I know it won't matter. He knows I'll be hungry and too tired to cook. Our history has proven that any hot food sitting in front of me after work is quickly devoured.

I walk to my car and recheck my phone; I notice that my husband never replied to my message about Chinese food. I vacillate about stopping for milk.

I catch my reflection in the glass of the elevator, and I give myself a good talking-to. I'm tired. I am tired and hungry; tired, hungry, and unfortunately still wearing a bra. I love my husband, but I'm most assuredly not stopping for milk.

I waver because I know he loves his latte in the morning. After another short debate with myself, I succumb to my desire to be home, and with a tinge of guilt, realize that—worst-case— he can hit a coffee shop on his way to the airport.

I start my car and wince at the radio. It didn't seem that loud when I parked this morning. I love this song, but I need quiet and turn it off.

I love the sanctuary of my car. As much as I enjoy a loud radio sing-a-long, with the radio off, I can listen to my heart. In the quiet, I can dream of a little boy going home. I breathe and try to lighten my heart by feeling my husband's joy as he proves his model is correct. He calls it his big dream.

Dreams for me are not big or small. They are dreams. I believe dreams are the rails that my life rides into my future. I do my best imagining in the car and the shower.

I have learned to keep my dreams to myself. I, in turn, try to be kind to the people that shared their hopes with me. I am never sure if I will receive kindness in return, so unless I know you well, my dreams stay inside my heart. Too often, I've been informed that my dreams are impractical. I now dream for me alone, or with a handful of people I can trust with the fire in my soul.

I try not to judge anyone following their dreams. Instead, I celebrate their path. I believe we are all working to reveal the highest expression of our lives. I know how to allow others to do this without my judgment about the path they are taking or the means they use. If I can help, I do. Mostly I cheer them on and stay out of the way. Celebrating everyone's path set me free to follow my own.

I turn out of the hospital's parking lot and remember the trials my husband endured to stand where he is today. I am relieved that, for now, my husband's theories are mostly being validated by a community of scientists which had, twenty years earlier, called his ideas unfounded and radical. His life has been a challenging of the orthodoxy of quantum physics, and the established intellectuals in his field made him pay the price.

When the pressure by the dean of the physics department to give up on his hypothesis became intense, he almost resigned from that university and considered becoming a high-school math teacher. The people in power made it clear that his job and life as a scientist might be in jeopardy if he continued to pursue his current line of inquiry.

Life soon offered us two tangible options, we chose the one to move here. The four of us started a new life here. We were told it was a lesser job at a lesser university. It is home. For the year prior, he and I were awake at 3:00 a.m., staring at the ceiling and wondering what was coming next.

It was a slow and painful process for his theories to gain

acceptance by the scientific community. I watched him suffer the doubt of following his path, no matter where it led or with whose ideas his own conflicted.

During one particularly bad week, he lifted his face from his palms and said, "I disagree with Einstein." I stood and held his hand and asked, "What was the theory of the creation of time and space before Einstein's? He had to have wrestled with the same dilemma you have now. You are in good company. Albert followed where his path took him, and so are you."

He smiled weakly and hugged me. I kissed him and watched him as he walked like a man defeated. He walked past our bedroom and into his office, where he closed the door. I remember waiting to hear music that never started.

My heart broke. I did not see him until the next morning.

While sitting alone in bed, I chose to double my effort to be there for him. I remember concluding that we needed to face our demons together; I needed to support him through his doubts. To do this, I needed to overcome my shyness. I needed to become the best advocate I could for him, my family, and myself. We both grew stronger. I know he still has doubts at 2:00 a.m. He has learned not to show them at 2:00 p.m. anymore.

My walking with his doubt gave me the courage to subdue my desire to shy away from people.

That was a dark period for us. Its darkness required me to build my fire. I needed to find the strength to follow my path. His travels and work left me to stand my family's ground alone, to be bigger than my timidity. I have struggled to try to learn how

I could live my dreams while supporting my family in theirs. I do my best. I am still not sure this is 100% possible. I am always adapting, always looking for a way through.

I long ago stopped playing second fiddle. I now believe the best way to honor my life is to live fully. After years, I no longer apologize for the things I love and have loved. I no longer ask permission to express my passions.

I have been down more than my share of rabbit holes, from conventional to crazy, and wouldn't trade any of them—because as I drive home, I am in love with the driver. My struggles have made me into a woman of substance, a woman who finally enjoys her own company.

As I turn onto my street, I am thrilled that tomorrow I can spend my day with one of my best teachers and friends: my dog. She is always happy and joins me, without reservation, in whatever madness I cook up.

As I walk through the garage door, I hear him working through the final details of the challenge ahead of him. He perseveres, knowing this is what he is meant to do with his life, and it has given him the strength to stand on the edge of an achievement beyond his grandest dreams. His tireless work and dedication to detail, combined with relentless curiosity, finally overcame most objections. He has paid the price.

I quiver when I realize the man standing in my kitchen is on the verge of winning a Nobel Prize.

My *La Te Da* is going to be a Nobel laureate.

Chapter Eight

MY AWE SUBSIDES AS I HEAR him talking to himself. Familiarity is funny that way.

He mumbles to himself because he hasn't heard me come in. He has a ritual that drives me crazy, but there is no rushing him at this point of trip preparation. He will be up for hours, checking and rechecking what he is going to bring. *Be prepared* is his mantra. He has sticky notes everywhere and will make sure that he has everything he plans to take.

This process started weeks ago with yellow notes appearing all over the house. He is now making sure each note has a corresponding item in his bag. Years of adventure travel has made him meticulous when packing.

I take a deep breath as I hear my name called before having

a chance to get my shoes off. I have learned to try to stay out of his way and wait for him to finish, but I know he will call me every few minutes, asking me to find something. I look at him standing in his office, and to my surprise, he is down to a small pile of notes, and deciding if he needs each of the items sitting on his office table.

Maybe we can do Netflix and dinner in a bit.

I drop my bag at the door and make my way to the Chinese food still in the takeout bag. He tells me he waited for me to eat. I smile; he is predictable. I am hungry enough to eat anything, so I guess I am too.

I open the bag and am delighted that he picked my favorite. He went to the place that makes the best sesame chicken in three states. Sometimes my body needs to eat food with questionable nutritional merit, but great flavor. It is the perfect start to the culinary debauchery the next few days will be. I always go a little food crazy for the first few days on my own. I am content as I serve the food, I call to him, but he is lost in preparation.

I go down the hall to physically grab him and drag him to the table in the backyard. We sit and devour it like we are teenagers. Each bite is a wonder. I have no idea why, but it is the best sesame chicken I've ever had. I want to save some for tomorrow, but fail. We play rock-paper-scissors for which of us gets the last bite.

We finish and clear our dishes. We stand together in the kitchen, reminiscing as we start to clean up the mess. He reminds me of *my cheating* that had resulted in a permanent reminder of my duplicity on his office wall.

I climb onto the countertop and reach toward him, like God toward Adam. He laughs and calls me a scoundrel. I reply, "You know I stomped you fair and square, call me Slumdog. I have always remembered the strangest things, and that was not the first time you bet against me." He scoffs out of habit. "I've learned." he mumbles. I let it go by with a smile and tell him I was just thinking about that poster earlier today.

We clean up the little mess there is. He is washing our plates, us standing side by side. We have a dishwasher, but it is how we have done dishes from the time we shared a tiny flat in college. He readies the coffee for the next morning, as I sweep the floor. We used to talk more while making the kitchen ready for the morning. For the past year, as soon as we finish dishes, he does what he has done since the Switzerland experiments started—he turns his attention to his computer on the counter.

He is always reviewing the real-time data stream from CERN, and he mentions another blip. He is not sure if this one is different than the one before or, was it the same anomaly getting larger? He mentions his concern to me. He has no way of knowing the cause. He concludes the energy output is at such an insignificant level it isn't worth calling his friend to discuss.

He makes a note of it, then turns to me and says, "See this blip?" I look but have no way to make sense of the data. "It shouldn't be there." What he points to has no meaning to me. He tries to show me another set of numbers on a spreadsheet.

I shrug, and he laughs. I only notice that he uses the word *blip*.

He has spent over thirty years in increasingly prestigious university settings. He and his fellow professors are the definition of intellectuals, and the only word he has for an irregularity in an experiment designed by a Nobel Laureate is *blip*.

He had wanted to name the dog Blip. He called her Blip for a few days, to both her and my displeasure. For old time's sake, he turns to the dog. "Come here, Blip."

I smile, the dog sighs and leaves the room.

"Dork." He and I hug tightly. "I'm going to miss you." He nods and kisses my forehead. He knows I love him. He then picks up his computer and goes back to his office to finish "one more thing…"

No Netflix tonight. I will be going to bed alone.

I check the clock and think, twelve hours. In twelve hours I will be on my own. It will then be the dog and me for months. I love my husband, but I have learned over the years to enjoy the quiet, too. I sigh; I will miss him greatly.

When my children first left, and the house was quiet, I avoided coming home.

I quickly became comfortable with it. I now relish being with myself. My work is stressful. I find that silence to be restoring. I will spend tomorrow taking a hot soak, eating takeout, and reading from the stack of books on my nightstand. There's one, in particular, I have been waiting to read. Spending a day like this is a sure-fire way to recharge my critically low battery.

He is going away. I know what to expect. I have lived

without him regularly over the years, occasionally for months. He started decades ago, frequently traveling to speak to the physics community.

As his hypothesis for the creation of the universe became a theory backed by mathematics, his critics became more vocal. The louder the objections became, the larger the number of requests for him to speak and consult. In the beginning, he never said no to an invitation. He was always on the road, defending his work against the proponents of more established theories. He slowly won over a number of his critics.

His goal back then was to leave no doubt—to either prove his theory true or false. He wanted to rely on the scientific method to decide.

He is still working toward that goal.

CHAPTER NINE

BEFORE I GET READY FOR BED, I change to comfortable clothes. My dog is waiting by the door. It is time for our nightly walk, and I am ready for some fresh air.

For the last two years, I have been helping to plan and facilitate my husband's latest adventure, but now it's my turn to plan. I haven't put any effort into preparation for my day to myself. Truthfully, as far as I have gotten was thinking about turning my phone off all day tomorrow.

That's not true. I heard an interview on my way to work with a woman that shuts off all her electronics. She calls it camping at home, and explained she says she does it to re-wild.

"Re-wild" seemed overly dramatic, but I liked the idea and have been romanticizing spending twenty-four hours like this ever since. My dog and me with no screens, no phone, no contact.

Twenty-four hours of relaxing in my backyard with a fire in the pit, a bottle of wine, and a book I have been saving so I can read it uninterrupted. I hope to become completely lost in *Zen and the Art of Motorcycle Maintenance*. I haven't read it in more than three decades. I wonder how I will find the book's message rereading it at the other end of adulthood. Seeing it on my nightstand makes me smile.

I am looking forward to watching the birds and squirrels using my backyard for parkour. Maybe I will be surprised by a fox or a hawk; I have seen several unexpected animals over the years. I recall meeting a raccoon eating a tomato off my plant, who told me that the wild didn't go away because my kind installed street lights and have doors that lock.

That night he stared at me, and we could both feel my heart beating. His wildness was stronger than my society. At this moment, I realize he planted a seed that has grown. A seed that has had me often sitting in my backyard in the middle of the night, with the moon for comfort, and the sound of the mice in the brush causing me to tense up. In the darkness, I can some-times feel the raccoon, but he never lets me see him. He leaves half-eaten tomatoes and broken bird feeders as a touchstone to wildness.

I have grown tired of wrestling with my husband's world view. He stared at me like I was a crazy woman when I told him about my encounter with the raccoon. He asked if I wanted to call someone to manage the pest. I said, "No, we can all share this space." I like having the wild so close.

I am so ready to be with my dog. We will settle in together and recharge our batteries. I plan on wearing baggy clothes, eating delivery food, and napping. My dog understands the feral side of me; she has hers, too. We are a pack of two.

My husband takes a lot of energy; my job takes a lot of energy; my house takes a lot of energy; hell, living my life takes a lot of energy. I'm getting excited about enjoying my freedom. I hear him call my name and realize I'm getting ahead of myself. He is not out the door yet. My planning can wait.

Maybe I already have all the plan I need. I laugh, thinking *it is relaxing*. I can wing it.

We have one more night together. I wait and wait; then, I surrender to my tired eyes and the clock reading an hour past my bedtime. I breach his office and kiss him goodnight. I know I will have to wake him in the morning. He will be asleep at his desk.

I'll enter his space with a cup of black coffee and push him to toward the shower. He will drink the coffee, mention that he prefers lattes, shower, and run out the door as he always books the first flight out in the morning. Tomorrow he will be at 38,000 feet in the air, moving at 500 miles per hour toward his next goal. I will be sitting in my yard under a tree with tea and a book on the sentience of plants or "*Zen*," I haven't decided. This is as apt a metaphor for our relationship as any.

He's living the life he wants to live; so am I. We tried to teach our children to do the same. They are still young, so how successful we were with this lesson remains to be seen. I wish they were here to share in my home camping experiment. My kids and I used to have so much fun together when they were young.

Tomorrow is going to be just my dog and me. She needs downtime, too. I laugh out loud at my goal for the next day. My husband is pursuing a Nobel Prize. I want to live the day as part of my dog's world, not making her live as part of mine. I love that dogs are always in a good mood; they never complain about what is for dinner. They love the simple things in life. I like the idea that tomorrow I will be as canine as possible. She has been patiently teaching me her ways since she was a puppy.

A few years ago, we were driving together when I saw a bumper sticker that said: *One day, I hope to be the person my dog thinks I am!* I remember her turning to me, cocking her head to the left, and asking, "Is that what you want?"

I laugh and give her a scratch behind the ear, as I say, "I hope that one day I can live with one-tenth of the joy and enthusiasm for life that you have. You have taught me more about joy than the Buddha, and more about living in the moment than Byron Katie. You are a master sent to show me how to love every bit of my life. Thank you."

My dog wags her tail and lays her head on my lap. I hear a familiar riff on my radio and turn it way up. We sing along.

My mind is restless, and I sit in bed and reminisce about that day. My mind is flitting from memory to memory like a butterfly in a spring meadow. That day changed me a bit. I was so grateful for a perfect fall day, the roof of my car was down, and my dog in the passenger seat. I was filled with love as I started to think about my parents.

I was headed to drive by their house, their dream house, their last house. It is a small country home with big trees and a stream running through the property.

I was reliving my youth and exceeding the speed limit on their backcountry road. I remember petting my dog softly as I began to sing along with the radio: John Lee Hooker and me singing "Boom Boom Boom Boom."

I am back as a kid in my parent's house, remembering the first time I heard Etta. I began working on my Delta blues voice that day. I was with my dad when I first heard the blues, and I was hooked. That man shaped me in so many ways. I'm missing him more than usual today, and I remembered the music, his music. My emotions soared, filling me with tears of gratitude. I love you, Dad.

I can hear him saying Beethoven, blues, and Motown are proof that music is the manifestation of magic that can change the world. I wish I could hug him.

Thoughts of my mom then fill my mind. She was the driving force for my love of music. God, I miss her, too.

She would pick us up from school with a new album, never buying more than one. She had a ritual about opening and play-ing pure vinyl. My mom would insist on giving it a good listen; it was one of her favorite things to do. Her stopping for forty-five minutes was one of the few things she did for herself. She gathered anyone willing to be quiet to join her in the living room as she played her new LP through on both sides.

She would close her eyes and listen. You were quiet, or you were outside.

She had three categories: keep, listen again, and resell. She loved all music, but she loved blues the best.

I hug them both tightly in my mind, thanking each for their gifts to me.

I feel aloneness roll over me. I miss my folks. I miss my husband. I miss my kids. I hold on for a minute savoring the salty taste on my lips. I look around my house, my life, and say thank you. I sigh as sleep overtakes me.

DAY TWO:

Walls

Walls have replaced the rhythm
that everything is both predator and prey.

I live with the expectation that with each sunrise
I will surely see sunset.

Life becomes lessened
because hunger does not lead me to be
face to face with the life
I must take to sustain my own.

Nor the knowing that my scent
may give me away.

I can count on one hand
the times my life relied solely on my next action.

The times I had to directly fight
at least one of the forces of nature to survive.

For this safety
I have traded knowing the names of the wind,
the tides,
the clouds.

I have lost the patience to sit quietly.
I am deaf to ten thousand sounds.

I am not free to feel the sun on my face.
To bless the rain,
To move without constraint.

I do not know the ecstasy
of a berry patch
after a couple days of hunger.

Community to sustain my life
has been replaced by an economy.

I live in the shackles of comfort.
I am dulled by plenty.
I am warm.
I am dry.

CHAPTER TEN

THIS DAY IS MINE, and I'm exhausted. The car to the airport leaves. Into the darkness, I watch as it drives away. I then sit in the bay window with my dog. His leaving always makes me melancholy; I finish my coffee. I then putter around picking up and putting away what he left in his wake. I finish cleaning the house and feel spent. I sit on the floor and ask my dog to help weigh our options.

We decide a nap is the most reasonable course of action. We have been up a full three hours, and bed is calling. I have a book to read. I know I won't make it two pages.

I crawl into bed and feel the soreness in my feet and back. I'm no longer a young woman. I sigh. Being a nurse in obstetrics is a young woman's game, and I am seasoned. Days when I feel like this have me contemplating retirement, but I stay resistant.

I resist for one main reason, a reason I came upon while chatting with a friend. We started our profession over thirty years ago. She regularly asks me why I keep doing it. Last year at lunch, she asked me again. I sat quietly, thinking, and finally said, "I like being a superhero."

She said, "I do miss that feeling, being the defender of women and their babies. Doing everything I can to keep them both safe. The joy of seeing a baby's first breath. I loved calming new parents who can't breathe, can't think, and can't imagine what to do next." We laughed.

She paused, "Being there when the pain..." Her words caught in her throat. I took her hand and said, "Yes." We both knew that giving birth was dangerous. We sat in silence, both of us with more war stories than we wished we had.

The human body is a wonderful thing, but birth taxes a woman's body to its limit. As a nurse, I have seen the best and the worst of the process. Every day I was reminded that child-birth is precarious.

Despite all of our medical advances and with nearly all births taking place in a hospital, delivering a child is the sixth most common cause of death for a woman aged 20 to 34.

My peers and I will always be superheroes, doing our best to make delivery as safe as it can be. Only a nurse, indeed! I struck a pose, my hands on my hips, and standing tall while I imagine myself in tights and a cape.

Then in my mind, I hear Edna Mode say, "No capes!" I play

along with the mini-drama in my head. I stand face-to-face with the epic super-suit designer and apologize. "Edna, I understand your reasons not to have capes on your superheroes, but I am exposed to much less daring-do than your typical clients. I'll be safe." She calls my cape a rag and disappears into my mind. I smile. I keep my imaginary cape because Superman has one, and every five-year-old does too. I swirl around so my cape will fly. My friend called me a dork. I hug her, and we settle into a lovely glass of wine to catch up.

My memory is interrupted by my dog's paw on my foot. I open my eyes to my dog, staring at me. She wags her tail and jumps into the bed. She barks, waiting for me to pull back the covers. She is so spoiled. I laugh at my life as I crawl back into bed. I love the slowness of a day like this. My dog snuggles in. I crack my book, not caring what, if anything, I accomplish today. The quiet of my space is perfection.

I read for a minute before my mind starts to wander. I'm delighted I am going to be traveling soon. My children are long grown and well on their own. I wonder if either of them would like to come along. I choose not to ask them. I know they have their own lives, and I will not be alone on this trip.

I have my airplane ticket, and I'm going for my own reasons. I will join my husband in Switzerland.

By *join him*, we both understand that he will be delighted to be buried in his work while I will be going to meet some friends. I will be a tourist. I am sure I will see him only to give him the items he forgot to pack.

I am happy his dreams of conducting experiments at the collider are coming true. He will be with kindred spirits, others of his ilk that he can talk to for hours about all thirteen dimensions. I have found myself regularly caught between nodding my head to be polite publicly, while at the same time shaking my head and wondering what's the intrigue of the banality of thirteen dimensions. It all seems too gee-whiz for me.

He and his team are over the Atlantic; I am now in control of my day. With no work and no husband, I take a deep breath to celebrate. I can rest a bit before I start the planning I need to do for my trip. The reason I want to make the trip to Geneva is that it is the perfect opportunity to drink wine, enjoy as much cheese and chocolate as possible, explore, and share the company of the couple I fell in love with a hundred years ago on my first visit to Paris.

The day I met them, I was sitting in a dreary conference hall waiting for my husband, even though I knew he was not coming. I decided to leave and wander on my own. I was lost, hurt, and angry. I was full of self-pity and unsure of how to take the train back to my hotel. I say they ran into me, but it was me looking at a map and walking when I literally ran into them.

I was visibly overwhelmed on the train platform. They tried to calm me and offered to help. I was relieved that I had met someone who could decipher the train schedule. I was doubly happy that fortune had them heading in the same direction as me. They asked me to join them. During our short train ride, they asked me why I was in Paris. I responded to them about the unfairness of being in Paris without my husband. I blamed him and his work for ruining my first time in this grand city. The husband looked over the unfolded train schedule, smiled, and said, "The perfection of the universe, is whether you like it or not."

I bristled a little and began formulating a challenge to such a broad statement. The doubt in my mind must have been clear on my face. He smiled and asked me to pay attention to my day and see if his supposition wasn't correct.

Noticing my need to challenge him, his wife changed the subject by asking if I would like to join them for lunch. Soon after, I was thrilled for the blessing of their fantastic company. They both had *joie de vivre*, and it was infectious. We strolled into a local park and ate a simple lunch of wine, bread, cheese, and olives from Spain. We chatted about a hundred subjects and had ice cream twice as the hours passed.

They adopted me for that first afternoon, and together, we explored the city. It was not so much what we did that day, but how they did everything that made them a joy. They expected good things to happen, shared what they had, and adapted to any obstacle that presented itself without judging it as good or bad. We enjoyed the city until our feet couldn't take another step.

We had gotten lost in the day. Night had fallen, and we were worn bare, and it was too late for them to make their way home. They had just missed their last train.

I was thrilled they could share my hotel room. Their staying would allow our conversation to go later into the night. Since that time, I have tried to remember what we talked about and can't specifically say. What I do remember is that when I was in their company, I felt like anything was possible. They placed a spark in me that I have nurtured ever since. As the night grew late, I was wondering what my husband's reaction would be to finding strangers in *his* room when he arrived.

This happened in a time that was pre-cell phones. I had no way to contact him. My husband has always been a private man, and paging a hotel to contact him would not have been to his liking.

They assured me it would all work out. We drank wine and read about the sites of the city we could visit tomorrow. As the hours passed, I was becoming increasingly concerned about my husband. Each time, both of them smiled and said, "It will be fine," and returned to the maps and guide books.

Too soon, it had gotten very late. The hotel phone rung to have my husband apologize for the lack of contact. He told me he was going to stay with his mentor at the conference hotel so that they could continue to catch up. I smiled and told him to enjoy himself. I mouthed the word "Perfection," as we finished our conversation. Speechless, I placed the receiver on the hook, and I looked at them.

I told them the hotel only had a room with two queen beds when I checked in. I had booked a single king and had acted like a brat when I didn't get my way. They smiled, not saying anything. The subject changed to a late dessert, and whether another bottle of wine was reasonable. We had fruit, a macaron, and chamomile tea, and were soon sound asleep.

The next morning, I had expected the three of us to embrace the day we had talked about, going to the Louvre and then maybe Montmartre. The mood changed during morning coffee when they explained they had to go home. They had called their son, and he told them that they were needed at home. It was not an emergency, just life getting in the way.

The change saddened me because I had hoped for a different day than I was going to have. I resisted this change; *NO* resounding in my brain like a dripping faucet. Back then, I resisted what is, trying to hold on to what I thought my life *should* be every time that change was not to my liking arrived. I stood against the universe, and she gently made way for herself despite my objections.

We ate a small breakfast, and we walked together to the train station. We exchanged numbers, addresses, and hugs. Then they were gone. My life felt empty, and I had to choose how to spend my day. The introvert in me wanted to go back to the hotel, but I could hear their spirit as it challenged my nature. She had said, "If you want what you have not, you must do what you have not."

This idea erupted in me as powerfully as when she had said it the day before. I decided to take this as a sign to go to the Louvre by myself. The worst that could happen was that I wouldn't like it. If so, I could leave and find something more to my fancy. I was in Paris, after all.

As I came face to face with the glass pyramid, I felt

trepidation. I then laughed, after traveling across the city, I was nervous about going into the Louvre by myself. The inside of the Louvre was undoubtedly one of the safest places in the world.

I strolled the museum at my own pace, stopping when I wanted, returning to the pieces I love, eating when I was hungry, and leaving when I had had enough. I didn't have to worry about someone else or having to work to please anyone but myself. I stood awestruck in front of the Sphynx of Tanis. It was there, face to face with her, that I first thought of myself as my friend.

Over the years, my wandering couple and I have met many times. They have taught me so much by watching the way they have reacted to the challenges of life. After all these years, they still teach me about the joy of spending a day with people who were living their sauce. *Sauce* is my term for people who live in such a way that they make the lives of everything they touch more delicious. Enjoying that which they love, that which is their passion in a way that everything around benefitted.

I enjoyed and continue to enjoy the experience of exploring on my terms so much that now I don't think twice about visiting a wonder of the world alone. I now meander wherever suits me, and mostly now expect the best from every situation. Being content in my own company is a gift. It still makes me feel sad and alone sometimes, but I don't let that stop me. My life is richer for the things I've seen and the people I have met while adventuring out on my own.

I feel the glow in my heart at the recollection of our first meeting and the joy I have had every time we are in the same room. My eyes close as I sit still and enjoy the breeze coming through the window. I snuggle under the covers, and for a change, steal the place my dog has warmed. I then roll to my side and breathe deeply to quiet my mind. I will call my friends to make our plans in a minute.

The next thing I remember is feeling my dog's nose on mine. It is how she has awoken me since she was a puppy. I sit with the sun on my bed and gently move my body. I coax myself awake, more deliberately than my dog cares for; her plan B is always to tug on the blankets.

I let her take them, and she seems a little put off that her ploy doesn't work.

CHAPTER ELEVEN

I MOVE MINDFULLY, awakening myself to the details of my bedroom, beautiful things I have placed with care, each designed to welcome me into a new day gently. Sadly, I mostly don't see their beauty anymore. Today I move slowly and notice.

I do this because today I can. My life rarely affords me this opportunity. I usually trade slowly waking for a few more minutes of sleep. Pressing the snooze button, then laying quietly while preparing myself for the harsh racket created when the alarm crashes in again to steal my dream. It startles me awake. I vow tomorrow I will start my day differently. I promise to start my day with yoga and meditation. My dog laughs at me.

I understand to be a better caregiver, I have to become a more engaged student in the practice of taking care of myself. To do this, I have to understand who I am more deeply. I want to let my consciousness and my body come together slowly and at its own pace. I do love starting a day like this. I lean to look at a clock that reads 10:46.

My observations have led me to the conclusion that my life moves faster than my body is designed to go. Modern conveniences make my life comfortable, but they do so at a price. To maintain a world with ever-increasing technology requires me to live at an ever-increasing pace. We are walking-speed beings in an eighty-mile-per-hour world.

If you don't believe me, visit my hospital.

A large proportion of the services provided by a hospital are to put bodies and minds back together when someone goes from 100-miles-per-hour to a complete stop unexpectedly. We are, as a people, uneasy with the speed of our lives, but we have few other choices.

I either keep up or get run over. Day after day, I race from one place to the next, from one idea to the next, from one role to the next. The internet, TV, and radio tell me how I can do it faster and more efficiently. I push myself to keep up because I'm afraid to slow down or, even worse, crash. I have watched so many others hit the wall, and they reinforce to me the high price those who crash pay. Our society has little regard or caring for people who can't or won't go at least ninety in an eighty zone.

For today, I will do my best to slow down. I am convinced that humans are meant to walk, and the human mind is designed to pay attention to nature at that speed. My hypothesis for life is that we survived as a species because we learned to stop and listen. We paid attention to the birds, relying on their songs. Like other prey species, we learned to be wary when their songs changed and to be on guard because it might be dangerous.

We once had hundreds of names for and the meanings of the colors of the clouds, the changing wind, the way the tides flow. We knew the language of nature because our lives depended upon this understanding. We had not been taught to see ourselves as separate, as having dominion.

We learned our place in the grand everything from our grandparents and their peers. Elders taught their people how to cooperate as a tribe and with the environment because they knew that if everyone acted as individuals, the clan could not be sustained. The clan was life. They learned lessons that had been passed down from generation to generation for millennia. They learned while joining ten thousand species all following the migration, how each sustained life, and each creature found its place amongst the vast herds. They knew when and where the Earth would bear fruit, where water was sweet, where they could rest.

Not long ago, we as a species began to move faster and decided we no longer needed the herds to survive. We traded this vast community for an economy. Now, I am enslaved to continually chasing what is new. My elders trained me on how to pursue what, by design, fades as quickly as it appears. Their lessons focused on how to be productive. They stressed teaching how to stand alone, how to thrive as an individual. To assess value in terms of money. All undeniably valuable in this age, but I wonder how long it can be sustained.

My house is overflowing with yesterday's fads. I now move too fast to have a connection with the land around me. I no longer need to prepare for winter or have the capability to roam. I can't be free in the cage of this society. I have no choice but to live with the illusion I am separate from nature. I am the fifth generation without the vast herds, and as a result, I have no connection to that way of life. My primary environment is a screen and four temperature-controlled walls, not sun and soil. I no longer see the face of the animal that dies to sustain my life; my food is no longer fresh; my legs no longer strong.

The closest thing I have to a herd is the twice-daily traffic jams that can send me into despair. I now have to rely on technology in the same way my ancestor's survival depended upon flora and fauna. I can't imagine that ancient way of living. I am comfortable in this modern way of life because it is all I know. The land around my house is no longer able to feed me. We both feel empty. I sigh and tell myself to stop. It is time to enjoy my day.

Today is my day off, and I am making a conscious effort to live as close to four mph as I can. I know I won't come close. My dog reminds me that I promised to emulate her today. She asks me when I plan to start. We have read each other's thoughts for years. I can't explain it; I simply know I love it. She is wise and helps me to sort out my life.

I chuckle with her and ask if spending time in our backyard

is okay. She turns and heads outside. I ask her to wait for a moment. I have things to do before we can sit under the trees and watch the squirrels. I will first try to slow my cycle to match my dogs. If that works, I will try to slow and cycle with the trees. The large cottonwood is best at restoring me and has long ago proved more trustworthy with my well-being than my phone or my doctor. I need to be with her to be myself.

My dog is glad to see the rant in my head has stopped. She knows that my daily routine usually starts with a walk, so she has not been far from me as I pad around the house. She knows our walk is about to begin, and she sighs with impatience. She knows I move at my own pace, and she can't change that.

I put my cup in the dishwasher, and head for the door. She is running back and forth, and I tell her I am coming. I push the button to open the garage door and see the front of my neighbor's houses, but seldom a neighbor. I am an introvert, so I do not mind this fact.

My dog's tail is wagging with pure delight. Every day one of the great gifts I give myself is trying to share the absolute joy my dog shows every time I take down her leash. I have nothing in my life to which I bring half the enthusiasm that she has for a simple stroll. She is a patient teacher and seems pleased by me trying to share in her eagerness to explore the day.

The best I am usually capable of on most days is to sing a bit as we take our walk. Unlike myself, my dog is curious and excited about everything. I am usually aware that the clock is ticking and that I have to be to work in less than an hour. I then rush through our walks—or worse, wish my husband was doing it instead of me.

Today, however, is my day off, my husband is on a plane, my friends know I am out of contact, and my kids are living their own lives. My pace can be my own, so this morning I will have the luxury to pay close attention. I promise myself to slow my thoughts and focus, but I always find I am not good at it.

Although I try to bring my attention to what is around me, I am having trouble slowing my feet and my mind. My world demands I move quickly. It is a hard habit to break. I usually am thinking about what I need to do, so I am unable to be as curious or excited as her. As I pet her, I discover when I try, I have no idea how to be unhurried. Even on a day like today when I have no place to be. I still rush.

My mind is obsessed with a myriad of things that are not pressing now and likely never will be.

This society pushes us all to be racers. Racing is about fearlessly pushing to the edge and hoping to survive one more lap around the track. Survival seems an apt description for most of my days.

I intentionally slow my feet, but my mind refuses to brake. My dog stops, her attention focuses on something unseen. I walk oblivious until the leash snaps taut. She looks up at me; her eyes are sad. I apologize and promise to slow my pace. I start by standing still until I notice something that has been there for a long time, but that I have never seen. I wait and look until I see a piece of yard art that takes my breath away.

I have been this way a hundred times, how have I not seen it?

The difference between my dog and me is that she is always curious. As a college student, I realized that curiosity is the force that brings ideas into existence. Creativity is the flash of inspiration that gets all the attention. Still, curiosity is the steady dynamic force that energizes the process for the long-term effort.

I am curious with an agenda. My dog is curious without one. She only wants to manifest joy. Watching her examine a thousand things while we walk has trained me, on my best day, to look at a few things a little more closely.

I have caught glimpses of what a slower pace might allow me to see. I remember the day I watched a snail climb my back door. I sat still and watched as the snail taught me that tiny incremental steps in a set direction would take me wherever I want to go. Every time I stop and pay attention, I learn something new. I rarely do.

Today, I begin to ponder on the possibility of obtaining a goal at a snail's pace. It is the model I will try to bring about changes I want in my life. So far today, my half-hearted attempt at slowness has allowed me to watch a butterfly visiting the last blooms of summer. I noticed the beauty of a leaf devoured by Japanese beetles. I stopped to look at the progress of the last peaches of summer ripening on a tree along my route. I ask the squirrel if she will leave one for me. Whether I get to eat one or not hardly matters—it is the exercise of being curious that has brought me a morsel of peace.

Slowness is teaching me that there is beauty in everything,

and as a result, I am more profoundly noticing the beauty in myself. I walk rejoicing that my body is fit enough to carry me through another day. I resist the thought that I am old, finished, and wonder why I am having this fight with myself for the hundredth time.

My mind asks me how much I have to give any new adventure. I wonder who I will be when nursing no longer defines me. I start to feel defeated when I tell my mind that I don't care. I do so love this version of me. I know I will be enough for whatever comes next.

Instead of fighting what is, I nod and agree. I have seen a lot of years. I am not young anymore. I see my wrinkles as a symbol that I have made it this far into my journey. They are proof I have always been enough. My extra pounds are a sign I have plenty; that I have enough to share. The pain in my knee is facilitating reconciliation with myself that I am finite and need to enjoy what is because tomorrow will surely be something new.

I am most at peace when I am moving at the pace of clouds or the sun across the sky. I try to be quiet and slow and still, and I usually fail. Maybe I am too hard on myself. I pat myself on the back for living fully if only in one moment. In the next second, I succumb to something as trivial as my stomach rumbling. I hurry home with none of the high-mindedness I had a moment before.

I remove the leash as I cross the street and ask my dog if she is hungry. She tells me she is a dog and wants to know what I have in mind. My practice in slowness is gone. I move quickly toward my kitchen. I am hungry.

Our walk ends with the decision that this is an ideal day for bacon. Bacon is everything food should be. Crispy and salty, it compliments everything and is perfect all by itself. Eating with my fingers, my dog reminds me to share. Together we eat most of a pound of bacon, a peach, kibble, two cups of coffee, and half a bowl of water.

I have no idea where my phone is, and neither do I care. I am camping and am enjoying my day. Nothing with a screen is going to interfere. The hardest decisions I still have to make in the next twenty hours are what to order in for dinner, and which wine is for today. Wine first. On my way out to my chair, I stand in front of a collection of great bottles and am tempted to drink something wonderful.

I reach for a bottle of Ridge Monte Bello I have been saving and then consider an everyday bottle. I reach, then stop. What the hell. I grab the Ridge. It is early, but I am not going anywhere today. Today is a day for me to do things I don't ordinarily do. I pop the cork and smell a hint of it as I pour it into my glass. I take it and breathe in its essence. I swirl it in the glass and admire how striking it is.

Wine is, for me, one of the perfect connections to soil and history. It is a touchstone to the Earth. I feel the relationship to history, knowing Caesar, Shakespeare, and Jefferson all felt the anticipation of the first taste as I do now.

I know deep down my dog would love wine as much as bacon. The way she is looking up at me, I know she wants to try it. As much as I love her, I have little doubt that her acquiring a taste for a big cabernet would be a monumentally bad idea. I asked my veterinarian about dogs and wine once. He called my dog spoiled and told me wine is bad for her. My dog knew I asked because I know she would love it. I let her know I would love to share a glass or two with her. She thanked me, and I promise to take her to her favorite dog park as a compromise.

She has highly refined tastes. She looks at my glass and then at me. She knows I am keeping something incredible from her. She once found the chocolate I had gotten from a local chocolatier. She ate it and now knows I have things she would love that I don't share. She told me she loved it, but remembers she was sick for a couple of days and would never look for it again.

She is trying to be a good sport about wine, but I can see a bit of wondering, hurt, and jealousy in her eyes. I give her the last piece of bacon as a peace offering. She wags her tail in acceptance, and I stroke her soft fur and apologize. I am pleased when her jealous eyes are distracted by a squirrel, and she forgets about my glass.

She jumps up onto the chair next to me, spins around twice and lands upside down, paws up, and head on a pillow. She will soon be snoring. I caress her as her eyes close completely. I settle in, knowing we are not moving.

CHAPTER TWELVE

I OPEN TO THE FIRST PAGE of my book and know I am about to lose a few hours of my day. I escape into the story as a chorus of birds sing in my tree. A few have gathered in my birdbath. I stop reading to enjoy their splashing.

The breeze is soft as the last flowers of the season are keeping me company. The birds and squirrels are readying for the cold by eating their body weight in seeds from the feeders. The sun is a perfect temperature, and I close my eyes to listen as a cricket joins in harmony with the birds.

I knew I was tired but was not expecting to doze off. I wake to my dog missing, my wine glass shimmering on the table, and page 31 of my book lying on my chest. I believe my bladder was installed solely to get me off this chair or out of bed. I get up, and

I call out. My dog emerges from the shade of the tree. She yawns, stretches, and then gives herself a good shake. I have yawned and stretched, but never the latter. I do my best dog shake and find it lacking. She is used to my silliness and is moving toward me, wondering what game I have in store for her.

I have read wolves pick their leaders by their ability to create interesting play. If it is true or not, I don't care. It is a story that makes me happy, and for me, in this case, that is better than the literal truth.

My dog is looking at me. She and I are a pack of two with no alpha. Sometimes she creates the play, and sometimes I do. After our walk this morning, it's my turn. I decide on ice cream.

She wags her tail in approval even before I say it out loud. I grab my keys, and she jumps into the passenger seat. I put the roof down and turn the stereo up. She loves car rides. I turn it on to see what KGNU is playing.

Community radio is a smorgasbord, good or bad. I never know what I am going to find. This station will move from a blues show to an hour of talk in Japanese, to a guy talking about local food. It was on his show I discovered my favorite ice cream shop. It is a little piece of perfection and a destination when we have no other place we have to be.

Sweet Cow has doggy ice cream. She eats her cone in a single bite and looks to me to share. We have talked about this. I am going to eat all of mine. I love her, but I won't give her any of my oatmeal cookie ice cream. Once we found this shop, it quickly became a ten-dollar-a-week habit.

I am sitting on a bench under an umbrella. I take the last bite of my cone and am content that I am spending as close to a perfect day as a nurse with tired feet can hope. The remainder of my day is a massage scheduled in an hour, Pho delivered later, reading more, maybe some TV, and then only a hot soak stands between bed and me.

I sigh at the thought of it.

We arrive back home, and I am startled that I have left my wine and book sitting outside. I never do that. My dog smiles at me. I hear her think ice cream has made us act like teenagers. We are both content. I pick up my things and head into the house. I set the wine bottle and glass on the counter, and for the first time, I check my phone.

No calls.

It seemed strange that my husband didn't attempt to call me. He is the absentminded professor; forgetting to contact me when science or fishing are concerned is well within the normal operating parameters of my husband. After thirty years, I have a pretty good idea that he is fine and beside himself with joy as he is either in or close to the world's largest science fair project.

I text him and wait, staring at my phone. Still nothing. I text him again and wait with great impatience. No reply appears. I feel a twinge of nervousness mixed with annoyance. I watch my screen. He isn't responding. I shrug and give up.

The smartphone has changed communication so that people expect a response to their texts or calls instantly. Now when I send a message to someone I care about and do not receive a prompt reply, it can cause my heart to race a bit. I wonder if something is wrong. I get impatient waiting for a response. My issue, I know, but I can't break the habit.

My parents lived their lives being available only when they were at home, and the phone rang. My grandparents and the rest of my lineage to the beginning of civilization were mainly not available to the outer world. Their voice was limited to the distance they could yell that dinner was ready.

I love and hate my phone. It overcomes my legendary lack of any sense of direction. It answers the weird questions that require an immediate answer, like: "Who won the 2016 World Series, or can dogs drink wine?" Beyond that, it keeps me in touch with my husband, kids, and friends, but it does so at a price.

It is the most intrusive of all modern devices. It has become a necessity, joining keys and my purse as the things I can't leave the house without making sure I have. It is a constant companion, one I am not sure I invited into my life. It is more like an in-law that stopped in for lunch and never left.

I have to make a specific plan to not have it with me, so people in my life don't worry about my well-being. It is like childcare in reverse; I need to inform people when it is not taking care of me. When I was twenty, I drove across the country, calling my parents every few days. Today that lack of contact would likely have police in three states looking for me.

I text my husband again and wait. Nothing.

During the Cuban missile crisis, communication between world leaders took twelve hours. In comparison, I ask, "How was your flight?" and am agitated that I am not getting an instant response. There are days that I have checked my phone every five minutes for hours, waiting for a response to the last message I sent. It is Pavlovian how I have been trained to respond to a chime.

My husband is a man who has trekked across much of the world. He has rocket scientists calling him when they can't solve a problem. He survived the raising of our children, many grand adventures, and living with me. Despite knowing this, an unanswered text on a work trip to Switzerland has me nearing panic.

I smile as I remember our first trip. My husband is the son of a man that saw no need to go any further than downtown and the farmer's market. "This city has everything I need," his dad would say.

I remember how anxious he was when he first boarded a plane. I held his hand as we taxied toward takeoff. I told him how I love the feeling right before the flight takes off. That single second when all is still, the planning is over, the anticipation peaks as the engines rev up and then the adventure begins.

I asked him if he was all right. He nodded, not hearing a word I said. As the plane sped down the runway, he gripped the armrests like he was giving birth. His fear lasted until the wheels touched down, and we set about exploring a new city. He loved the excitement of faraway places, loved that everything was new to him, and reveled in exotic foods.

Soon he was using his not-insignificant intellect and charm to garner speaking invitations from all over the world.

In the beginning, he fit in as much touristy stuff with me that he could, but mostly he spent his time working on his presentations and debating his latest findings with anyone who would listen. As his reputation grew, I became a widow on these trips. I resented being left alone.

It took years to accept my reality, and to become grateful for the life his profession allowed and allows me to live. I learned to make the best of the situation by becoming what I call self-ful.

Self-ful is the art of nurturing my complete self during all of the interactions I have in a day. I wanted a place between selfless and selfish that I could live healthfully within. Selfish is me first; selfless is me last; self-ful is me being equal in my interactions. It is me being equally true to myself and everything else in my life. Putting love, beauty, and joy at the forefront of making the choices life requires.

I began to see and savor what interested me. As a woman traveling *alone*, I felt I stood out. I soon learned travelers are people that always have room for one more. Divergent groups have adopted me. I have been whisked around in buses, boats, cars, cabs, carts, foot, and twice on a camel to see the wonders of the world. I usually meet at least one person who is excited to share the same things that fascinate me. When I was fortunate, I found someone that loved discussing the wonders of the world I had researched and would share time to go and experience it.

As I got better at seeking out what interested me, I would use my husband's connections in academia to track down and hire a professor or graduate student to act as a guide and to share the exploration of a local wonder or two. I would bring enthusiasm and hours of reading, and they would hopefully bring expertise, joy, and conversational skills. I have seen the world with poets, princes, and a Pulitzer Prize winner.

As my confidence grew, I would venture out on my own and see what the day held. On my own, I have been lost, anxious, and afraid. Through this, I became emboldened and exhilarated to venture out with only myself as company. I learned to trust myself, to enjoy the company of strangers, to be less timid with my life.

This was when I have, more often than not, met people that love something so much, they have to share it deeply with others. These experiences have shifted my understanding and my approach to my day and my life. This understanding has been the cornerstone of my becoming a woman I love. Force, fate, and opportunity have worked together to help me find my path. Now that I am on it, I explore it.

This travel arrangement worked for me until our daughter was born. One of us had to stay at home. I was jealous and angry for the first year about my husband continuing to traipse all over the world while I raised our child. I missed the exploration, seeing what new facet of myself exploring a new culture exposed.

As a young mother, I decided I could either remain bitter or find my way to satisfy both of our travel needs, given the demands of each of my family members. To deal with my envy, I needed to confront my concern that his need to travel was secretly a need to be away from his family in general, and from me specifically. We talked about my concerns, and over time, I grew to understand that adventure fed his soul, cleared his mind, and allowed him to focus his attention. Travel was a job requirement, and he was unbearable to live with if he didn't have regular journeys.

His needs still left me at home, taking care of my family as a single mom. I missed my travels, too. When both of my children were very young, I had to figure out a way to feed my need to explore, given the constraints of a stay at home life. After some trial and error, he and I worked out a way that I could explore with him and still be able to drop and pick up my children from school. I got both the adventure of travel and of sharing my life with my children.

I had to modify my life. I sought a way to have some of the aspects of travel I loved most. I began reading about a location where he was about to explore. I would have him seek out a local expert that was willing to have conversations with me about that interest. We would then chat over the internet or phone; some conversations lasted minutes, while others have lasted for years.

Over thirty years, these conversations about local treasures and lore have led to a number of them speaking at the university. Many have eaten at least one meal at my table. The closest ones have stayed in my home. He had to experience his adventure directly, while for this time in my life I became perfectly happy in my garden, with my children, reading numerous books and enjoying many exceptional nights in dialogue with some of the most interesting people in the world.

Once our children became self-sufficient, we returned to travel. I watched as our kids grew with each exploration we went on. Whenever possible, our children came along. My husband and I feel these travels were the best educational experience we could provide. My kids are now intrepid nomads who have seen large swaths of the world.

Every time we boarded a plane, my kids and I found the world to be a smaller and smaller place. Soon they were dragging me out of my comfort zone, giving me new eyes and a new heart for the world.

My children watched me, and quickly they began studying on their own, then seeking out their passions. At relatively young ages, they copied my model. I had little choice but to let them go in the hands of people I had talked to on the phone, so they could explore what called their hearts. They would leave on grand adventures with no hesitation. I had told them to pursue their interests and had to let them do so when they did. We—mostly I—had to learn to trust each of their choices and paths. Every adventure brought perspective and joy beyond what I could have imagined. Best of all, through our experiences, we have made friends all over the world.

I have, on a few occasions, turned the tables and left my husband behind with them, while I accepted return offers to visit individuals whose company I enjoy. The first time I went, I felt awful, feeling I was abandoning my family. I came home to a mostly clean house, kids that had too much pizza, and a dog that was delighted I was back.

My husband and I have been good together. We have made a life we are proud of, children that are a pleasure, and examined many passions deeply.

Chapter Thirteen

FOR ME, TRAVEL IS STRICTLY for pleasure. I have heard adventure defined as when you are standing in a place you planned to be, and are wondering why you are there.

In the interim of our kids growing, my husband had stopped traveling exclusively for work and started going on adventures. He would go for weeks to jungles, deserts, and high-mountain terrains. The rawness of the experience was an addiction.

Once, early on, he was lost for eight days. It was the longest and hardest time I have ever spent. I didn't know for sure but had good reason to believe he was dead.

I was home with two small children and lots of fear. I was relieved when he was found. After he was rescued and recovered enough, he returned home, but he was never again the man that

I married. He said for those days, he was fully alive. He lived on bats and grubs, and the water dripping in a cave he found.

He was sure he was going to die there. He didn't. He was never so reckless again, but soon after he recovered, he was planning his next escape.

I assumed he would be more cautious in choosing destinations after almost dying. He wasn't. I could either adapt or leave him. I adapted.

After this event for him, the more remote the location, the better. He craved places with no creature comforts and not a place to buy a thing for days in any direction. The rawness of the setting would clear his mind and allow him to see the essentials of the creation model he was championing more clearly. He said he would come back refreshed and ready to tackle his work with renewed energy. He claimed his most significant breakthroughs happened during these trips.

While on an excursion in the wilderness a few years ago, I asked him why he thought it was that these trips renewed him. He sat quietly, gathering his thoughts, and finally said, "Surrendering to the unknown, out here, teaches me to recognize and surrender to the unknown in my work-a-day life. Making my way through a place that has no maps helps me refine the art of finding and being comfortable taking the next step on a path that is uniquely mine. Following my life's path from here back into the city allows me to be truer to my life when I'm at home."

"Everything out here has its unique purpose, and I recognize that this includes me. My life is mine, and only mine. I have learned how to trust myself out here. In the wilderness, the stakes can quickly become life or death. Being comfortable here teaches me to trust myself back in the city. These lessons carry over when I'm home, when the most real danger I am in is that my ego will get bruised."

"To live well means living my life as an adventure, not as the guided tour our society is designed to sell us. Every time I am out here, I learn my life has to be mine. It is the way I have found to have the courage and curiosity to do the things only I can do. Some people seem to get this life view by instinct. I have had to learn it one trudging step at a time."

I hugged him and asked why he had never shared this with me. "You never asked before, so I never had to put it into words until now." He kisses me and returns to tending the fire.

I smile and sit quietly, comparing his life with mine. I live with the unknowns of life and death every day. I come out here to see a sky full of stars and become enlivened because I can't be sure what is around the next bend. At night, I love to sit by a fire and listen to the wind in the trees. Some say simple pleasures. I think not simple at all.

My world at home is defined by screens and hype; out here, the world is defined sitting under a tree, in a forest, under a sea of stars. Knowing tomorrow I will be at the mercy of nature makes me feel alive.

I am always happy for the renewal of being outdoors and learning the lessons I have learned. I did grow tired of the ordeal of getting my family to—and home from—very remote places. I found I was still curious and loved the conversations with some of the people that joined us on the excursions, but became less tolerant of being wet, or cold, or both.

Nature used rain to convince me to rethink going on his adventures. A five-day walk in a monsoon, with my rain hat safe and dry on the kitchen counter, persuaded me that he had to explore his way, and I could return to the idea that had worked for me for years.

I no longer needed to go on every trip.

CHAPTER FOURTEEN

FLOATING FROM MY MASSAGE, I find that I still have no reply from my husband. I stare at my phone and start to worry for real. He ate bats in a cave, I tell myself, he is fine. I grab the leash and decide to try an evening stroll to calm my nerves. A walk usually helps. "I am supposed to be without screens today," I tell myself. I told him this was my plan. Everything is fine; he is honoring my request as he has done in the past. I feel something is different this time, but I can't change what I can't change.

Who am I kidding? He is lost in the science equivalent to Disneyland and has forgotten about me. *La Te Da,* you never change. I can't even get upset anymore.

I feel my heart ache. I can do nothing but walk with my dog. My energy is drained, I take a shorter route than usual. We rarely use this path. I like to think of myself as a complex and nuanced person, but today as I walk, I realize I am not much more than a collection of habits. While I hate doing the same thing every day, I am not a big fan of change either. How am I supposed to find peace, given that set of life parameters?

I like this route because it has beautiful flowers and no traffic, but it is not long enough to be satisfying. My heart and stomach growl. He stole my mood, but not my appetite. I call in and pay for my food delivery order as I head for home. Modern technology does have its advantages. I have a few blocks to go, but I just want to be home. My legs and heart are heavy. I check and find I still have no response from my husband. I text *Hi.*

It's a school night; I plan to make tea, and I eat while watching two episodes of the new season of my current binge-able TV show. I hope to get lost in this show. It is a guilty pleasure. It is beautifully written, and the story makes me always want more. I struggle before I talk myself out of watching a second episode. One is plenty. I instead go to take a nice long soak.

My tub is my sanctuary and has provided more peace of mind than any other thing in my life. I need it right now. I settle into it, and in twenty minutes, I'm still trying to relax. The peacefulness of the night air is coming through the open windows. It should be perfect, but my husband hasn't contacted me. I surrender and decide to head to bed.

I text again as I settle in under the covers with my book. Nothing. I read a bit and am nodding off when I hear a noise downstairs. I instinctively call out, "How was your day?" I receive no reply. I wonder if I remembered to lock the door.

Years ago, my house was noisy. Kids make noise constantly. For years, I longed for quiet. Now I long for any of the racket that once drove me crazy. My house is too quiet. I wish for all the noises I now miss so much. The patter of my kids' feet and hearing "Mom" shouted every few minutes. The drama and the laughter. The asking for rides, then car keys and money. The sounds of them living their lives. All I have now is quiet.

I look for my guardian and find my dog sound asleep. How is she able, at forty pounds, to fill my husband's side of the bed? She should be up and barking. She should be racing downstairs to see what was happening. I lean over and nudge my protector awake. She stares at me like I am crazy and tries to curl back into her warm spot. I curl up, too. She goes back to sleep; I don't.

I'm fine. So much of my life has been me wanting for my current circumstances to hurry and change into something I thought I wanted more. Then, once it was gone, I found myself wishing for days lived long ago to come back, or at least allow me to visit like a tourist, enjoying only the aspects I remember loving.

I usually live each day like nothing is going to change, but sooner than later, it always does. Then I am surprised, even depressed, that I can't go back to yesterday, and usually, for a while, regret the opportunities I've missed.

I am in my house with my dog. None of the people I love most are within a thousand miles. The place each of my family refers to as home is only home in their memory. I am feeling silly about the noise downstairs and return to the safety of my blankets and open my book again.

I check my phone, and text my husband goodnight, and wait. It is tomorrow there, and he should be drinking coffee and responding to my texts, but I receive nothing. I feel a twinge of emptiness, then anger, then sadness. Sad I am not important enough for him to contact me back. I remind myself that school-girl drama is not entirely gone from my empty house.

I roll over to sleep. As my dog snores, I am even more awake. I surrender and reach for my phone. I stare at it and try willing the damn little screen to do what I want. I try to settle into the fact that for tonight, I am alone. Alone in my now quiet house. It is late, but I text my children goodnight anyway. I get no reply.

I consider texting a few friends but decide against it. I don't want to answer the questions they would ask. My dog is chasing something in a dream. I am sure sleep will be a while in coming. I am worried. I turn the page of my book, trying to recall where I am, and leave the phone in a place I can see it.

Peace gives way to panic as I hear a thump in my kitchen. My heart starts racing as my mind fills with a laundry list of horrors, each one ending with my family crying in despair.

My trauma management training kicks in, and I catch my next thought, trying to slow my panic. "Are you okay right now?" My mind says, "Yes…but." I ask myself again, "Are you okay?"

I feel my heart pounding as I remain motionless, deciding what I should do. I stay still, hearing nothing but my heart beating. I want to hide under the covers, but I can't stay in bed. I am the only adult in the room, so it is up to me to see. I stand. I listen. I am now hoping I am alone.

I imagine an intruder standing quiet, listening for me to move. He is wearing black clothing with a mask, holding a bag full of my stuff. I am sure he is considering if he should climb the stairs or sneak away.

It is completely silent.

I sit still waiting for another noise. I picture the intruder, following a training I sat through years ago, I try to imagine the menace in clown shoes and a tutu. I see him three feet tall. I picture his ominous presence in my front room.

I listen. It is quiet, and I am getting braver. I tell myself I need to go downstairs. My five-year-old self asks me why.

I wake the dog again. I decide to act like I did when I was a teenager and check every room in my house. I grab my phone and consider calling 911. My dog inhales deeply and stretches as she jumps off the bed to join me. She's unsure of the game we are playing, but she plays along. She is my friend.

I move as quietly as I can, listening. Silence persists as I turn on the lights of my bedroom. I creep slowly, my heart pounding, nervous as I proceed. I feel fear increasing as I move down each stair. The lights are on upstairs, so I have no choice but to continue. The menace knows I'm here. I listen for anything moving but have not heard a sound for a while.

I don't sense anyone in my house. Do I slink slowly or move quickly? I decide to hurry. I half-run through my house, turning on lights as quickly as I can, leaving them on as I go. I have the same feeling as I did when I was ten years old and watching an Alfred Hitchcock movie. I know I am being childish, but I can't help it.

With fear sitting on my chest, I move from empty room to empty room until I am standing in my kitchen. I am thankful I do not have an unfinished basement. I double-check the locks and begin to feel ridiculous.

Embarrassment escalates when I see my purse on the floor; it must have fallen off the counter. I pick it up and sit on the stool it must have hit on the way down.

My heart is still beating too fast. My dog sits in front of me. She is wondering what I am doing. "I'm silly," I say to her. I feel safe again. I look at my phone and wonder why I thought it would protect me. Did I think the foreboding presence in my house would hold on while I call 911?

With the mystery of the noise solved, I start to calm down. I am now sure I am alone in my house, and for the first time, this fact makes me happy. I stand and look around.

My house. The sound of it still makes me smile. I decide to make a cup of chamomile tea to drink with my book. I hope the combination of these two will help me find sleep well before the sun rises again.

I start water to boil and open the refrigerator, looking for a snack I don't want. I begin to turn off lights while listening for the kettle to whistle. Soon I have a cup of tea in hand and my dog is nowhere to be seen.

I sit on the stool and take a sip. This is the first house I can call my own. For years I had lived in housing that we rented or a place provided by the university. Some were lovely, but it was not my paint on the walls. It was not my dirt in the garden. It was not my space.

I was not having that again when we moved here. I told my husband if we move, I had to have my own house. I made a list of what the property had to have.

I searched for months, standing my ground until I finally found this neighborhood full of trees. It is a classic Craftsman bungalow with roof supports, stained glass, and a huge garage. It didn't have a great porch, but it does now. It has a cottonwood tree that's seventy feet tall, a fireplace in the bedroom, and a kitchen built with Jacque Pepin in mind. I love this house. It's everything I wanted.

I stare at a closed freezer door and ponder ice cream. I look around for an accomplice but my ever-faithful dog is sleeping upstairs, so I have no partner in crime. I don't open the door.

Room by room, I turn off the lights as I make my way back to my bedroom. I finally return to my bed, moving my dog over so I can crawl under the blankets. I need to get to sleep. Tomorrow is not far away, and sleep is going to be elusive.

Back in bed, I read my book, drink my tea, and regularly check my phone. It pings once. It is from my son, and he loves me, too. I smile and choose not to respond.

I text my husband, as it has always been the best way to reach him. He hates talking on the phone. I check it until I can't. I hope he is okay. I am restless, but I am more tired.

DAY THREE:

We are on a journey without maps.
I cannot be the first to come this way.

The first to hide my heart,

The first afraid to stand
in the full light of the sun,

I remove my shoes
knowing the space where I stand is sacred,

Sacred because I am
and it is.

I bow and the Sacred tells me to stand
"Stand tall and follow the example of the ancient tree"

A wave of doubt broadsides me.

Why, how, where and when prove meaningless,
The compass directions of a child.

I am awake and alive.

I have made it this far.

Well beyond any place I could have dreamed.

*Today, I sit sure that there is "More" for me,
a "Next" to embrace,*

All while sacred redefines what "More" means.

What is "More" when I have everything?

What is "Next" in the infinite?

What is the question curiosity can't answer?

What step too frightening to take?

CHAPTER FIFTEEN

NURSES DON'T WORK MONDAY through Friday, eight to five. We work strange schedules because neonatal units require staffing twenty-four hours a day, seven days a week.

Unlike yesterday, this day starts with no bacon, has no massage, no backyard reading, and no nap. I check my phone to find a message from my daughter. She loves me. I smile. I text my husband good morning, but I have very little time to wonder about him right now. I get dressed and have just enough time to take my dog out for a short walk.

I rush out the door. My mind is racing. How is it that I have used up all the relaxation from yesterday? My dog reminds me of my antics of the night before. We both laugh.

I go to check my to-do list and panic when I realize I am

phoneless. I feel naked without it. I stop to weigh if I should go back and get it. I know if I do, my walk will not happen, and I will spend the time staring at a screen instead. I move on, knowing this way I can explore with my dog. We walk.

I want to spend my mornings differently, more slowly, but I don't. We end up walking our regular route, and the whole way, I am wondering if my husband has contacted me. Wondering is almost as bad as having my phone in my face as I walk. The beauty of the day is wasted either way.

I stop and breathe deeply. My dog sits and waits for me; she has her back against my legs. I tell her I love her. I think about yesterday and sigh to myself about the unfairness of having to work. I sometimes feel this way in the morning. Once at work, I am happy I am there. Work makes me feel valuable.

I hurry home, shower, and dress. I feel like I am running late, but when I check the clock, I see I can have a second cup of coffee. *Bonus*. I am having trouble finding motivation this morning. I hope more coffee helps.

I never understood why the clock in the morning moves faster than at any other time of day. In what seems like five minutes, I go from being early to running ten minutes late. I jump up and move like I am on fire. I drive to work like I'm Batman.

A light stops me, and I take the time to scroll through my phone. I still find nothing from my husband. He is starting to concern me. As I hurry to work, I wonder if I should involve my kids about their dad or be patient a little longer. This long without contact is out of the ordinary, even for him.

I make a left onto the main thoroughfare and turn on the radio. I am hoping music will change my mood before my workday begins.

I hear the end of a news story about *"a small glitch with the Large Hadron Collider."* I am shocked and wonder what is going on. I drive to work searching for news about CERN. I get nothing other than the most superficial coverage.

I am becoming anxious as I drive. I get to work, and the parking garage is full. I circle, trying to find a parking space and wish I had left five minutes sooner. I go up the parking garage, level by level.

In those few minutes, I hear additional information about a power surge occurring at CERN. I remember being told by the experts that built it, including my husband, that CERN is entirely safe. Officials say that they have it completely under control, and there is no need for concern.

The same sort of officials told the people of Bhopal and Fukushima the same thing. Officials are always telling people like me that they are a step ahead. They say it in front of cameras, up to when the thing they assure me they control bursts into flames.

That thought makes me chuckle and shake my head. My mom always called me a pessimist when I was younger. Despite my best efforts, sometimes I revert. I spy a car backing out, and I wait for them to move. I check my phone; then I scurry as fast as I can to the entrance of the hospital.

I want more information, then realize I will hear the whole

story, in painful detail, tonight. I slow my pace a bit. My husband will call, and I will get the rundown when we talk.

Like in the past, he will say he is sorry about not getting back to me, but life kept getting in the way. I will say that everything is okay and will be relieved to hear his voice.

I enter the hospital, hurrying to get my day started. I round the corner and am startled to see a large group of people standing in front of the waiting room televisions watching the news. This size of a crowd only happens during the direst of news events.

I stop to hear the same thing the radio had told me. *Science's finest experts are on the scene. First responders are poised to take action if it becomes necessary. Militaries from many nations are on alert and offering technical assistance. Dear viewer, please rest assured that there is nothing to be concerned about.* Blah blah blah.

I see my boss among the crowd and tell her my husband is in Switzerland at CERN. She asks me what I know. I say I haven't heard a word from him. She looks at me a bit skeptically, then her manager's face takes over. She tells me to do what I need to do. She asks that I please keep her in the loop. I turn to leave when she asks me again if I know anything more.

I tell her I found out myself ten minutes ago. "I'll let you know when my husband lets me know." I notice many people stopping to eavesdrop on our conversation. I say goodbye to my boss and weave through the crowd and move to the elevators. The doors open, and I make my way through a maze of hallways to get to my station.

Every hospital I have worked at makes me feel like a rat in a sociology experiment. I joke with new employees that for the first year, I half expected to find a piece of cheese and a man in a lab coat and a stopwatch every time I had to find my way through a new section of the hospital.

I check the clock as I start my computer. *Made it.* I look at my phone and see messages, but none are from my husband. My son is checking in with me, and I have a text from my daughter asking me to call her when I have a minute; no rush, she says.

I go to find her number, then stop. I am full of adrenaline from playing beat the clock and not thinking clearly. I call, text, and email my husband: "*What is happening? Call me!*"

More and more, I feel like I'm sending my messages into the ether. He has only been there one day, but it feels longer. A wave of panic rises, and I imagine him trapped, or injured, or dead.

I am starting to become scared. I text him again and wait.

No response.

Bastard.

I picture him working, his phone muted in his pocket or left on his desk as he is off doing God knows what. He has done this to me numerous times.

I feel anger rising toward him even though I have no information as to why he is failing to contact me. I wish he would call. I don't know what he is in the middle of, so I choose not to interrupt him.

My computer is now running, so I sign in. I surrender to putting my hands to the work in front of me. I text my daughter that I will chat with her later: *I am at work*. My phone will have to wait.

I move into work mode—the seamless transition from wife and mom to nurse occurs instantaneously, as it has for years.

Chapter Sixteen

THE FIRST THING I DO IS CHECK on my little patient. I see his name on the board. He has made it through the last two nights. I am thrilled and can't wait to see how he is doing. I hope to find good news. I would love to have something hopeful to say to his sleepless parents.

I check his chart and talk to the nurses leaving for the day. I will be able to tell them he is getting stronger; he is getting close to being able to breathe on his own. I can ease their minds as his oxygen levels are nearing normal. The doctor's note says he thinks he will be able to discharge him soon.

His parents did not imagine ever standing in this room when they saw her pregnancy test had a plus sign. They expected a perfectly healthy baby, and the worst of their problems being the adjustment to having an infant in their lives.

Since Paris, I have been running an ongoing experiment with my life. I look to see if "the perfection of the universe is, whether I like it or not." Some things are harder to find perfection in than others. This little one is testing this theory. I try to refrain from judgment and look for the lesson the universe is teaching.

Ideas like how many people are still alive because the Titanic sank have been the fruit of this examination. The Titanic sinking forced governments globally to take steps to make ocean passage safer. Thousands of people have lived full lives because such a high-profile ship sank.

Is that perfection? I don't know. The capricious nature of life leaves much of this examination in a gray area. Perfection is a high standard. Rarely does time reveal any of her secrets. It seems only by accident that a bit of the perfect becomes visible to me. Even when I have seen it, living with any definition of perfect can be difficult. I searched for another word, but none works for me as well.

One truth I have found is that the worst days of my life always seem to be the foundation for the best days of my life. Perfection? Again, I don't know. It takes time and distance to be able to see the path life has used to bring me to the place I am standing.

I live with the theory that if I see it or not, I know perfection is there. Over the years, I've had several frameworks I've used to explain my life. Of these, *perfection of the universe* has served me best. Some of the people I've shared this with have scoffed at me. When they do, I change the subject and move on. I know I, and every other person on the planet, is crazy. It's just the brand of crazy that is different.

I have now read through all my patient's charts and am ready to start my rounds. My phone pings. I have a message from both my kids: *Call me.*

I step into an empty waiting area as my phone's battery reads one percent, then goes black. I shake my head. I can't plug it in right now. I hear a patient's call button, and the professional me takes over. The call will have to wait. I have my job to do.

I see my boss. She asks how I am doing. I thank her for being empathetic. She smiles, tells me she has come to help on my floor, and then enters the room with the call light going off. I like her, I am thankful for her, and I love that she is good at her job.

I walk into the room with my little guy first. An exhausted set of parents look up as I greet them. I run through the checklist in my head of my things to make a note of while I respond to the mom's request to adjust her bed. We ask at the same time how the other is doing.

I reach into the incubator to check on my little patient's condition for myself, and only then do I turn my attention to the tired eyes and wounded hearts of his mom and dad. "He is improving," I say. "His color and breathing are strong. His lungs are sounding healthy. You have got yourselves a fighter. We will keep a close eye on him, but the doctors think he is close to being able to go home." They listen as best they can, but they are in the middle of a crisis and are barely holding on.

"How are you two?" I ask again. "Have you eaten?" I get no response. I ask the mom if she has any discomfort beyond what you would expect from giving birth. She says no. I can see the pain in her eyes. I saw what she went through. It was a traumatic birth.

I turn to her husband. "You should take time to shower. If you would like, I'll find scrubs that will fit each of you. Little things are important when big things are out of your control. Clean clothes and food will help."

He hesitates. I say, "Don't argue. I have been at this longer than you have been alive." I point him to the shower as he looks back at his wife and heads for the bathroom.

I go to a cupboard where I hide sets of scrubs. I drop a large-sized top and pants on the chair by the bed and ask her if she would like some, too. She says she is fine. She has clean clothes packed. I check her vital signs and see if she can shower. She can, and I try to persuade her to shower next, and to change into clean clothes.

I tease her gently. "The scrubs are ugly, but they will get your husband a discount in the cafeteria." We laugh. I take her hand and say, "Send him down for food and coffee from the coffee cart on the other side of the hospital. He needs something to do."

"I was thinking of sending him home to get a few things for me. Mostly to get him out of the hospital," she says. I reply, "Good idea. He needs to feel useful. He will go crazy if he sits here."

I fuss a bit over both her and her son. She is getting restless from being bed-bound; she wants to hold her son. "Your son will be fine. He is getting stronger, and we have a close eye on him. Your doctor thinks you three are not far from being sent home. Don't hesitate to call if you need me," I say as I leave the room and move to another family under my care.

The typical pattern of my day starts to take shape, and I spend the morning running all over, trying to meld the realities of an extensive hospital system and the needs of each of my patients as best I can. My work motto is: "It will all work out with a little luck, grace, patience, and my foot on its throat."

The morning hours go by in a flash when I see it is close to lunch. I check in on my little guy before I go downstairs to the cafeteria. I find all three asleep, in clean clothes, and well-fed. Two half-full cups of coffee sit on her food table.

"Good woman."

Chapter Seventeen

I PURPOSELY WALK BY A TELEVISION in the waiting area. All of the hospital rooms I was in had TVs on, but I have learned not to pay attention to them. People in the hospital want me to give them my full attention.

I am stopped in my tracks by a scrolling headline that says: *CERN may be worse than first reported, information from the research lab is sketchy. Breaking news will be shared as it becomes available.*

I check my phone. I want to call my kids. I hit the button and then remember it is dead.

A wave hits me, and I am paralyzed. I am utterly helpless. My world spins, and my mind is reeling. I have no idea what to do. I grasp for understanding as my life feels like it is unraveling.

All I can do is grab ahold of a chair and sit down.

I watch the news report and ask the man next to me if I can borrow his charger for my phone. We sit in silence, watching the TV together.

The story is nearly the same as the one four hours ago, but now authorities are alerted, and the Swiss government communication officials are speaking to reporters. They are saying words that mean nothing and are promising to provide more information as soon as it is available.

Given the nature of the work at CERN, I guess it will become public in about 35 years.

I turn to the TV across the room to watch a different channel. I wonder how every channel's news reports are, word for word, the same. Only the newscasters are different. The news reports are painfully lacking in specifics.

I need to know about my husband; I need information I can use. I recheck my phone. It has a bit of power, and I hold my breath as it boots up. I look for a message and find nothing.

I text him and then call his boss. I get voice mail. I am unable to speak, so I hang up. I will call again in a minute. I don't have enough charge in my phone to call my kids. The screen goes blank.

I forget that I was hungry. I forget about my little patient. I forget about being professional. I sit numb to the cacophony of the hospital. I can hardly think. My mind has stopped working.

I see my boss. The next thing I know, she is standing by me and I am standing by my car. She asks me several questions, then asks me if I think I can get home safely. I nod. She tells me to go home and take care of what I can. She tells me to call her if I need anything, and like a whirlwind, she closes my car door, and in a moment, she is gone.

I sit in my car and listen to the same news reports again and again before I find the strength to consider driving. I become disgusted with the radio and turn it off, then on again.

I need to hear; it makes me feel closer to my husband.

I finally have the strength to start my car and begin to make my way home. I run into traffic and am disoriented about how to get home from work. I plug my phone in and become frustrated waiting for it to come to life. When it finally does, "Home," is all I can mutter. Traffic is unbearably slow.

I am anxious, and my body feels like a coiled spring. I need to move. I honk my horn for the first time in my life. It seems to increase my anger and cause the person in front of me to flip me off. I snap and, in a rage, roar at the idiot in front of me.

The fabric of my heart is fraying, and I want to be safe at home before I implode. I think to call my children, but I can barely drive as it is, so I choose to wait.

My husband is God-knows-where, but he is absolutely in the middle of a massive global crisis. My mind is in a frenzy, forming one tragic scenario followed by another.

I am in full panic; he may be dead.

He hasn't been there long enough to know where the bathroom is—how can he already be part of a nightmare like this?

I yell at the car in front of me, looking for a way around. I am stuck. My heart is racing. My brain is bouncing. I am trying to find one thing that makes sense.

At a stop light, I rock impatiently, waiting like a drag racer for it to change.

When I look out my window at a tree in a yard, I roll down the window and become startled that everything on the street is continuing as if this is just another day.

I turn off the radio. I hear a bird singing and a dog bark.

I want to yell at them to stop. Doesn't the universe know what is happening? The birds, the dogs, the trees, nothing has changed. I am confused by how peaceful the world is, given my state of mind. I am lost in this place when the car behind me honks. The light has changed.

I release a verbal barrage that would startle a construction worker. I exhausted my vocabulary on a personal best rant, a tirade which was remarkably satisfying while I was doing it, and ineffective once I stopped.

I try to stop and think about what else I can do. *Who can I call?*

I remember not leaving a message for his boss. I call to get his voice mail again. I ask him to call me, hang up, and I let loose with another shorter, but equally toxic barrage.

What else can I do?

Why doesn't my husband call me?

I think to call my kids, but I need to regain my senses before I do that. I'm almost home.

The light turns red again; I haven't moved. I am having

trouble concentrating, and I can't decide which one of my kids to call first. This only compounds my anxiety. I should not be driving.

I don't remember how I made it home. I turn into my driveway, and the next thing I know, I'm standing in my kitchen. Yesterday this was my sanctuary. Today, it feels like a prison.

I check my phone. Nothing. I am a mess. My dog is barking. She never barks. I feel trapped. I'm a pacer. In a panic, I move like a cat in the zoo. I'm in and out of every room of my house. I rush around, trying to find a way to change this new reality with my willpower.

I keep opening, looking in, and then closing the refrigerator door. I'm in full panic mode.

What do I do?

My dog is pacing with me. Her tail is not moving, and her pace perfectly matches mine. She knows I am in trouble.

On my third lap around the house, I see the light flashing on an old answering machine connected to the landline my husband kept for our parents to contact us. It is the single phone number that is universally remembered by my family. My husband was too sentimental to cancel it. I think he hoped it would ring one more time.

I had forgotten we still have it. I press the button on the machine and hear my husband's voice. My husband is not a prankster, but what he said next made me wish he was. The dog sits and stares when she hears my husband's voice.

"God, I hope you get this. My phone is dead, and I can't

remember your cell phone number, I did remember this one. I don't have much time, so please listen. The issues at CERN are far worse than the media is reporting. The Collider was expected to make micro black holes for nanoseconds. It has, however, created a feedback loop that has formed a stable black hole. It is growing and will most certainly swallow the Earth. No matter what you hear to the contrary, this is going to happen. We have no way to stop it. My guess is it will take a few days."

"As the electromagnetic energy increases, it will first cause a total power blackout in Europe. It will eventually shut down the power grids everywhere in the world: no power, no phones, no modern anything. Cell phones and the internet will stop working soon. Pull out the camping gear."

"The black hole will continue to grow. It is expanding slowly right now. It will eventually consume everything. I have seen it through a...let's say, microscope. It is remarkable. It looks like... It is far different than anything I imagined. It is..."

He hesitates as I hear words catch in his throat. "Know that I love you and that I love the kids." Choking up, he struggles to continue. "I will never see you again. I love you more than you can know. I love the kids. Please tell them I love them." He pauses for a second and says, "Thank you for a hell of a ride. Be sure to..."

He is cut off. His message to me ends.

I'm not sure when, but I am sitting on the floor. My brain is swirling.

My husband wants me to pass on his love to my children because the world is coming to an end.

I wonder where the camping gear is. I shout, "Where is the fucking camping gear?"

My mind is racing with questions. "Be sure to what?" I scream. "Be sure to what?"

I hit *69 and see if I can't get him on the same line. No ring. I can hear no noise on the line of any kind.

Shit.

I try to call again. Then I try his cell phone.

It is silent.

Is he gone?

I remember that the sleeping bags are in the closet in the den.

I find myself in a place beyond panic. I am confused because the life I have come to expect has stopped. I have no basis of reference from which to find my bearing or to form a rational plan.

I play the message again and again. Repetition allows me to hear a few sets of words: "A black hole that will most certainly swallow the Earth. It will take a couple of days. Find the camping gear."

What the hell does that mean?

I call his number again. Nothing.

I yell at my phone, "Work, damn it. I need you to work." I try it again. Nothing.

I can't stand to pace because my legs are frozen. My mind is looking for a single thing that makes sense.

My body is shutting down when I remember the rest of the camping gear is in the garage.

I am lost and trying to find anything to hold onto. My chest is tight. My fists are clenched. My heart is pounding.

I have forgotten how to breathe when my dog licks my face. She startles me. I focus on her as she does it again.

Immediately I am back in my body. The suddenness startles me. I find I am holding on to her as if my life depends on it. "What do I do?" I bawl, as she squirms away. "What do I do?"

I stand and check for my phone. I need to talk to my husband. My mind is in overload, and my body is frozen in terror. I am now standing, but I am unable to move. I feel the air fill my lungs as my mind is slowly starting to form one coherent thought.

My kids.

I forgot to call my kids.

I grab the old phone receiver and realize I have no idea of either of their numbers. I hear the phone's tone change from dial tone to a busy signal. It has been forever since I have heard these sounds. For a flash, I am a teenager again when the phone was a lifeline. The busy signal is both familiar and foreign. My legs give out, and I crumple to the ground.

I place the receiver on the hook and cry uncontrollably.

What the hell am I going to do?

My dog grabs my arm and tugs me. I find my feet and rush around like a crazy woman looking for my phone. I am lost in my own space. I hear my dog bark and follow the sound. Finally, I see she is sitting next to it.

"Oh my God, I love you," I shout as I make my way to her. I take a deep breath and look for the number while holding on to my dog. Fumbling, I can't seem to find my daughter.

I am nearing tears when I realize I can ask my phone. I mutter for my phone to call my daughter. It asks me if I want to call a local pizza place.

I snarl as I am unable to form a word.

I force myself to focus and find my daughter's contact information. It rings, and she immediately picks up. She starts speaking so fast I can't understand a word she is saying.

I realize I am talking as well. I try, but can't understand her through her tears.

The line goes silent. I freeze. I can't take much more of this. I shout, "Are you there?" Then I hear a clicking noise.

I am confused when I hear my husband's voice. My mind is racing, trying to understand how is it he is at my daughter's house.

I go to speak when I hear him call me *Mom*, and the reality of the situation causes me to become a bit more coherent. She must have three-way dialed my son.

The thread I'm grasping onto is barely holding me.

They are both physicists, and I hope they can help me understand anything about what is going on. We all start to talk at once. It is chaos.

The three of us are babbling incoherently, each of us with too much to say. My children stop when they hear me say I have heard from their dad and am going to play the message he left.

The line quiets. I hit start and hear: "God I hope you get this." I let the whole message play. When the message finished, I ask, "What do either of you make of that?"

I have snapped. Hearing it again has made me become hysterical, and it takes some time for me to regain enough composure to hear what my kids are saying. I finally understand they are asking me to play it again.

When it finishes, I ask, "Can either of you help me understand?"

My daughter says she has heard the same thing, that from what she knows, nothing can be done to stop it. I am barely able to hold my head together. I am lost trying to grasp what she is saying.

My son begins to speak when the line goes dead.

I shout, but they are gone.

I redial. Nothing.

Text. Call. Nothing.

I try again and again. Nothing.

"I really need you to work right now!" I shout at my phone. "I need to hear what my son was saying. I need to tell my kids I love them. Work, damn it!" I yell at my phone to work. I plead with it. "Please!"

I try it again. Nothing.

I try the landline. It is working. I dial both numbers and get nothing from the other end.

My son and daughter, my grand-children, my husband are gone.

I am alone, standing in stunned silence, and try to find anything I can hold onto as the world spins beneath my feet. I try to steady myself but find nothing but air.

I am aware that I am falling, but I am barely conscious until I feel my head and shoulder hit the floor. My ears ring, and the pain is enough to cause me to black out.

I awaken on the floor, badly shaken. I had thought I was able to deal with any crisis. I'm not even close to being ready for this. I had no idea how to move, much less how to go forward from here.

I am not sure what forward even means.

I remember loaning the camping chairs to my neighbor.

I try to sit up but fall backward again. I am crying uncontrollably and realize I am staring at my now-useless cell phone.

"Camp chairs, I don't give a crap about camp chairs!"

My neck is killing me. My shoulder is throbbing.

My husband is gone. My kids are gone. I can't breathe.

I can't think. I can't move. I can only stay still.

I cry out, "Help me."

I wait, knowing I am all alone.

Alone sucks.

Chapter Eighteen

MY MIND RACES AS I TRY in vain to turn back time. I am completely helpless.

I try to call them again, knowing I am sending a message into the void.

I will never hear my children's voices again.

Never hear my grandchildren.

Never hear my husband.

I sit and try to let reality sink in. I am fighting to try to make this moment align with my life as it was yesterday. Full of the people I love.

Feeling the loss of them overwhelms this fantasy.

I didn't get to say *I love you* to any of them. I didn't get to say anything but gibberish, and now I am powerless to do anything.

I trusted technology to do what it trained me to do. I believed that whenever I wanted, I could push a button that would connect me to anyone, anywhere. I assumed that my phone was always going to work.

I stare at it and see I texted the word *Help* to my husband. I am astounded by how feeble, how powerless, how abandoned I feel.

A wave of regret hits me. Regret for all the hours that I had let pass before I called.

I wish for one hour back, one where I could embrace my children and share my love with them. I picture my family trying to contact me, feeling the same frustration, the same betrayal, the same void.

How is it that I don't get to say goodbye?

I have had all day today where I worried about my work, about intruding on them at their job, about scaring them for no reason. They hadn't done the same, as my phone shows numerous attempts at contact from them.

I tell myself that I didn't hear a single one because my phone was dead. I don't forgive myself. I should have done something more.

I am too sad to cry. I sit, feeling like an absolute failure.

I look up at a municipal court coffee mug my husband got as swag at a local government gathering that included the college. All I see is *It's Muni Court: Everything is Just Fines*. I gasp like I've been kicked in the stomach.

Everything is not fine. My kids are gone.

How will anything be right again?

I am an idiot. I did nothing to contact them until hearing my husband's message. I didn't reach out to them in trust, as adults. I chose to treat them like children.

I didn't call because I assumed I had all the time in the world. I have always been able to contact my kids whenever I wanted. Well, now I want to more than anything, and I sit holding a useless screen.

I break down even further, feeling loss and love mingle in equal parts. My heart breaks as my mind explodes.

My aloneness is palatable. I have no husband and no kids.

I have me, and I'm sitting on the floor. I feel desperate, and out of habit, I look at my phone again. Nothing.

That a tiny screen represents my hope makes me snarl at myself. *Stupid.* All my messages are unsent. They sit, waiting for a massive unseen system to work again.

I know it won't, but my optimism will hear none of it. I cling to hope for no other reason than it is all I have. *I'll try again in five minutes* goes through my head.

My muscles no longer work as the battle in my head rages. Something about five minutes brings me comfort for a second, then fails like a dam holding back a flood.

I refuse to move. I sit, and over and over, I replay each moment of my last phone call with my kids. I stay still, knowing when I shift, the bubble of this moment will be lost.

Tears start rolling down my face. I gasp for air.

I feel my loved ones slipping further away, no matter how tightly I try to hold on.

I am lying on the floor, trapped between hope and reality. I look for a way back, but I know that the future has other plans, and going backward is never one of them.

The universe shoves me into my new space when I notice my dog tugging at my arm. She knows I need to move. Our eyes lock; she is afraid for me. I don't budge.

She barks, trying to get me to my feet. I know she is guiding me into my new life; one I'm afraid will be stone quiet. Empty. Unloved.

I sigh, knowing my life will continue. I have no control over anything. I am afraid of how this version of life will go. She tugs on me, and I yell at her to go away. "Why did you bark? Why did you tug on me? Why didn't you leave me alone?"

Alone? What the hell is wrong with me? I am alone, and I am yelling at the universe for more. She comes over and sits eye to eye with me. Reality has found me, and there is no going back.

I put my hand on her and remembered the first day my daughter brought her home. She was tiny and frightened. Her eyes are looking like they looked back then. The look she has must be close to the look I have. Terror.

As a puppy, she wailed for the safety of her mom. Her longing for yesterday with her six siblings made my heart ache. She was feeling lost, scared, and alone. She howled for a life that was no more. She cried and moaned for love that was too far away to hear. I was all she had. We were falling in love, me and my little girl. We sat together all night. I fed her warm milk, we played, and she fell asleep on my chest.

I called into work on Monday so I could be with her for one more day. Somewhere in the middle of our first night together, she became my dog. We seem to be able to read each other's mind ever since. She looks at me and says in the way you do when you have no idea what to say, "We will be fine."

I stare at her, knowing she doesn't believe this to be true. I pull her close; we are face to face. We lock eyes. We are jumpy, startled by every single thing. We wonder, "What can we do right now?" She hugs me, and I hug her back. She softens in my arms, her being there makes me feel less alone and less scared. She says, "Let's go have bacon, some coffee, and a walk."

I can't hear any of it and say, "I'm alone."

She pauses and looks at me. "You are not alone. You have me. Your family, they all love you. I love you, and you love all of us. We are bigger than a black hole." I hug her tighter. She melts into my embrace. "We will be fine," she says, trying to mean it. "Let's go eat something and see what else might be fun to do next."

I am still in a panic, but now I have a purpose. I can breathe; I begin to walk, moving like I am in a dream. I am fresh out of any other ideas. How am I supposed to respond to the ending of the world? Not me, or all people, but the whole damn thing is going away.

That thought is too much, and I decide to try to take my first steps into this life when the magnitude of everything I love disappearing finds me. I try to ride it out, but I am without direction. I don't know where up is. I am thankful that I have bacon frying on the stove, but can't remember starting it. My next actions are simple because simple is all I have.

I look out the window. *Disappear.* I turn it around in my mind. *To make not appear.* I stand at my window. It looks exactly as it always has. My mind is lost and searching. I move to my front window but see nothing out of order. How can all of this go away? My mind won't let go, and it can't move forward.

I have no way of making any sense of this. I remember David Copperfield making massive objects disappear. Why am I thinking about David Copperfield? I suddenly laugh out loud. The dog startles; this was not what she expected from me next.

I look at her and say out loud, "I do have another idea. I think you are going to like this." I walk to the wine cellar and announce to her, "It is time for you to try a great bottle of wine." I open the cupboard and take a crystal bowl and a wine glass. I pour a bowl and glass of Insignia. I set the bowl in front of her and clink my glass. She looks curious and inhales deeply.

I tell her the nose of a wine is essential. It is like a first kiss. It tells you everything you need to know. She sniffs lightly, waits, then deeply inhales the bouquet. Finally, satisfied with the nose, she drinks. She rolls it on her tongue, then swallows. She is a natural connoisseur.

We toast. "No matter what comes next, we have great wine." She waits for me to drink, then she follows. She laps at her wine with enthusiasm; her tail is wagging like mad. We laugh and drink until the bacon is crisp.

I divided the bacon up and put half in her food bowl. We sit to eat when I notice again that outside the birds are singing. The world is ending, and the birds are singing. I am not sure why I keep finding this to be so odd. Life always goes on, my dog says. She then finishes her first glass of wine and asks for more. I divvy up the rest of the bottle.

I finish my food, and for the first time, I have a chance to relax a bit and think clearly. I'm alone with the knowledge that the world is likely coming to an end.

CHAPTER NINETEEN

WHAT DO I DO WITH THAT? Who do I tell? How do I tell them? Should I tell them? What the hell do I do now?

I imagine the interaction: "Hi, we have been neighbors for years and never really talked. My husband is a physicist, and he told me the end of the world is coming in a couple of days. I was wondering if you would like to have dinner tonight and listen to the message on my answering machine."

I am stunned. What the hell? *What the hell?! WHAT THE HELL?!!* How did I get here? I did everything I was supposed to do.

"What the hell do I do now?" I ask my dog. She looks at me like she is ready for a nap. "I need a plan. I like plans, and right now, I have none." I pace around; she wags her tail amused by me. Relax and drink some wine, she says.

I think through my dilemma about telling people and find I am agitated at all the fanatics that have proclaimed the end of the world. They were citing nonsense and speculation. I have facts. Their ravings about repentance and doom will make my credibility that much harder to earn.

I picture myself wearing an *END IS NEAR!!!* sandwich board and watching people trying not to make eye contact with me; or better yet, they give me a dollar and move away as quickly as they can.

Do I tell people what I know, or do I sit at my table, eating bacon and drinking wine with my dog? Bacon and wine are easily winning this debate question. My initial reaction behind me, I weigh the situation more heavily. I ask myself if I would want to know, or would I prefer to be going along with my day and have it end? I think I would want to know.

I need to think about it more. I grab the dog's leash. Walking always helps me think through problems. Can the end of everything be defined by a word as ubiquitous as a *problem?* I don't think so, but right now problem is as good a word as any.

My dog sees the leash and hesitates between walking toward me and finishing the last bit of wine from her bowl. She decides, finishes her wine, and checks again, making sure it is empty. Only then does she join me. I reach to put on her leash. She steps away and looks up at me for a second. Her eyes seem a little different, but I chalk it up to my crying for hours, or that she is drunk. I move to put it on her again, and she backs away a bit. We look at each other. She then stands still and lets me fasten the lead.

I take one step across my kitchen as the full burden of what I know falls upon me. I feel anger rising in me. My jaw tightens as the thought that everything is doomed begins to force its way into my reality. I think about being swallowed by a black hole and can find nothing in my experience to relate to it. The dog has stopped and is watching me. Her eyes grow stronger as she tugs on the leash, pulling me toward the door.

My mind hits a crossroad, and I decide to try a strategy taught me by my grandmother—prayer. I close my eyes and ask God to stop this. It is the strangest prayer I have ever uttered. I wait. Then I check my phone. It is still not connected to any service. Apparently, I will have as much success asking for this miracle as I did when asking for help on a high school chemistry exam.

I try again, thinking that perhaps my appeal was not worthy. I try to strengthen my earnest plea by adding *Please*. I wait. I try not to look at my phone as a sign of faith. I quickly break and check. Nothing too much happens except I am calmer as I chuckle at my effort. I thank God for the diversion and follow the tugging on my wrist.

All these years living with my husband and I am not sure what a black hole is. I think it is funny that God would take Stephen Hawking a year before a black hole destroys the planet. It seems Stephen, more than anyone, should have been able to see its fury up close. He had thought about them for more than thirty years. He has written books about them, given lectures about them, and has created mathematics to explain them.

I had heard him speak about black holes and his theories of time on three occasions. I wish I would have paid more attention. His passion was apparent. It strikes me as unfair that I, who care nothing about this event, will get to experience one firsthand. "God irony" always makes me laugh.

I feel a tug on my arm as my now-impatient dog is pulling me toward the door. The crisp night air replaces my thoughts about Mr. Hawking. I begin to walk across my street. The night air makes me feel better. I am pleased to see no one for me to talk to.

Maybe God was listening. I say thanks. Even though nothing in my reality has changed, a crisp fall night has plenty of magic. I feel grateful for the perfect night for a walk.

I am still working on if I will share what I know, and if I decide to, how to do it. I'll take a lap around the park and think about my new role as the messenger of doom. I think through everything I have read on being the one chosen to tell people that their world is coming to an end.

I think back to Sunday school and realize the unfairness of my situation. Moses had tablets of stone written by the finger of God. I have a phone message. Clear proof that technology doesn't improve everything.

I laugh as I think of the situation in which I find myself. How is it that I became the voice of the fates? I curse my husband.

Walking has always helped me figure out solutions to many of my day-to-day dilemmas in the past. To solve this one, I will need to take a very, very long walk. I chuckle when my dog reminds me that I don't have that kind of time.

Then my dog says, *Noah*.

Noah? Then her meaning hits me.

Noah is the only person that we know of that has shared my dilemma. I muse to myself that I know what it feels like to be a Noah the day before he starts building an ark in his front yard. Thinking I know the truth, but not knowing if it is true. What if it doesn't rain? What if I tell the neighbors about global destruction in a week or so, and it doesn't happen? Will they think less of me?

I shake my head and steel my spine. I scold myself for driving myself crazy, as the ridiculousness of this situation swirls in my mind. I wish this weren't happening. I know, like Noah knew, neither of us was ready for the task.

Noah had at least two advantages over me and my current impasse. While waiting to see if animals do begin to appear in pairs, he could always tell his neighbors he was building a funky house. He could tell those who inquired that he has a passion for boats, and wants to live on one. He, however, is a farmer, and moving to the water would be impractical. He could say to his wife's chagrin; he started the work as a lark. Thinking further, he had another option they could use to explain the behemoth structure being erected in the neighborhood. I chuckle thinking about the HOA board's reaction to this blatant violation.

If the first explanation seems too unreasonable, he could say that the ark was a boat for Mediterranean vacations that had gotten out of hand. He could justify his project by saying that he had bought plans out of impulse and started work without doing much research. Who knew 300 cubits was so big? He could rent it out as a party boat if it never rained.

He had years. I have no such luxury. I get to tell people that their life has a few more days. My husband, not God, said so. Another point for Noah. My proof is a phone message on a cassette tape from a man they have never met, captured by a twenty-year-old answering machine. To hear it, they would have to accompany the crazy lady back to her house as I did not record it on my phone. My credibility might be an issue.

I can see the recipients of my news, putting themselves between their children and me and slowly backing away. They will mumble "Thanks" as they guide themselves and their loved ones far away from me.

I feel a tug on the leash. Distracted by my insanity, I have lost track of where I am and where I am going.

CHAPTER TWENTY

MY DOG KNOWS HER ROUTE and heads to her favorite part of the park, the area that allows her to run free. I am not paying attention and continue to follow her. I notice too late she is heading straight toward a couple standing by a picnic table with a stroller and their dog.

I regain myself and hear the husband say, "Switzerland…" I continue to be pulled by my dog until both faces turn to look at me. It is too late not to engage them. My dog's tail is wagging excitedly upon greeting her canine counterpart. The little brat looks up at me and smiles; she so enjoys pushing me out of my comfort zone.

Reluctantly, I take the last few steps into their circle, I look down and smile at their baby in the stroller. I see little feet bobbing, and for an instant, I feel joy. Then too many thoughts hit my head. I cannot and will not process the fortunes of this child. His little toes are making the scale of this reality too large and too real.

Instead, I smile. I notice for the first time that infants in our society greet the world with their feet. This little one, with one shoe on and the other foot bare, simultaneously makes me smile and sad.

I stop my train of thought again. I stare down at the baby and am afraid to hear what the next words to enter my mind will be. It is about how cute those little toes are, and I am thankful.

I regain focus as a muffled voice behind the stroller says a set of words, and then, "Isn't your husband there right now?" I say "yes" before I stop to think. The second I answer, I realize I am about to be asked a hundred questions. Questions for which I have no answers. Do I share what I know or not?

I recognize the woman. She works in the physics department at the university with my husband. I am ready to say hello when she says, "The last I heard from my friends at CERN is that the collider is out of control and that the formation of a sustainable black hole is imminent. Have you heard anything?"

I am startled at first by her abruptness, but more, I am relieved that I am not alone. Like all professional endeavors, the physics world has less than seven degrees of separation. I realize that thousands of people work at, or in support of, the collider—so of course, I am not the only person to know.

My thoughts stop as I sigh in relief. I no longer have to hide a secret. I am no longer Noah. I look up from the baby, while my heart slows and my body lightens as my imagined burden dissipates. I am pleased that I don't have to live with any of the "she's a lunatic" judgments I had feared.

"My husband left me a message saying the same thing. I can't contact him. He was mid-message when the connection ended on a voice mail he was leaving. You probably know more than I do. Have you heard anything about my husband?" She looks at me and measures what she is about to say.

Looking me squarely in the eyes, she shakes her head *no*. I don't believe her.

She picks up her baby and says, "As a student, I worked on the collider. I was there during the planning phase, and I know the potential for a major catastrophe is minuscule. I also know that people I have known for years are telling me the situation is critical. The experts are at a loss to explain what has happened or how to stop the reaction."

I nod. "I can add the black hole has formed; my husband in his message said he saw it through a microscope of sorts and that it is growing." I see her head jerk slightly, she swallows hard, looks down at her baby, and then takes a series of deep breaths.

She is fighting tears as she sits at the picnic table with her daughter. She holds her close and cries. The couple says nothing as they try to come to grips with the enormity of this new reality. I think of my children when they were infants, and we cry together.

This is an unexpected punch in the face brought about by baby toes. Seeing her hold her son makes me wish I could hold mine.

We then stare at each other in disbelief. I turn away as the pain of looking at her child becomes too much to bear. We lose ourselves and tears engulf us again. It feels good not to be alone, even though what we are sharing is horrifying. I fight against the realization of what the end means. I want to stay composed because I hate crying. It messes with my body and gives me a headache.

I recover slightly quicker than they do and stand quietly, waiting to hear the rest of what she is thinking. "Can you call or text?" I am shocked that this is the first thing she asks. I shake my head no, and suddenly, I feel alone again. I wait for another question, but neither she nor her husband is in a place to form thoughts that they can speak or want to share.

I ask, "Who else knows?"

The professor dries her eyes and says, "The people I work with do. I think the news is spreading, but I haven't seen or heard the latest broadcasts. We had to stop watching it," she says, glancing at her daughter. "At work, we discussed if people would want to know. Is it better to meet your fate with your eyes open or closed?"

"Open," I say. They both nod in agreement.

She says, "Some made a good argument for closed, but I think that option has sailed."

She gulps, and her brusque nature returns when she says, "The electrical grid is not far behind the phone system. We decided that people not knowing would cause a greater panic than if everyone was informed."

I respond, "I know my husband, and I am still having trouble believing his story. I am having a hard time imagining that the world is going to come to an end. He understands how and why this is happening better than anyone. Regardless of this, I can't fully believe it."

In mid-sentence, I startle as I don't feel my dog, and look around to see where she has wandered. When did I drop her leash?

I forget our conversation, and I whistle and call as I see the two staring at me. I return my gaze to them, and say, "Sorry." Still looking for my dog. I continue, "I would rather know and be able to face what is coming with my eyes wide open. Not cowering in fear, but being active and alive for my last days." They weakly smile, and we stand in silence.

I look at them both and ask, "What do we do now?"

The physicist sighs. "No one and nothing can save us. I am going to spend my time with these two." she says as she kisses her baby and turns her back mostly to me.

Her husband agrees and then suggests that the park should become the central meeting and information distribution point. All of our houses face the park. A fire on the baseball diamond would bring out our curious neighbors.

"We can all share what we know and support each other through what comes next. We can decide if we want to share resources and talents and do what we can to make the time we have left as comfortable and safe as possible."

I nod in agreement, still trying to ingest her news. "Good idea. What are you two going to do now?"

"Nothing," he says, "It's a beautiful night, and we are going to enjoy it." He reaches for his son, and I watch her mother turn her shoulder to him, too, and break down in tears as she kisses her child on the forehead.

I don't say *goodnight* or *thank you*, but turn and start heading for home. I think to myself that I have things I need to put in order before I can give my attention to others. My mind is numb, but I am relieved that I am no longer Noah.

I whistle again and hear my dog running to join me. I glance back to see them both sitting motionless with the baby now between them. I can hear them both crying. I continue home.

Nursing has taught me about human nature and how people react in a crisis. I am finding out how I react. I realize I have been a bystander in crisis for years. I watch as the body initially mends, but I am not there a week, or month, or a year later. I don't get to see the shattered pieces of their lives, or how well the shards go back together. I am there for a small window. We meet at the beginning of the trauma. Work is how I intersect with each of the thousands of lives that have impacted mine. As a nurse, at the hospital, they are more their injury than a complete person.

They then start to remake their lives, and how they repair themselves is something I never know. I don't see the strength it takes to face another day in bed, fifteen days after the accident, trapped in a body that is no longer a friend. I am not awake at 3:18 a.m. pondering how many unknowns still lay ahead. I have not been the one sitting in the dark fighting a private war with a reality they didn't plan to live. A fight that I am finding happens primarily alone. The battles are brutal, with trials as intense as the redefining of your self-worth inside a society that has no time to spare for the broken you. You alone to help yourself when the reality of the struggle and pain take over.

Knowing that my life will never be the same is inescapable. For me, this is not a global crisis. It's me coming to grips that the illusion I created that is no longer sustainable, and my life must now reflect what is ahead of me.

Every person, every plant, everything will face its end.

I turn to ask one more question, "How long do you think we have?"

She looks up, "Given that the hole has formed, I would say no more than three days. I would guess it is more like two."

Seventy-two hours? I have, at most, seventy-two hours to live.

I turn away because I can't watch them together anymore. I have heard doctors tell a patient's family that their loved one would not make it through the night. I think of when they were wrong, then recognize how often they were right. I have never been on the receiving end of such news. I try to resist, but I have to ask her one more thing.

"Do you agree with my husband that this is inevitable?"

"I have known your husband's work for twenty years and moved to the university in the hopes that I could work with him. If he says he saw it, he saw it. If he saw it and it is growing, then yes, I would agree. No one on Earth is more credible on this subject than him."

CHAPTER TWENTY-ONE

I NOD AND LET the news find me. I breathe in the night. My dog walks under my hand. I feel her fur, and I follow. I am not sure what will happen next, but I know I will need food, water, and shelter at a minimum. I have no control over anything, but for my peace of mind, I need to do an inventory of essentials.

Do I have enough for three days?

I have no idea what the next three days will be like and how people will react. Will peace take over as striving for a tomorrow becomes pointless, or will the worst of human nature take over? My guess is both will combine, but I have no way to predict how it will be. I wonder if thinking in terms of having only three days is useful. It doesn't matter, as a clock has started in my head that I am sure I will not be able to turn off.

As I get closer to home, I know I have plenty of supplies to last three days, but I need to see, to touch what I have. I plan to lock it away so that I can continue to live in the artifice that I'm safe. I feel a growl, a rawness in life that I have not known.

My dog looks at me with the slightest snarl on her lip. I curl my lip to see how it feels. It feels good.

I wonder if my eyes are changing as fear and freedom are mixing inside me, making me into something new. I step forward and stroke her back, and she startles and snaps at me. I feel the hair on my neck rise as I growl back. I drop the leash and ball my fists. We lock eyes.

She moves a step back and crouches to pounce, then in a second, her eyes clear, and she stares up, as surprised by my reaction as to her own. She sets her feet, glaring at each other freezes us. I am ready to erupt; then, her tail begins to wag. My fists stay balled.

She relaxes and is soon back to being excited by whatever comes next. I am still feeling primal rage. She has moved on, and I feel a snarl coursing through me for much longer. I still want to fight. To roll in the dirt with her and see who is alpha. I watch her walk away, tail wagging. I let go as my need to prove dominance subsides.

I have never felt like this before.

She moves forward without a hint of a grudge. The thing I love most about dogs is that they always seem to be sure that the very next thing that happens will be the best thing they have ever seen. They are delighted by life, and their joy is infectious.

Her tail is wagging. I am still full of adrenalin and fury. I breathe deeply and try to settle back into my usual self.

After the last few minutes, I more than ever wish I could share her joy for life. I decide to let go and be like her. I wiggle my butt and howl into the night. My dog barks and shakes her head, then begins to bounce around me. I laugh and bounce around her. I remove the leash she is dragging, and we walk together. She is thinking about play, and to my delight so am I.

Then, I start thinking about how little time I have left. Has time stopped, or is it running faster? She looks at me and then quickens her pace for home.

How was time measured by people who lived 10,000 years ago? Did they even care? As I think, I understand I have no idea what time is. *Time is money* finds its way into my mind, and my brain is off to the races.

Yesterday, time and money were vital external forces in everyone's lives, but now they are irrelevant. The more I think, the more I am sure that time and money are business constructs. Business. Business is pointless now, too.

With time and money becoming meaningless, for the first time in my life, no for the first time ever, all of the people on the Earth are on a genuinely equal footing. No one has a way out or an advantage.

All of us have, at most, three more sunrises. I stop my next thought, deeming myself a nerd.

What the hell does it matter? My stomach rumbles, and although time and money may be obsolete, hunger is not. I am famished, and I have incredible food at home. As I walk, my intellect starts again trying to understand what is happening and, more importantly, what to do with the days I hope I have left?

What am I going to do? Then I am struck; whatever I choose. I don't have one idea about tomorrow. I know everything has changed. Tomorrow has always been a mystery, one of the great wild cards in life. What tomorrow will bring is still a mystery, but how many tomorrows I now have isn't. I have the answer to one of life's unanswerable questions.

I chuckle when my inner voice says it is the same as the number of licks it takes to get to the Tootsie Roll center of a Tootsie Pop: three. I shake my head and hear an old college roommate saying, "Living inside your head must be tiring."

What is worthy of my tomorrow is a question I have pondered for years. I remember talking about what is life, and love, and time in my dorm room with my friends when we had all gotten way too stoned. I now have every reason to believe that the Earth will soon be gone. Humanity is free, as free as my dog, the squirrels, the birds.

What is worthy of my tomorrow?

I then question myself, asking if this means war, poverty, crime, and wanting have stopped. No tomorrow means that nothing needs to be gained. Nothing needs to be hoarded. Nothing needs to be protected. Everyone having only a few hours to live renders moot our entire social system which is designed to regulate human interaction.

What will happen next? I don't know, and right now, I don't

care. I am free! I spin on my heels and laugh out loud. The sight of it delights my dog.

I am suddenly glad we took that loan to go to Spain last year. I still have many great bottles of wine from that trip. I will open one when I get home. I was saving them, but now nothing that includes being ready for tomorrow matters. The thought of that makes me skip with delight. I haven't skipped in years; it feels great.

I am free from ego and acquisition because it doesn't matter. All of us face the same fate. There is no running away because there is no away. I can't stand and fight, because everything is about to disappear. I am relieved from panic, as this is turning into the next great adventure of my life.

I want to explore it. There is no fun in turning away.

This is my eight seconds on the back of the bull, and I want my last ride to be incredible.

CHAPTER TWENTY-TWO

I AM FREER THAN I HAVE EVER BEEN. I am ecstatic in not having to be responsible for the first time since I was six years old. I loved being responsible for my family. I feel despair for my kids and husband; all are too far away. Joy and grief seem to be like a braided knot. One is not far from the other. I feel a wave of loneliness and sadness wash away my joy. I have no one to play with. I then smile because I have my dog.

I feel the next wave of grief hit, but I know that the pain goes deeper than that. I stop on my lawn and open my heart. I see a perfect rose, and I savor its beauty, knowing this joy will be accompanied by the arrival of ever-deepening waves of despair. I force my feet to keep moving. Right foot…left foot. I make it to my front porch when a wave of love for my family overtakes my pain, and I begin to cry hysterically. This merry-go-round is exhausting.

I remember the day my mom planted that bush. We had such a great day. It was one of the last days the woman I love so much was able to garden. I smell the rose. I will never see those who I love most ever again—no goodbyes or hugs, nothing but silence and a heart that is about to explode with grief.

I shout into the nothingness, demanding an explanation. It is silent in reply.

How grateful I am for this pain. I am blessed that love has frozen me in my tracks, and has brought me face to face with itself. I can't breathe, or see, or moan. I can't do anything but feel wave after wave of love and loss as it tumbles me like the surf of the ocean. I can't do anything, as the love I have for everything fills me. I smell the rose again, and its beauty drops me to my knees.

Overwhelmed by several emotions, I am stripped from my body. All that I love seems to have gathered around me. Time and distance are irrelevant. I am spun. I intend to let go and let it take me where it will.

Right then, my dog puts her nose on my face. Tears turn to laughter, then back to tears again. My heart is naked, and in front of me is my dog's face. She has concern in her eyes as she rubs against me. I hug her with all my might. I am so thankful she is here. She lets out a small howl and squirms away from me. I tell her I am sorry and cry even louder.

We sit on the stoop; I am dumbfounded by everything that

is happening. How the hell did we get here?

My dog sits still, not even her tail is moving. A parade that is my life passes in front of me. I had this happen both times I lost control of a car. I am surprised it is happening now. I am a shattered mess, baring my heart to the universe. I say "I love you" and "thank you" to each and everything I can think of that has taught me a fuller understanding of myself.

I see people, places, and things I had long forgotten. As they arise in my consciousness, they are letting me see how their touch shaped my soul. I understand people who had hurt me, and whom I hurt. Times in my life I could not have despised more are taking their turn to show me they taught me to love, too. This love formed this version of me.

Time and distance disappear as I lay beside the rose bush and sob. I am grateful for my life and all the things that have shaped it.

I do not know how long it took to regain myself. I wipe my nose on my shirt and wait to see if another wave is coming; it is grueling. I want it to stop, but I don't. Grief and love are dancing with me. I have no choice but to let them.

My hair and clothes are a mess, but I feel better. The universe decides to return me to my body. I feel my dog's nose against my cheek, then her fur in my hands.

I sit up. "Oh, my God," I cry; my strength is gone, my body purged. I gulp the air, thankful for this connecting point. I feel her, and am elated she is here.

I have taken the earth under my feet for granted. As my feet are finding ground, I am thankful for Gaia in a way I have never been. I steady myself, realizing how loved I am. I put my hands in my pocket, hoping to find a tissue. I have two.

From here, each step, each tic of the clock, becomes more and more precious. I have only a few hours left. I walk inside my home, drinking in my world, savoring it. This place is delicious.

As I pass through the door, I hear the end of a newscast reporting that the power grid in Europe has collapsed. I had forgotten to turn the television off. I stand still and listen, but it is all nonsense to me. I understand the words, but they seem to be coming from another reality. One where I no longer live. They are talking like we are preparing for a hurricane or a blizzard. The newscaster is talking about steps to take to protect yourself. I shake my head.

In my stupor, I walk over to turn it off. Endorphins are coursing through my body. I am not thinking clearly. "Experts are working to stop this. What can we do to be ready for it? We will tell you how in fifteen minutes." This was the last thing I hear some man on the TV say before I hit the power button to shut it off. I can't process another sentence. I laugh at how ridiculous that set of words is.

I am okay with what I know. I stand in the quiet and start to plan. I thank my husband for the heads-up and turn my attention to opening the windows, taking off my shoes, changing clothes, and finally washing off the very last application of makeup I will ever put on my face. I have both a hundred directions to go and none. I feel so lost, then ask myself if that is true.

I look at myself in the mirror and am having trouble placing who I am. The face looking back is beautiful. I smile as a wave of raw emotion overcomes me. Not joy or fear, not anything with a name, just emotion hits me. I grab the counter to steady myself. Another wave hits, then another, even harder. I have no choice but to let it. It feels like a purging as I begin to accept that I, my family, everything, absolutely everything, has been given a death sentence.

I breathe deeply and narrow my direction to one. I look down at my dog. *A death sentence calls for a proper last meal.* I know it is dark, but nurses, warriors, and cops have similar humor. We bear witness to the worst that people and nature can do. We have to protect our hearts. Using black humor is one of our favorite tools.

She is looking at me when I ask, "Number 577523, what do you want for your last meal." She wags her tail and says *ice cream*. I frown as I know the freezer is empty of that delight, and Sweet Cow is most assuredly not an option. I apologize and ask if she would be willing to have me improvise. She puts her tail between her legs; she is teasing me about my cooking.

"Come on. I'm not that bad. Would you settle for a rare steak and a big red?" She lets out a small bark, and we laugh together. I go to get the crystal bowl and think about which wine to drink. It seems that her wine habit is quickly growing out of hand. Luckily, I have enough wine for a few months, so mine can, too.

I begin to gather my favorite foods and am working on

dinner when I start to remember some of the people I have seen die. Would I die well, I wonder. Death is like birth in that no two are alike. I have seen more than my share of both. I feel uniquely experienced in how human life begins and how we go in the end.

I have had people tell me that this was their last day, that tomorrow they would be free. Those that do this nearly always pass as they predict. I have talked to many who see and talk to deceased friends and family members that "are coming to escort me home." They chat with the unseen, then when they are ready, they cross over.

Some I have known to become quiet and then slip away when no one is looking. Others hold on waiting for someone special to arrive, holding on for one last kiss, one final goodbye. I have watched some people wrestle to stay alive, fighting until nature wins. I feel my end is coming, and I wonder what route I will take.

It being my turn strikes me as odd. I look at my hands and wonder how is it that this manifestation—me—will stop being. I'm lost in this place in my mind. I am going to die very soon. I am startled when I touch my hand on the stove. I am instantly back in my body as the pain pushes all of my thoughts out of my head.

I go to get ice, but the smell of the tenderloin getting too hot creates an urgency that overrides the burn for a second. I move the pan, and the pain creeps quickly back. I head to the bathroom for ointment and a bandage. I tend to my burn and smile as a bandage on a dime-sized wound might be the last injury I ever treat.

I hear the dog moving and wonder if, for the first time in her life, she is helping herself to food I have set out. I return to the kitchen, unsure of what I will find when I get there. She has jumped on the counter and is trying to look innocent when I ask her what she is doing. I feel a roar surfacing as I grab her collar. She looks at me, and she refuses to jump down.

We stare eye to eye. I grab her legs, flip her onto her back and hold her down by her neck; my teeth bared just enough. She squirms and then stops fighting. I picked her up and set her gently on the floor. She slinks to the corner, and I am happy she is gone—the little thief.

What the hell is going on with me? I get eye to eye with her and start to apologize. I stare into her eyes and can see we are changing. Wildness is replacing civility. We stare at each other unsure and unapologetic.

She quickly regains form, and soon my old friend is drinking wine and waiting for dinner. I am not used to my reaction; it is unsettling. I plate my steak with a salad from my garden, then make a bowl for my impatient dog. I make her wait. She is staying closer to me than my shadow. I am not sure what is coming over us; she is not sharing what she knows.

I pour more wine. Then we start to talk about the time we got lost in the mountains, our two-hour hike that lasted over six. We were exhausted, but in retrospect, we had a great day. She apologized for the rabbit she chased. I smiled and reminded her of the sunset we watched once we found each other again. "I love you." "I love you, too."

Dinner is ready, and we settle in with a bottle of Artadi Viña el Pisón, a fantastic Rioja. I remember buying it during our trip to Spain. We got the last three bottles they had available at the vineyard. The chief winemaker joined my husband and me for a picnic in the sun. Wine, cheese, tomatoes, and lamb from the vineyard was the fare that day. He beamed as he watched my husband and me become overwhelmed at how wonderful his wines tasted.

We shared two bottles, unspeakable beauty, brilliant conversation, and delicious food. It made for a perfect day. I wasn't expecting to drink this bottle for a few more years, but now I have no intention of letting them go to waste. I take a drink and remember that time has made it better. It is smoother, more complex, an absolute pleasure.

I wonder if those who know me would say the same of me. I hear an old song about what others think of me. I hum thinking, oh well. Oh well is right. I always did my best, and my dog seems to like me again. I am not sure what I am anymore.

I return to my wine as the lyrics of that song keep repeating in my head. I drink deeply. It is tremendous and will go impeccably with tenderloin and vegetables from my garden.

I open my kitchen windows so I can relish the sounds of nature in my backyard. The birds, the wind, and the first chirps of a cricket are the chorus that enters my space. I pour the last of the bottle. The wine agrees with us, and we drink the last bit together.

She thinks I should have started doing this a long time ago.

I tell her it is not good for her. She disagrees.

I serve the food and sit at my patio table. My mother would be shocked to see me eating with the table manners of a barbarian. We eat every bite and open another bottle, an Andrew Will. The temperature is Goldilocks, my stomach is full, my chair is comfortable, and my dog is asleep. I should be content, but I am restless. I need a refuge from all of the madness that today brought. I have had enough.

I walk inside, strip off my clothes, and head to the bathroom. A hot bath is one of the great havens in my life. For years I have used hot water, wine, bath salts, a book, and candles to restore me. The sanctuary of the act soothes me and rarely fails to ease me out of my everyday life and into a tiny bit of magic. Lavender and Epsom salts have helped to keep me grounded during the hardest days of my life.

Finding balance has been tenuous for me in my best times. I have no idea what balance means when seventy-two hours is now closer to forty-eight.

The hot water hits my feet as the tub fills. I think about adding bubbles. I'm not sure why they seem right. My son used to love bubbles. I have some that have sat on the back shelf of my bathroom pantry for years. They always reminded me of my son when he was a small boy, and that bit of joy was more than a fair trade for the shelf space.

When he was little, he would try to get lost in them. He would scoop them in his hands and try to make a beard on any living thing that got close enough. The dog we had then was always a willing victim, as was I, but not his sister. I smile and listen for echoes of the squeals of delight this activity generated. I hear them like they are just happening.

I am filled with melancholy as I retrieve the box from the shelf and pour it all into the tub. I expected bubbles, but not the white explosion of joy that envelops me. It makes me laugh as the sheer volume of foam expands and can no longer be contained in my tub. I understand why my son at five would have a bath no other way. I call the dog, but she was never a big fan of this game. She was a puppy the last time bubbles filled the tub. She remembers and sits well out of my reach.

A candle flickers, and I surf a wave of nostalgia that accompanies each of these memories. My children's faces fill my mind. I see them at all ages. The memories come, and I try to hold on. I love them. The music of the night fills my space as I realize that all the humming sounds of electrical devices have stopped. It is very late, but I have no idea, nor do I care to know the hour. The night is dark on this street for the first time in nearly a century. Only the tallest trees and rocks can remember the last time the night sky looked like this. I open the shade and am thrilled to see the stars in a magnitude unimagined.

The crickets are in full courting song. I hear dogs howl. The night is alive.

I notice my phone and can't remember how it ended up here. I turn it on out of habit to check for messages. My battery is near dead. Old habits die hard, and for a flash, I am concerned about not being able to charge it. I go to set it down as it has been useless to me for hours.

It is of no value to me anymore. This morning I couldn't be without it. "You are yesterday's news." I go to set it down when I remember the text threads I have saved. I open ones from my husband, my kids, grandkids, my parents, and my friends. I read them telling me about our love for each other in a thousand ways. *"Can you get milk?"*

I have 18% power left on my phone and spend it hearing the voices of people I love in text form. *"Can we talk?" "Meet you at 7:00." "Goodnight."* Kissing emojis and pictures. All are saying, "I love you."

I feel that bit of panic as I see 1% on my screen. Today has been about the balancing act of holding on and letting go, surrendering to the end of things I love, and embracing what is new. I am accepting of this for the same reason a mob client does; I have no choice.

I read my daughter telling me about my granddaughter when my screen goes blank. I drop the phone on the floor and add hot water to my tub.

I rejoice, thanking all the people that passed through my life. I love my granddaughter so much. I hold on to her last words to me until I nod off.

I wake in total darkness. I usually would be unnerved, concerned about a hundred things I would try to take control over. I have none of that now. Black holes seem to be a cure for worry, the need for control, and cause of stress. It is glorious.

I hear my dog snoring. I wonder if I should wake her. I know

I have another candle and the lighter that I use for soaking and feel around until I find them. I light the candle and make my way to my bedroom.

CHAPTER TWENTY-THREE

I PUT ON A SWEATSHIRT and some leggings and notice the bonfire burning in the park. I am still tipsy, and this is why I decide it is an excellent idea to walk over. I start that way until I open the door, then I turn and go into the backyard instead. I want to observe the sky in peace. The sky has more stars than dark, and it is wondrous. I have never seen it like this. It feels so close, like the Milky Way and the rest of the universe is pulling up a chair to watch the show on planet Earth.

I wave my hand and bow like an opera diva. I am a smart-ass at heart. "Hope you all enjoy the show."

Until today, a black hole was the stuff of faraway places, far away as measured in light-years and revealed in photos taken by the Hubble telescope. I always felt space was a novelty item, a topic that little boys talked about, like dinosaurs and racing cars. I would say that space exploration is an expensive frivolity. My husband and son would balk and regale me with all the great discoveries the space program has made possible. Little boys who never grew up. Mine are no different from the rest.

Tonight, space is a spectacle. I sit looking up and embrace it like the ocean. They are both grand mysteries, but then so is the tree and the moth that flutters up to my candle. Me—I am a mystery.

How did I end up in the way of an out-of-control black hole? Now that is a mystery. I chuckle. The wine is in full force. I am looped enough to think of myself as both funny and philosophical.

I wish I were Superman. Then I could reverse this. I lift my glass and drink, knowing Superman is not coming.

I drink my last bit of wine and realize I have had more in the previous two days than in the two months before. I set the glass down and sit in the quiet and stare at the sky. The end of things will be an intimate affair with me and the universe in attendance. What kind of apocalypse is this?

I embrace the night as I wander over to the bonfire to see how everyone is coping. This apocalypse has people of all ages with bare feet and fine wine, cakes, beer, and chocolates. Everyone is telling stories around a huge campfire. It is a circus of hugs and alternating waves of delight and despair. Stories punctuated by tears of loss or the ecstatic laughter of celebrating our new-found sovereignty. Sovereignty because very little matters. The rest of our lives playing out to the crackling of the fire and kids making s'mores. I haven't had one in years. I grab a stick and quickly remember the joy of it.

I take a seat and hope my family is enjoying their night as much as I am mine. Grief is a hide-and-seek artist. With that thought, it is my turn to ride the wave and settle into the embrace of strangers. I find myself crying on many shoulders, and as many are leaning their head on mine.

My dog arrives, looking a little hungover, and irritated that I wasn't there when she woke up. She plops at my feet and is back to sleep in seconds. I so love her. I eat my messy treat and survey the gathering. Every emotion is on display; I sit and watch.

One by one, we tell each other our stories of love, of joy, and beautiful things we know. We honor the lives we have led. We are sharing our most important memories. With each story, individuals are becoming a clan, my tribe.

A man sits in silence and shakes his head in disbelief. I ask him to share, and he talks about his pain, his loss, his fears. I hear myself telling him of my dreams that will never come true. We are all we have, and we are more than enough. All we can do is hold each other and cherish what is going away, and what we have. Our numbers are growing. The gathering is becoming a cross between confessional and street party. People need to share the impact of knowing these might be their last hours. Dread is not the prevalent air of those gathered; a feeling of unfettered joy is. We are free.

A man I have seen in the park for years as I walked my dog,

has in a few hours become my priest and me his. We speak like people with nothing to lose. With nothing to gain. With nothing to hide. My heart is lighter than it has been in…in ever. This day is nearly over, and the night and the wine have me thinking about kissing him. He's a handsome man.

My imagination is working overtime on how I should live my last days. I contemplate one last romp before the end comes. One romp with the man on whose shoulder I have been crying. As I ponder, I realize I don't want a romp; I want to make love to someone I have spent hours and hours, years and years, getting to know. Somebody I have seen sick, and joyful, silly, and amazing. Someone I love, someone I know loves me.

I want to see a lover's glow in his eyes. I want him to see my love for him in mine. I look into his eyes and see nothing but kindness, and talk myself out of one last kiss. I know that if I did kiss him, we would explode and I would moan. My mind takes over, and like a hamster in its wheel, it works at a frantic pace.

I wonder if he is good in bed. Can he curl my toes? I wonder how it would be to touch him. Would he be gentle, or would he take me? I speculate if he would be receptive or be put off by my advances.

I play the scene in my mind and see myself, a middle-aged woman, and am soon feeling foolish and embarrassed. I feel my courage leak out, like helium leaving a balloon. In a moment, I see myself as less. The world turns black and white as I find myself with my feet firmly on the ground as any thought of flying has become laughable. My introverted nature has won again. He lets go of my hand, and the thought passes to another.

I stand with a mixture of regret and relief as he walks away.

My dog moves in to take his place. The magic is gone, and I hear my bed calling me. It is time to go home. I wave to those standing close and say, "Good night, I've got work in the morning."

Stunned silence greets my words. "I am a neonatal nurse, and babies will be coming tomorrow. They haven't heard the news." I see the group nod with approval.

"Are you going to walk?" someone asks as I turn toward home. I think that is an odd question; walk where? I guess home, but that is silly, she must be talking about work. I am going to drive like every other day. Why would I walk to work? I never have before, why would I tomorrow? I dismiss the question with the thought; I won't have time to walk.

I whistle for my dog. She has wandered off, and I want her close as I try to make my way home. It is pitch-dark in front of me as the light from the fire fades. Finding my house is not a simple chore. I stop and stand, listening to the waves of noise and wait for my eyes to adjust to the darkness. I need to find a flashlight. I have an aging wine buzz, and the darkness makes me unsteady. I want to keep moving, but the night holds me still.

I have found that when moving, sorrow has a harder time finding me. I stopped because of the dark and have no way to escape from being caught by any number of random emotions. My knees go weak as my heart tosses me. I try to resist facing them again. I am tired of this cycle. I look for a way out, but can't find one. I surrender and let them have their way. I surf. Oddly, what I have found is inside my grief is joy. How much worse if I felt nothing?

I open my heart and invite the next wave and am surprised by what I am grieving. Of course, I grieve for my husband, my kids, and my friends. I was not expecting the depth of feeling I was having for the rose bush that reminds me of my mom, my husband's heirloom teapot, Grandma's cookie jar, a clay pot made by my daughter, a painting done by a friend. I am blown sideways by the inevitable loss of the tree that has shaded me for years. I love the chair beneath her, where I sat to read as my kids played in her branches.

CHAPTER TWENTY-FOUR

MY BOOKS. I had not expected another wave of loss, but this one forces me to try to hurry home. A personally autographed *Grapes of Wrath* from the day I had met Mr. Steinbeck as a young child. A hardback copy of *Walden/Civil Disobedience* I kept in my purse as a teen and read again and again whenever I had a minute. I smile recalling a copy of *Mr. Pine's Purple House*, the first book to delight me as a child. It is in tatters, but that makes me love it all the more.

I wince, thinking about my family's five-generation Bible. It tracks my lineage. I remember the day my grandmother added my name; her penmanship is exquisite. I watched her closely when she added my husband and each of my children.

I remember the day she gave it to me. I feel the pain of

knowing I will not be able to give it to my son. He used to spend hours looking at the names and asking me questions. I loved sharing what I knew.

I whistle again and wait. Then I whistle again, as she comes out of the darkness. I wait as she runs to see if I'm okay, she apologizes for not being by my side. I pet her and tell her I am grateful for her. She goes to move, but I stay eye to eye with her. "I love you." She kisses my cheek.

We move together. I am more able to see her now that my eyes have adjusted to the darkness. We walk into the night. I know that my old life is gone and that my new life means relying on my dog to walk the short distance home. I bow to this reality and thank her for being there when I need her. I am hardly able to see her, and she can find the way.

She moves slowly, waiting for me. I am relieved. I find myself wanting to hurry because I have two books I want to see. I try, but I can't go any faster. They are my absolute favorites, a well-used copy of *Charlotte's Web*, and a beautifully bound copy of *Call of the Wild*. Some pig and Buck.

Upon arriving home, I light a candle and make my way to my bookshelves. I have a flashlight and a camp lantern, but I want to have a candle burning as I sit with my books. Reading like Abraham Lincoln, as I remember making my brother read by a candle when we were little and camping in the backyard. He would say, "This is stupid." I would growl indignantly and say, "This is how Abraham Lincoln read, do you think Abraham Lincoln is stupid?" Being nine to his six, he knows "no" was the only suitable answer.

He is now my confidante and friend. I share my heart and secrets with him, and he with me. I lock his most private thoughts away in a safe place, away from prying eyes. We face our fears together. I feel much less alone, knowing he is a phone call away. He is my champion, and I am his. I love him. I caress the chair he made for me when my oldest was born. It has been the perfect spot to read on nights that I can't sleep.

I set the candle down on my reading table and pick up three pictures I want close to me. On my table, I have a picture of my grandmother reading *Charlotte* to me, of my mom reading it to my daughter, and the third of me reading it to my granddaughter. Each un-posed, but all nearly the same. All are of a grandmother sitting in bed with her granddaughter in her lap, picnic food on the bed, hot chocolate in mugs, and us in pajamas. I savor each of those days. Perfect sheets and a warm comforter are setting the stage for the sharing, one generation to the next, of a story we all love.

We are intertwined like cats, curled together. I am looking at the picture and can still savor this time spent with someone I love more than anything. Women embracing the youngest member of my clan hearing E.B. White's story of love for the very first time. I carefully crack the book and read the listing of each first reading.

I stop at mine. I remember it as deeply as I can. I can feel my grandmother holding me. I flip to the first page and hear her voice reading. I remember hearing the story and going from wanting to be Fern to becoming her. My grandmother's voice was transporting me to a magical place. This story changed my way of being in the world. Radiant became my focus, I tried my eight-year-old best to be radiant.

All of the women of my family shared this celebration with her mom and grandmother on her eighth birthday. Hand-sewn pig pajamas are the attire of that day. Turning eight was a celebration that lasted a week, but "Charlotte Day" was for women to be women. A special day for generational women to share their love for each other. These are some of my most cherished memories. The joy they hold is strong enough to hold back the grief to which I have become accustomed.

I set the book down and head to the kitchen to make hot chocolate. Some of my most favorite things are books, my chair, and a cup of hot chocolate. I am delighted that I have one more cup of a cocoa mix, the recipe for which my grandmother had first put on paper over a hundred years before.

I made it for my granddaughter's eighth birthday less than a year ago. A few minutes on the BBQ grill with a pan, the mix, and the last of my milk, and it is ready. I change into my latest set of pig pajamas and am soon heading back to the bookshelves with a candle and cup in hand.

I feel the three women I love most gathered around as I open the book and take a sip of my grandmother's delightful concoction. I taste *meraki*. *Meraki* is a Greek word for the magic of why my grandmother's cookies always taste best. It is the love and pieces of herself she gave away, knowing she was baking them for me.

"One pig is a runt..." I close the book, and then my eyes. I open my heart and use it to hug each of these women gathered for this sacred moment. "I love you, and thank you," I say to each.

I'm joined by all of the beloved women of my family. It feels like a hundred are in my space. I say to each in turn, "You taught me it took no courage to be myself fully. I had your love as a path to follow." It seems so right to toast my women with a mug of hot chocolate. I lift my cup and drink.

"Some pig," I shout into the darkness, "Some pig," I hear return on the wind.

I cry tears of joy. I open the book again and read until tears stop me. I savor the last drops from the cup. "I love you all," I sigh and carefully put Charlotte back in her place on the shelf.

I wish the women I love a good night, knowing I will see them all soon.

CHAPTER TWENTY-FIVE

I NEXT PULL THE BOOK I bought to share with my son, his version of Pig Pajama day. I open it to read. I remember as a kid being afraid for my dog the first time I read it; fearful my husky would go missing. Heidi living Buck's fate in the Yukon kept me on edge until my dad showed me the gold rush was over a long time ago.

I look at the cover and remember the struggle of this book. The battle of wills that my son and I fought. The perfection it produced.

My eight-year-old son experienced the world differently than my daughter. He was and is a mystery to me. He was always trying to prove himself. For his birthday week, we did what he wanted. We got dirty. We drove go-carts, played video games, camped, hiked, and looked for mischief. I dove in, thinking I was open to spending seven days in the chaos that is an eight-year-old boy's dream week. He loved it. I survived it.

In those seven days, I formed an appreciation of what being a young boy means, and how hard it is. When I was eight, I found boys my age to be foolish creatures. Having spent a week immersed with one, I can tell you he was more like a caged wolf than I could have imagined. I was surprised by how uncomfortable he was in the surroundings of our modern world.

He shows me through his actions that he's locked in a society that is more worried about his safety than he was. Security was not one of his concerns. He and his friends wanted to roam free and satisfy their unexplainable need to come face to face with the very next thing. To see how they measured up to everything around them. To test and see if it was strong and how to break it. I watched him take these lessons to heart and explore himself to find where he can be broken. He then fortified himself against any newfound weakness, adding another layer to his shell.

He broke me several times that week. I was unprepared for how strong my little boy had become. I had promised it was his week, and he took me at my word. He allowed me into his world and showed me what it was like with all the innocence and abruptness a young boy can have.

He looked to be a skinny sixty-pound kid, but in his mind, he had to prepare like a warrior readying to take his place in the arena. He had to be strong in front of his friends. Period. His peers and media socialized him that weakness is an intolerable sin. Surrounded by other young boys all learning the same lesson, he lived in a ring that would tear him apart whenever he let his guard down. I tried at first to make it soft for him, like my daughter's week, and couldn't understand when he didn't know how to be in the space I created with pajamas and a book.

He challenged me. If I was to share his world, I had to live by his rules, not mine. This was his week, and he was hoping I would adapt to him. He knew he couldn't make me. He had learned to hold his tongue because this was what he had been taught in a myriad of different ways. Sharing his feelings made him vulnerable and weak, a doe surrounded by wild dogs. He held his tongue and learned to be invisible.

He had been taught by life that he was voiceless. He understood fully that no one listens to an eight-year-old boy. Fed up with me, he told me I had promised him a week, and I wasn't fulfilling my end of the bargain. He demanded to be seen, to be heard. He used his voice, and I gave him the reins. From then on, I did my best to make his week his own.

He made sure I lived in his world, or the one he wanted to live inside. It hurt me at first, but as I opened my mind and heart to him, I quickly grew to love that week, because I learned to love my son more deeply. I learned to love him, and his father, and my father, more deeply too. I understood them differently. Back then, I left the comfort of my rocking chair and moved the reading of *Call of the Wild* to the light of a fire ring outside. He fidgeted as I read the book's first chapter inside, uncomfortable with the comfort of the indoors.

He asked to go outside. He asked for fire. The spell of that book read by the light of fire cast magic I will never forget. I can still see him that night sitting by the flames, searching for anything he can find to throw in it. He asked for a tent, which we set up. I had to explore being uncomfortable to put him at ease.

I was unsure what he thought of the book until I went to close it, and he asked for a bit more. He scooted next to me, and my heart melted. I continued to read him this masterpiece. He later told me it is the only book he ever loved. We didn't get through much of it during his week.

He asked me to finish it, sitting in camp chairs by the fire pit in the backyard. It took the whole summer to share the story. He told me later that he would stop our reading because he enjoyed my undivided attention so much. He said he tried to read other books I bought him, and always found them wanting to this experience.

He asked me to read it to him again when in college. He broke his leg and was recovering at home. He wanted to hear it, but only if it was by the fire in the backyard. I cherish both readings.

I can still smell the smoke on the pages. I breathe it in as a tear hits the page. Some dog and some pig. I love *Call of the Wild*, but in a different way than I love *Charlotte*.

I replace it on the shelf next to Charlotte. I consider stopping with these two, but the light fell on the spines of my library, and I can't say no.

CHAPTER TWENTY-SIX

I HAVE BEEN A READER ALL MY LIFE, and the books in this room are the ones that affected me most profoundly. Many are the books of my youth. The words on these pages largely shaped how I see the world. These authors taught me to think, to question, to love, and to dream.

I grab a tattered gray hardback that looks exceptionally well-worn, and open to one of the dozen bookmarks left over the years. Circled in pencil is: "Live in each season as it passes; breathe the air, drink the drink, taste the fruit, and resign yourself to the influence of the earth." I remember *Walden* giving my teenaged heart words that helped me to understand my world. I pull one book after another as a pile begins to grow around me. I read a bit of each to taste them again.

Tolstoy's, "All happy families are alike; each unhappy family is unhappy in its own way." I have pondered on this line many times in my life. To see it in print still gives me chills. It is brilliant.

I have always been confused about what happiness is and why it was so sought after. I understand peace. I understand joy. I understand content. But happy? Happy always seems to be a concept made up by somebody trying to sell me something, like a Coca-Cola ad. Happy has been as elusive as the gold I might find at the end of the rainbow.

I wrote in the margin of the book: "I am giving up on trying to be happy. I will do my best to be at peace." I read those words and sitting here thirty-five years later, and I am not sure I am closer to happy than I was back then.

I am thinking about heading for bed when the light flickers on *East of Eden*. I saw those three words flicker in the candle-light, and I remember both times I have savored its pages. Cathy Ames was my introduction to an unrepentant and fierce woman. I don't remember any other character from the book, but Cathy Ames was an awakening for me. Ferocious and broken in equal measure, and each of those measures is immense.

Steinbeck wrote of her that she was "born with a malformed soul." For my younger-self, her character transformed what a book could be. She appeared in words that are bigger than the page. Unlike every other character I had ever read, the arson fire of her personality was something brand new for my sixteen-year-old self to digest. She wasn't looking for redemption and wouldn't have taken it if it was offered. She knew it for the scam that it is.

She made me challenge more assumptions about life than any other character I had read. I never read a book the same way after this one. When I reread it a few years ago, her impact on me was just as strong.

Evil is a simple term for a sixteen-year-old. For my forty-seven-year-old self, it was a much more complicated set of circumstances and lessons with which my soul chose to wrestle. She is unlike most women in literature. She is not safe and warm; she is an inferno. Dangerous to those who treat her as a pet instead of the cobra she is. For my current self, she challenged me to read about her actions without judgment or opinion.

I watched her unfold before me; her role written to confront my notions of right and wrong. I was able to read her actions without internalizing them, without forming opinions as I had done with every page when I was a kid. My older self read her as a lesson. A yield sign to be recognized and for me to move to a safer distance. Her fire burned me. It also soothed me. I warmed myself by it.

She taught me to detach a bit from what I was expected to be. Her path was absolutely not mine, but she illuminated a not-insignificant lesson about being true to myself. I learned to follow the light of my own company from her.

I flip through the book to find her, and I read a bit as I sip the last of my wine. I savor both. The beauty of Steinbeck's writing always melts my heart. I find myself wishing I could read it now. I wonder what she would say to me.

It is late, and dozens of books are strewn at my feet. I am

caught in that place between joy and tears. I wish I could have music playing as I stroll through my favorite books. Vonnegut, Rushdie, Orwell, Alcott, Swift, Barks, Rumi, Steinbeck, Hemingway, Hesse, Austin, Agatha, Salten, John Kennedy Toole, and so many more lay open on the floor. The books of my life.

The first candle burned completely hours ago. I have many candles burning now.

Books have been my constant companion. There was never a day since I was eight when two or three were not on my nightstand. Even when I bought a Kindle, I still had hard copy books with a bookmark waiting for its turn to be next.

I read until I read a sentence that no author would have written. Sleep has caught me. I surrender to it as I have many of the nights of my life, with gibberish words making me smile, as my eyes close for good.

DAY FOUR:

I sit on the loam
Completely soaked

I inhale

Everything relaxes as timpani
gives way to a single leaf's shimmer.

As the last droplets percuss in the puddle by my feet

I am in the moments before the rainbow.

Before time has made a way to look back.

I shiver like the trees.

Now that the wind has gone
I shake, creaking to fill an unfamiliar space

I am cleansed by the storm
but the lingering violence still marks my flesh

I inhale for the second time.

Direction is meaningless as I have yet
to find the balance to stand.

"What of myself have I lost in the torrent?"

I wipe my eyes
but still can't focus

Is it a tear
or a raindrop
that clouds my vision?

I sit on the loam

Waiting to inhale

CHAPTER TWENTY-SEVEN

I WAKE ON THE FLOOR, wondering where I am. The sun is filling the sky but has yet to break the horizon. I am confused and pick up the book that is open on my chest. I smile. It all started here, *Little House on the Prairie*. I was in second grade, sitting on the floor next to a rocking chair. My teacher was reading the words in this book, words that set a fire burning in my young heart for books. Not a year goes by that I don't thank her for that gift. Of all the teachers that impacted my life, her's has been the greatest.

Her reading the great books of youth to me for a year laid the foundation for who I am today. I never got to thank her. Like many other gifts in my life, by the time I realized the value of the present, it is too late to thank the people who made a way for me.

I start to move like this could be my last day. I pet my dog as she is watching me closely. She tells me she needs to go outside. I start toward the door when I stop. I pick up and look at the picture of me with my grandmother. Where did the time go?

As I descend the stairs, three pictures, an empty cup, and a wine glass in hand, I think back over my life and am sure that I never felt safer than I did when the picture with my grandmother was taken. Enveloped by love, I look at the picture of my grand-daughter with me. I hope her memory of her day is the same as mine, love, and being loved. Both of our lives are now measured in hours. I wish I could hold her and keep her safe.

My heart breaks, knowing my granddaughter's name will be the last on the inside cover of Charlotte. I hug the pictures because it is as close as I can get. "Put that picture down, it is time to be productive," I can hear my mom say. She tells me to let the dog out and to make coffee; that I have work to do. I feel the joy of coffee in the morning when I recall that I have no way to make it. I have yet to get the camping gear from the garage.

I have to see if I have ground coffee, or do I have whole beans. Beans that will mock my inability to turn them into a fine dust. I follow my dog back through my kitchen. I cross my fingers and turn on my kitchen sink. It is flowing water that seems clean and hot. I rejoice. I am learning to take nothing for granted.

I decide to leave the backdoor open and head up for a shower. I don't pad around my house as I would typically do. I have no idea how long the hot water will last. It is still working, and I am soon relaxing in the steam. Hot water is a delight. Nothing is better than a hot shower, and I am going to enjoy this one.

The shower is my place for setting the course of my day. I have one priority, to get to the hospital and see if I can help. I see many of the little faces that have taught me about life and perspective over the years. Holding a tiny body that is fighting to live while looking in their parent's eyes have always made all my problems seem insignificant. I am living with the thought that everything I do may be the last time.

Years ago, I hung a Thich Nhat Hanh quote on my bathroom wall, and I try to read it every morning. It is there to remind me to be attentive as I do things as simple as washing a dish. To fully live in each moment, because each moment is extraordinary.

I rejoice while standing in the shower. I am the miracle. I am the dish. I am the dessert. I am the savoring. Today I am preparing for work; as a young girl, I once readied myself for midnight mass. I allow the sacred to take my breath away as I ready for the day in silence. I can move at my own pace as I will not be responsible to a clock, rules, or productivity goals. It is me and life today, and I can't wait to see what it has in store.

I have no schedule to keep or boss to answer to. The time-clock's hands are frozen, and it will never be my master again. I surrender to my own pace, and somehow in the last twelve hours, I have learned how to slow myself from ninety MPH to about twenty-five. What a luxury it is, having control over my life. I have never been a very good slave to the clock.

I pull out my favorite nurse's scrubs and put it on. It is soft and worn, and it fits me just right. I do it slowly. I am moving today, like dressing is a tea ceremony. Each movement is precise as I am telling the story of my final day to myself.

In the time it usually takes me to ready myself and drive to work, I have prepared myself for my last day at work. I dress under my dog's watchful eye. I finally put on my shoe, and I tie my left shoelace. Finished.

I stand and look at myself in the mirror. I am ready. I grab my work bag, and with keys in hand, head for my car. Most everyone had abandoned their jobs the second they heard the end was coming. I love mine.

For over thirty years, I have given care. I have given my heart, my attention, and my skill to people on their best and worst days. After working in all kinds of nursing for years, I now greet newborn babies upon arrival. My graying hair and experience calm the new parents. I work hard to keep the mother as safe as I can. I am fascinated by the mystery of it all. It is what I was put on Earth to do. It is my sauce.

It, in large part, defines everything I do. I give care. Over my career, I have seen tragedy in all its forms. I have also shared in the glories of life. To a varying degree, I see both every day at work. The miraculous always comes with a price. I know today might be the last day I can be one of the things I have most loved in this life: a nurse.

Nurses see the violence of time and the capricious nature of fate. We see lives laid bare, and are witness to the spirit of people as they take each step required to forge their way back to a "normal" life.

As their body and spirit heal, they embrace that which broke them, the thing which exposed what is truly inside. Simple everyday items like cars, an icy sidewalk, and a bathtub are some of fate's favorite tools for changing a person's reality. I have been there to help my patients put their feet back on the ground, to cheerlead their hard work. To hold their hand as they search to find a new way to live.

I pull the emergency cord that unlocks my garage door and I open it. I get into my car, and it doesn't start. My vehicles always start. I turn the key again, trying to determine what is failing when I remember the women last night asking, "How are you going to get there?"

I get out and stroll to those crowded around the fire in the park. As I approach, I see the physicist with her family and am glad because I want to ask her a question. I see her drinking a cup of coffee and feel a tinge of jealousy. I look and don't see an available cup. She looks at me in my scrubs and smiles. "You weren't kidding about work?"

"No," I say. "I have every intention of going to the hospital today. Can I ask you how you knew my car is dead?"

She informs me that the electromagnetic pulse that fried the electrical grid also destroyed the computer in my car. She stands on a picnic table and asks if anyone has a vehicle that is pre-1985 and would be willing to give me a ride. No one does or is willing to speak up.

I thank her and start to change my plans, trying to decide between riding my bike or walking. I say to her that I'm happy the hospital is not far away, only a few miles when a man standing close says, "Not far by car can still be hours on foot." Although walking seems safer, riding my bike it is.

Halfway to my house, I regret that I didn't ask to get a cup of coffee. I am a little chilly, and it would have been a great way to start the day. I miss my coffee. I am afraid if I go back with a cup, I will not do as I have planned for today. I pout about it as I return home to change into clothes suitable for biking.

As I get closer, I see her looking at me through the window, and she doesn't look happy. She greets me at the door, wondering why I would go for a walk without her. She follows me as I quickly strip off my scrubs and unceremoniously stuff it into a backpack. I put on bike clothes and begin to ready myself for the ride.

No more ceremony; it is time to do.

CHAPTER TWENTY-EIGHT

I THINK ABOUT THE PEOPLE gathered by the fire and wonder why I am doing this. I contemplate staying until the thought of my little patient finds me. Curiosity takes over, and I resolve I am going to find out the fortunes of that little one. I am hoping that he has made it this far. Was his fight big enough? This question pushes me out the door.

Sometimes the experts are proven wrong. Were his doctors correct about his need for a machine to breathe? Did his lungs heal enough before the power failed? Does the hospital have power? Mostly, what tricks do the fates have up its sleeve? I have to know.

Over the years, I have been greeted by former patients that had received the news that they would not make it through the night. I wonder for a minute if Gaia has a card up her sleeve for all of us.

Time will tell, but for now, I have work to do. I grab my stuff and head out to the garage.

As I think about riding my bike, I feel afraid. I stop and weigh this day. I am petrified to travel into the unknown, but I have to see why the Fates will not let me sit and talk in the park. The Fates have gifts for those who face their fear. I need to embrace the miraculous adventure today, and I will only be able to if I face my fears.

I create a laundry list of things that could go wrong. Everything from marauding gangs chasing me like a scene from *Mad Max*, to pilot error causing a crash and me injuring myself. I picture myself lying helpless in a heap on the ground. My brain moves to the bike malfunctioning, leaving me to walk in the middle of nowhere.

Nowhere—I chuckle—it is three miles away. I am shocked by my need for drama. When did I become a 1920s silent film star when it comes to my life? In my mind, I hear my mom say, "When were you not?" We laugh together.

I tell myself to go, or at least travel half a mile before giving up.

I am going to do what I am going to do. I push through. I am going. I stand by a bike that has hung on the wall, unridden for too long. I love the sensation of riding, the miles rolling under my tires. It always makes me feel alive.

Today it is my lone means of transportation. I pump up the tires and put a small set of tools I keep in my car into my backpack. I put on my helmet and gloves, and I am ready for yet another of this new life's adventures.

I feel nervous. Although I have driven this route thousands of times, today it somehow seems unknown. "Beyond here be dragons," I say to the wind as I make final preparations for my ride. My mind is loudly asking me to forget this idea and stay comfortable and safe. Apparently, the end of the world wasn't a substantial enough threat to override my phobias.

The ride ahead of me brings to the surface anxieties that go back to when I was a young girl. Far too many years ago, I went for a ride across town to a friend's house, and on the way, I got lost. I rode and rode, becoming more anxious and disoriented the further I went. I had no money, no idea what to do, and no courage to ask for help. I had left myself as the only tool I was willing to use.

That nine-year-old's fear still grips me today. I am an adult, but the memories I had as a child still hold me back. The feeling of being all alone is palpable. Am I enough?

I need to overcome this if I am going to be able to be a nurse one more time; if I am going to be able to give care. I am going. My nine-year-old self did none of the things I would do now. As a child, I forget to stop, to assess my surroundings, and to calm down and plan my next step. I did nothing I now know to do when trying to solve a puzzle.

Back then, adrenaline had taken hold of me. I was in full flight mode. I had lost the connection between my mind and body until, in a total frenzy, I crashed into a parked car. The jolt of the impact snapped me back to a place where I could think. The owner of the car came out of his house and asked me if I was all right. I shared that I was lost, and he helped me figure out where I was and where I was going. I quickly realized I knew where I was and how to go back home or to my friend's house.

Fear likes to remind me about being lost, but not that I found my way, and mostly that I am not a child anymore. I remind myself that my nine-year-old self solved her childhood problems. This self will be all right, too.

Fear is the window to freedom, and I only have this day to live. I am going to see what destiny holds.

Out of habit, before I start to ride, I run through a checklist in my head. It begins with keys, wallet, and cell phone. I stop for a second until I remember it is dead. I want it in my bag, although I am not sure why. I ponder, then quickly decide I am not going back inside for a dead cell phone. Just move, and quit making excuses.

If I am going to be a nurse today, I need to get on my bike and ride into the unknown. As I roll my bike through the gate, I see my dog slip through, too. I try to put her back, but it is clear she is determined to come with me. I listen to my inner voice and am thankful for the company.

I wondered if she has the stamina for the trip. Hell, I wonder if I have the strength to make the ride. I scratch her head and jokingly promise to ride slowly. "I might even stop once or twice for you."

We smile at each other and set off into the unknown.

CHAPTER TWENTY-NINE

I WILL BE PEDDLING ON the same route I have driven for years. I know there is a bike route, but I have no idea where to pick it up. The plus side is that traffic might be light today.

My dog calls me a dork. I chuckle; my dog does, too.

I wonder if I will be okay without Siri to guide me.

You worked there for over thirty years; stop being ridiculous, and trust yourself, my dog says as she confidently heads off.

I start to peddle my cruiser bike. I love the wind against my face. I usually love the feel when on my bike, but not today. I have never been so unnerved on a bicycle. Today, the streets have no traffic lights, no rules.

I don't know what to expect. The lanes are blocked by the occasional car that died when the electromagnetic pulse hit.

Nothing is moving. The roads are littered with dead vehicles, and they make me feel even more vulnerable than when they were moving.

I am thankful the pulse hit late at night, leaving the roads easily passable. I don't get far before I again consider turning around. I tell myself to get to the next light pole, and then to decide, then the next one, and then the next. I am making the trip in ten-pedal increments.

I begin to breathe more naturally. The further I go, the less unsafe I feel. If my way had been jammed with deserted cars, I think the ride would be more dangerous. I still feel like I am in the movies, and I expect zombies will soon appear.

My dog smiles at me; we both know how silly I am being.

My mind is bringing the shadows alive. I catch movement out of the corner of my eye. That movement disappears when I look at it directly. My brain forms a bubble, and I am hyper-aware of every step my dog runs and every spin of the pedals.

I want her to stay close. I can feel her wanting to be close. We go from light post to light post together.

When my fear decreases enough to allow me to look around, I see I am making good progress. I am going to make it. I peddle forward, assured in my success when I realize I am pushing the pedals as hard as I can, but not moving forward very fast.

I can't be in this badly out of shape. I have not gone far, and this hill is minimal. I stand on the pedals to go faster but find that—no matter how hard I push—I am slowing. I scold myself for not riding harder, for being in miserable shape. Despite my effort, I am slowing to a stop. My bike has become unrideable. I dismount and find my back tire is no longer holding air.

The hospital is close but not that close. I resign myself to walking and continue toward my goal. Pushing my bike, I have to decide if I should keep it or leave it behind. Leaving it behind is reasonable, but with each step, I don't lay it down. I am unsure why. It is a burden that I keep carrying.

I look around and see I am walking through a neighborhood I had locked my doors to drive through for years.

I finally set my bike down, but as I walk away, I feel less safe. Why? I am rifling through my psyche, trying to figure out why my bike makes me feel safer. Finally, I decide I don't care why. Walking without it makes me feel lonely, leaving feels like deserting a friend. I have owned the bike for years, and leaving it out on the street is something I can't get my head around. It is now useless as transportation, but as a security blanket, it still has magic. I walk back, pick it up, and continue on my way.

I picture myself as the old Peanuts cartoon character Linus, and decide now is not the time or place to fight it.

Both my dog and I are catching our breath as we acclimate to walking. We are a few miles from my house. I have driven by here every day for years, but I have never been here. I have been warned by hospital administration that this place is potentially dangerous.

My mind plays games, echoing news reports, and warnings from well-meaning people concerned for my safety. Images of violence run around in my brain and down my spine, trying to make my feet move faster. I am in no way equipped for being alone out here; alone with what I've been told existed on these streets. I am sweaty, and I tell myself my heart is racing from riding, but I have been walking for a while now. I am sweating because I am scared.

I am listening carefully and am unnerved by how quiet it is. Ordinarily, busy streets seem more ominous when silent. Noiseless buildings and unlit street lights stand like an empty stage, awaiting the next performance artist to appear. They seem to be a theatrical backdrop, so I guess I am the performer. I smile, thinking of myself on center stage. I love being center stage, but only with a guitar in hand.

I am hyperaware of how slowly I am moving. I am getting the same feeling as I did when I was a kid in a haunted house. I keep waiting for something to jump out at me. Adrenaline is coursing through my system, and I am aware of my minimal abilities to either fight or fly if needed.

For no apparent reason, I feel like I am being hunted by something unseen, that a million eyes are watching me. I speed up my pace, trying desperately to get to the safety of the known. I know I am being irrational, but this knowledge doesn't help. My sole focus is getting to my hospital.

My mind decides to generate a random series of unhelpful thoughts. During stressful times, this was once a typical response for me. It seems old habits die hard. I try to stop them, but the impression that I am in danger is repeating over and over again.

I wonder if anything remains of the hospital. Is it still the institution I left less than two days ago? Do drug addicts or thugs overrun it? Am I going through this much anguish for nothing?

My dog looks up at me, shakes her head, and sighs. God, I love my dog.

I stop my next thought from coming and backtrack. I had not considered that the hospital might have changed when I left my house. A wave of alarm rolls over me. Why am I here? Why didn't I stay where I was safe? The unrelenting dialog in my head imprisons me.

My dog barks at me, and I find I am running. Running, trying to escape the unknown. I keep going until my dog slowly crosses in front of me. I yell at her to get out of my way. She slows to a stop in front of me. I am about to yell at her to move.

She looks up at me, gives me a dog whine, then begins walking in the direction of her choosing. It is not in the direction I want. It is not the way to the hospital.

I notice her tail is wagging and that she is headed somewhere with a purpose. "Where are you going? The hospital is that way." I stop. She doesn't. "We are going the wrong way. Where in the hell do you…"

I continue, and as I follow, I smell the most delicious smells. I look around at row-houses that look well-kept. I did not know this neighborhood existed. I yell at her to come to me, but she ignores me and keeps going.

I stop, and she turns to look at me, wagging her tail. Then she turns her back on me and runs away. She ignores me calling her, as she moves quickly down the street, and further into the unknown. I have no choice but to follow her. If I can't leave my bike, I am most certainly not going to leave my dog. I go deeper into the unknown.

She is well ahead of me now and not looking back. In my rush to get going this morning, I had not eaten. I had left food for her, but her bowl was untouched when we started this adventure. I did not plan on her joining me. I was used to eating at the hospital and had not thought about food.

She is now alpha, and I'll have to play her game. She is on a mission. I follow. She is still ahead of me, and I watch her disappear as she turns the corner.

I follow her, and as I get to the corner, I see she is halfway between a crowd of people standing in the street and me.

CHAPTER THIRTY

THEY ALL TURN THEIR ATTENTION to me as I approach. Another wave of dread hits as three men break from the pack and move to meet me. I feel the hair raise on my neck.

My dog arches her back, and I hear myself connecting with her as I never have before. She runs to my side. She is calm.

I feel a wildness that I am unaccustomed to. I feel trapped. If I had claws, I would be preparing to use them. I steeled myself and put on a smile as I move forward. My jaw tightens, and my legs twitch as they get closer, I want to run.

Before I can say a word, a large distinguished and gray-haired gentleman brusquely asks, "Where are you going?"

"I am a nurse at General, and I am going to see if anyone needs my help." I slow to a stop and carefully examine each man's face. I watch them like a poker player, looking for anything to tell me what they have in mind. I have never felt smaller in my life.

"The hospital is that way." He points.

"I know, but my dog came this way." I try to grab her collar, but she won't let me. The three, one older and two clearly younger men, are looking skeptically at me. I feel fire raising in me and try to keep it contained. I set down my bike and immediately wish I hadn't.

"Hospital? Would you mind if I look in your bag?" the most senior of the men asks. I move back as he moves forward—my mind races as I remove my bag from my back and begin to stammer. I then decide to stop talking.

I grip my bag tightly to my chest and think about ways to resist. I ask, "Why?"

The gentleman stops and looks at me, then moves forward. My dog has moved in front of me, and her back is against my legs. We both let out a small growl.

A look of concern crosses his face as he continues moving toward me. He says he would like to check it out before I go any further.

I come to my senses, realizing the standoff is in my mind alone. I tell my dog to sit and be still. She does, pushing hard against me. We both know I have no choice but to offer my bag.

He asks me to take my dog by the collar. I reluctantly do as he asks. Everyone is tense, or maybe it is only me. I feel wildness coursing through me, as another growl is rising in my throat.

My lip twitches, but this time, I keep the snarl inside. I pet my dog, hoping she does not have the same impulses. She follows my lead and stays still.

He takes my pack and returns to the others.

"It is my medical equipment," I stammer.

He looks up at me and back to my bag as he empties the contents onto the hood of a car. I start to protest when he gives me a look that causes me to fall silent. He carefully puts each item back into my bag. He looks at the scrubs, the medicines, and lastly, at my stethoscope. He zips it closed and calls me forward. He seems to be satisfied that my story is true.

"What brings you here?" he asks.

"My dog. She has a mind of her own." I say looking down at her.

His face is unmoved.

"That is why you are here; what brought you out in the first place?" He is standing and appears to be eleven feet tall.

My brain does a backflip as I start talking like an auctioneer.

I tell them about my calling as a nurse and babies coming when babies come. I am sharing more than I want to. I tell them that I am concerned for my little patients and am going to the hospital.

He listens to me ramble. He is trying to get a word in when he finally interrupts me to ask, "In what unit of the hospital do you work?"

"Neonatal," I respond.

He looks at his companions, then to me, and says, "She is

in the right place at the right time. Come with me." His mood is noticeably lighter.

I am hesitant, but I follow him and find I am walking quickly to catch up. He is waving me next to him. I hear my dog barking for me, but as I slow to turn, he takes my hand.

"We will take good care of your animal." His eyes are gentle but concerned. He grabs my hand tighter as he quickens his pace. I am sure he is evaluating me, but I am equally sure he's convinced I am the best option available to him.

For what, I don't know.

As we go to enter a home, I hesitate. He says, "Just a bit further. Please trust that you are safe and that I am delighted you are here."

I am both nervous and intrigued. *Where are we going?* I follow him. I become speechless. I hear the sound of a woman in pain, and her cry stops me cold. I refuse to go any further. He turns to me as I jerk my hand out of his.

I hear another shriek of pain, and I stare at the large gentleman whose eyes are now filling with fear. He seems impatient with me and asks me to please trust him. My feet are not moving, and I am deciding which way to run when I realize that what I am hearing is labor pains.

I catch my breath. Suddenly, it all makes sense. I follow the cries through a door into a master bedroom full of women. All their heads turn as I enter. A young woman in labor and four older women are all staring at me. I can see they are confused, wondering where I came from and why I am here.

I can tell she is close to having her baby. The women say nothing, and their attention quickly returns to the young mother.

"I have been an obstetrics nurse for nearly twenty years. Can I help?"

They all seem to be a little relieved that I am here. I also understand I am an unknown to these women, and they are on their guard. I ask them for details about how far she is into her delivery.

"Please tell me, is anything out of the ordinary I need to know?"

They start filling me in, and years of medical training take over, as I begin to ask specific questions. I need to get ready for the birth and ask permission to use the bathroom. The grandmother nods toward an open door.

I close the door and pull my scrubs out of my bag. I wonder if my dog is okay while I dress and wash my hands. I hurry back when I hear the next contraction hit. I take my stethoscope out and take out the medical supplies I have packed. I have been timing her contractions and am as ready as I can be when I return to the makeshift delivery room.

My attention focuses on my new patient. The women have readied as well as possible for their youngest member to give birth. I get to be part of another delivery and am grateful for a dog that didn't listen to me. I check the mother's heart, then the baby's.

A surge of joy and energy engulf me. Generations of people have been born at home, surrounded by women who will love them for the rest of their lives.

Her grandma says, "He is coming."

I nod. The pregnant woman is in full labor as another contraction moves the baby. She exhales hard and grips her mother's hand. Her mom tells her to breathe and that she is doing fine.

Birth and death are miracles, each a unique experience. I am delighted fate wants me to be part of one more birth.

I say that everything sounds as it should. We are going to have the baby the old-fashioned way. No monitors. No drugs. No doctors. No hospital. It is a woman and her baby surrounded by love. This is why I became a nurse.

The next contractions arrive in quick succession, and the women around her do their best to comfort her.

I am pleased my last birth is simply helping a young woman give birth, and her allowing me to be a nurse.

In all these years, I have never aided in a delivery outside of a hospital. I'm accustomed to being on stage and the family being an audience. That was not how this was going to go. Every woman in the room had given birth, so each knew what to expect each step of the way.

It is a thing of beauty watching these women take care of her. Natural childbirth is the only option. I am a bystander witnessing this birth with more awareness than the thousands that have gone before. A couple of hours into labor, we are spectators watching nature take her course. I check her vital signs and am listening to the baby's heartbeat when, without thinking, I begin humming Leonard Cohen's "Hallelujah."

It is second nature to me. I have been humming at work for years. It has become a ritual for me and superstition with my team at work. This song is our version of a rabbit's foot. I hear Grandma's voice start, then another, then all. We all quietly sing.

I'm amazed—thousands of births, and this is the first time my humming turns into a song.

The room feels sacred and extraordinary. We are singing "Hallelujah" not as a shout, but as a reminder. Harmony is a fitting way to welcome this new soul. I look up to see the young girl's grandfather watching us. He is silent, but his face is glowing. He wipes his eyes and pulls the door shut again.

The baby is ready, as grandmother positions her granddaughter, to allow gravity to aid in the delivery. The contractions are brutal, twisting her young body as she screams in pain. Generations of women are there to support her. The new mother's strength is waning as the last contraction hits. She pushes one last time, the shoulders clear, and he is free. Grandma sighs, and smiles as she holds her great-grandson in her hands.

He is 6 lbs. 4 oz. of perfection. His father kisses his wife, and then he cuts the umbilical cord. Her grandmother cleans him up, then holds him close to her. The room stops and is silent for a single instant as everyone stops to look.

I hold back my tears; he would usually be a promise for the future. Today, he is a gift to help us forget for a minute.

"I'll take care of him. Please take care of my granddaughter," she says to me. I turn and see the new mother and her baby being tended to by the people who make up a continual line of care. As a new great-grandmother she is holding the newest member of the family. It is an unbreakable web. I watch her place the little one on her granddaughter's chest. I stand back and see what my profession looks like when handled with love.

In thirty years of being a nurse, this is the first birth I have been afforded the honor to witness instead of work. She is in excellent hands, and I did not intrude. After twenty years of obstetrics, he is my last little one. I pause, realizing in waves that my life's work is over.

I wait until the energy calms a bit, then I check both the baby and his mom. Both are doing well. I say so, then step out of the way as I see I am no longer needed. I'm sure I never really was.

Now she needs her family. She is hungry, sore, and tired. Her clan is here, and I leave mother and baby in their loving hands. I thank them for the privilege of sharing this day and head for the door. I am hugged from all directions and share my gratitude with all of the people who I have just met. Each one has allowed me in.

I emerge to tell everyone not already in the room that it is safe to enter and see their new baby boy. They move by me to embrace the newest member of their family.

I stand in the doorway and watch as a giant of a man cups his great-grandson in one hand and welcomes him to the world with the softest of kisses. He looks intensely at the boy staring up at him. A tear from his cheek falls and startles the baby. Five sets of waiting hands fly in, and he hands him back to his wife.

He stands, wipes his eyes again, and makes his way toward

me. He kisses my hand and thanks me.

I tell him, "Thank you for allowing me to be part of his birth." He hugs me lightly and turns the rest of the way out of the door.

Chapter Thirty-One

I MOVE TO FOLLOW HIM, Grandpa, out of the door, but cannot until I get one more round of hugs. Grandpa points me to a second bathroom so that I can clean up.

I wash and stop for a few minutes to let my heart catch up to the events of today. I remember hearing my dog bark once during the baby's birth. I wonder how she has fared without me.

I wander down the hall to find her sitting calmly, smiling; she has been waiting for me. I take a seat as she puts her head in my lap. I relax and get comfortable. A man I have not seen before appears with a plate of food and says, "You must be starving, your dog ate enough for three."

I blush a bit. "We forgot to eat this morning." With the initial excitement of the birth dissipating, I realize I am weak from hunger. The smell of fantastic food fills the air. I close my eyes and deeply savor the aroma. I am content to sit. I thank the man for my plate and quietly give thanks for this day.

I am about to eat when Grandpa sits next to me, holding my backpack. I take my first bite and look up at him. "Oh my," I say, taking another bite.

He smiles. "I can cook a bit."

"You made this?" He nods as he leans back in his chair and says, "You appear out of nowhere, with that dog and a broken bike, looking worse for the wear, and announce you are a highly skilled neonatal nurse. Life never ceases to amaze."

I try to listen mindfully to what he says next, but his words are lost as I am shoveling food in like a rescued castaway. I eat and rest, and now understand why the fates wouldn't leave me alone.

For the first time, I look around the house to see where I am. I am in a lovely home, full of people who care for each other. I feel the nip of envy. My family was lost to me yesterday. I sit still and hold my emotions at bay. The house is full of people telling stories and talking about the preciousness of the newest member of their clan.

Grandpa gets my attention. Small talk is for typical days and ordinary circumstances. There is little desire for small talk. Behind the joy, we are still facing the end of the world.

He asks me if I have what I need for the next few days.

I decide to ask questions instead of providing answers. "I have been mostly out of touch for the last couple of days. Can you tell me what you know?"

He stares at me in disbelief. "You must be the only person in the world not to have seen the endless replays on TV. They filmed the black hole swallowing CERN. They showed that drone footage endlessly. How have you not seen it?"

I freeze as my plate falls to the floor. I gasp as a surge of understanding envelops me. I can't breathe. I can't talk. The realization that the world watched my husband die is hitting me. I feel like that moment when I miss the final step and wonder if I can catch myself before I hit the ground. I am in free fall. I have been unknowingly holding on to hope that my husband was still alive.

That hope disappeared as his words hit my ears. I burst into tears.

All the men back away, as Grandpa puts his hand on my knee and waits. I try to speak, but he shushes me and hands me a handkerchief. He sits quietly. I am inconsolable.

"My husband is gone," I finally sputter incoherently. "Oh my God," I mutter. I surf another wave of emotion that is tearing my heart from my chest. This wave is longer than the first and tosses me more violently. I am devastated as the pain of his loss racks my body.

Wave after wave crushes me as the news sinks deeper into me. My body contorts as the first understanding of how much I have lost overwhelms me. I am in too much shock to breathe.

Then the dam breaks again. Grandpa sits quietly with me. I fight to get above my pain, but am unable. I am inconsolable.

Crying is exhausting, and eventually, the waves of grief

become small enough that I am finally able to speak. He asks how it was possible that I didn't know.

My voice halting, I explain that I haven't seen the news. I tell him about camping at home. Then, I open up and tell him everything. I tell him a little about my yesterday, then who my husband is. He was, as far as I know, at CERN when it was engulfed. I tell him of the phone message and the timeline he has laid out for me. About my lost opportunity to say goodbye.

Grandpa sits silently listening and waits for me to finish. He finally says, "Oh my God, I am so sorry. I had no idea."

"How could you have?" I want to hug him. Instead, I thank him for his kindness and apologize for my outburst. I say I am sorry as tears again fill my eyes. I sit in the chair, my heart pounding, I'm unable to stop crying. I am getting so tired of this, never knowing when my emotions will disable me.

I hear a chair slide back and look up to see a young man coming toward me, his face scowling at me. "Your husband did this! Your husband doomed us, doomed that baby?" He is growing angrier and is pointing down the hallway. He points at me. "You did this?"

He is becoming more and more agitated as the men around him either try to hold him back or are starting to look questioningly at me.

One of the men that greeted me earlier now questioningly repeats what his son said. "You did this?"

I sit in shock. I feel alarmed by the aggression of the situation. A desire to fight back is overtaking me. I am having trouble holding onto my rage. My jaw tightens as I hear my dog growl.

My dog stands. I start to move, looking for a way to get her and me out of the house. I am ready to run when Grandpa stands up and says, "Enough. Did you not hear what she said? Her husband is there to help. Like she is here to help us. Sit down and be still or go outside. Better yet, just go outside. All of you go." He is not a man to be trifled with, and half the room clears out.

He apologizes and asks if he can hug me, and I am relieved. I hold on to him for dear life, trying to feel safe. I let go sooner than I wanted to. I am struggling to regain my composure. I feel trapped and try to excuse myself.

He asks me to forgive his family and has his niece make me another plate. I am scared. I want out, but I have nowhere to go and no way to get there. I am still broken to travel very far. I look down at my dog. She is staring up at me. She tells me to sit still and compose myself. She is right; exhaustion and hunger win. She doesn't move, and I am too tired to move.

My dog slides closer, acting like she wants to comfort me, but I can tell she is also looking for any bits of food missed in the cleanup. I call her a brat.

She looks at me with sad eyes, but I know it is her way of begging for a bite of the beef on my plate. I assure her that giving her food is not going to happen. I am starving, and it would be rude.

Three bowls, I say to her. I thought I taught you better.

She wags her tail. "I'm a dog," she says to me. I plan on

eating every last bit of what is on my plate. My heart has slowed, the room has quieted, and I feel safer.

As I savor my food, Grandpa and I begin to talk. We talk about life, babies, and the oddness of our meeting. His composure allows me to begin to relax into his space and feel at home.

I toy for a second about asking to stay. I don't. This space is not mine. My purpose here is over, but I don't want to go. I know I can't stay and need to figure out a way home or to the hospital.

The sun is in the west, and the clouds are turning pink as I ponder which way to go. I decide to go and see my little patient at the hospital. He forces his way into my attention. I see the clock and know I can't resist leaving anymore.

I look at Grandpa and say, "I do love your company, but it is time for me to go." He tells me I can stay if I would like. I shake my head no, wondering why, for the second time, I am pushing away from safety.

I stand to excuse myself and ask for my bike.

Grandpa says, "Your bike is broken, and I have nothing I can use to fix it. The best I can do is offer you a ride."

CHAPTER THIRTY-TWO

"YOU HAVE A CAR that works?" I ask.

He nods and motions for someone to grab my bike as he leads me to his garage. As I walk in, I look at him and say, "You own a 1957 GMC Stepside?" He smiles. I continue, "From the summer when I was twelve until I was fifteen, my father and I rebuilt one exactly like this one. I learned about cars turning a wrench on every bolt on that truck."

I look it over from end to end, then the inside. "This truck is perfect. I remember the day my dad said to me that I was too old to need a babysitter, and I had the ideal sized hands to tighten bolts he was having trouble getting to. He turned off the TV and made me go to the garage with him. I protested to deaf ears."

Grandpa laughs and waits for me to continue. "I loved spending time with him. We listened to sports or music on the radio, he let me drink my first beer, and slowly I became the son my father never had. In that garage, he birthed in me a love for classic cars, Motown, baseball, and beer. As I got older, I became more interested in my friends, but by then, I was hooked and was never too far from his next project. Dad was always building something in our garage."

"I would have liked your dad. My middle boy is the one that loves cars. The others only drive them." Grandpa and I swap stories. Sharing details about the cars we have owned, and the joys each one brought. He tells me this truck was his father's and that he rebuilt it once his dad had entirely worn it out. "He gave it to me in 1978. It has been my pride and joy ever since. I would scrape together a bit of money and fix something on her. Baling wire held that bumper in place for a few years."

I say, "I know the process, I've built a few vehicles in my life. I have a '63 split-window at home that is about seventy-five-percent done." He whistles with approval.

I ask, "Can I tell you something about that first truck?" He nods. "Being almost 16, I had convinced myself that the truck was going to be my dad's gift for my birthday. When the day arrived, I got a boom box and a pizza party. I said to my dad, 'What about the truck?' He said, 'What?' I said, 'Isn't the truck for my birthday?' He and my uncles burst out laughing. 'Oh no, darlin'. No, that truck is all mine.'

Grandpa exploded with laughter, and said, "Damn right."

I continued, "He said if I wanted a truck like this one, I know what it takes, and that he as my partner would love to help."

"What did you build?" Grandpa asks. I grinned and replied, "You are going to laugh. My son still has it." Grandpa looks intently at me with a half-smile, waiting for my next words. "A 1965 Triumph Thruxton Bonneville."

Grandpa laughs, "A bike? Your dad helped you build a motorcycle?" He shakes his head in disbelief. "Your dad is a better man of his word than I would have been. No, not ever, would I build a motorcycle for a sixteen-year-old child of mine."

I stare at him, and he shakes his head. "My wife would have killed me." I said, "He got a kick out of telling his friends I was building the motorcycle all of them envied. They would make excuses to come over and check it out. My dad had a 1969 Norton Commando he had just finished. Our project gave him a reason to take me out of school, borrow a friend's old TX500, and go for rides. He told my mom we were tracking down parts, but she knew it was because we both felt most free when motoring together down the highway."

"I love the memories I have from each of those rides. The summer we finished building her, we rode them across the country to celebrate. We considered going into Mexico, but my mom would not hear of it. 'It is time for my children to come home,' she said firmly to my father. She put her foot down, and we could not figure a way around her. We did ride home via the long route, arriving a week later than we promised."

Grandpa smiles. "Your mom sounds like a saint and a lot like the woman you met in there. She comes from a family of motor people." He then told about when he, with his brothers and dad, raced the dirt track circuits. "I learned how to build cars on a shoestring. In the week from Sunday to Saturday, we would put together a racer that would be destroyed in fifty laps. Win or lose, my dad would be all smiles. He would smile a little bigger each time—and there were many—that he beat my wife's father." He nudges me, noticing his wife is standing within earshot.

I smiled at him and wait for him to continue. "A couple of times a year, my dad would let me drive. You do the work; you should get some of the fun." He would say, 'My mom used to say my dad put a wrench in my hand before he gave me a bottle.'"

He points to a wall full of car photos. "I built and rebuilt them all." He takes a picture of a 1940 Mercury Coupe off the wall. "This is my favorite. It turned the head of my wife nearly forty years ago. All of this started with this car."

We both look at the photo and take a deep breath. I hold back tears. He doesn't. "So much is about to go away. The scale of the loss is overwhelming. That little one won't get any of this." I begin to cry. He hands me a fresh handkerchief, and we cry together. We hug until the tears stop, and I don't feel alone for the first time in days.

"Darlin', I could talk to you all night, but you have places you want to go, and I offered you a ride. Where can I take you?" he asks.

"Home, please, I can take my scrubs off in peace, thanks to you." I excuse myself to the bathroom to wash my face and hands. I look into my bag and decide not to change my clothes. As I leave the bathroom and I find him waiting for me holding his great-grandson.

"He wanted to say goodbye." I lean and kiss the little one on the forehead. He then kisses him too and returns him to his wife, who hugs me before she takes him back. We say a thousand words to each other with a glance and a smile. I hug her, and we whisper, "thank you" at the same time. She grabs my hand and holds it, fighting back her tears. She puts my hand into Grandpa's and says, "You need to go and hurry back."

He opens the door for me, and I climb in. He puts my dog into the back, and the three of us are ready for our last ride in a vehicle. He turns the key, and I'm reminded of my dad driving his truck. I am beyond sad, but I don't have time or the luxury to become lost in grief right now.

I dry my eyes and say, "Brings back great memories. I can't thank you enough."

He smiles and says, "You're welcome."

I can't believe I am looking out of a windshield of my dad's truck as we head out into the last sunlight of the day.

CHAPTER THIRTY-THREE

"CAN I ASK YOU A FAVOR?"

He nods.

"Can you please take me by the hospital? I have to see what is going on there."

He thinks for a moment, then says, "I will, but understand my priorities are at home."

I nod. Grandpa turns right and heads toward my hospital. We ride in silence. We are both far away; anguish and loss mixing with living fully in the joy of listening to the music of tires on the pavement.

The windows are down; fresh air fills my lungs and caresses my face. With the heat on full it is still a bit chilly, but we would have it no other way. Me acting like a teenager makes Grandpa smile at me as he plays with the air rushing against his hand. We enjoy the silence of sitting with a kindred spirit. Words would not have made it better.

We crest the hill, and there it sits, a massive building, dark and empty. I am startled, wondering how this can be. "It's dark?" I mutter. "Turn here, please go by the emergency entrance." He turns and goes where I am pointing.

The hospital stands like a shell. My mind is reeling. How can no one be here? Where are all the people? What about my patients? My little warrior? I need to see how he is doing.

I am having trouble processing what I am seeing. I never imagined my hospital empty. We ease to a stop well away from the building, and I point at what I perceive to be a hospital security guard. He is pacing, checking the doors, and trying to look in the windows. We both watch him. He is too preoccupied to have noticed us.

I turn to Grandpa and say, "I wonder if he is injured."

"He looks fine from here. Are we done?" Grandpa sees the look in my eye, and before I say what I am thinking, he grumbles a bit and begins to move the truck forward. The man turns and watches us.

As we near him, I yell out the window, "Are you okay?"

The man in the dark hesitates for a second, looking to us, then back to the hospital doors. He begins to walk to the driver's side window of the truck. It is dark, and he is nervous and is keeping his distance.

Grandpa says, "That's close enough."

The man in the shadows stops and says, "I'm fine. What are you doing here?"

I can tell Grandpa is ready to go, but is tolerating my concerns. He is a gentleman, but I am testing his patience.

"Where is everyone?" I say.

The young man says he doesn't know and for us to move on. I explain I am a nurse and have patients here that are my concern.

He says it isn't safe here and more firmly asks us to move on.

I refuse and ask him to explain why I can't go in.

He takes a deep breath and says, "There were three patients in the isolation unit of the hospital that are highly contagious. When the generators failed, the containment on the quarantine units failed. The hospital's management said they didn't know for certain that the world was ending. They decided they had to do everything they could to protect this community if our society doesn't come to an end. They ordered the hospital locked. No one inside could leave. No one outside can go in."

"People are locked inside?" I ask.

He nods and says, "Please go. I have work to do."

"Why are you here?" I ask. Illuminated partially by head-lights, I think I recognize him, but I want to be sure.

"My wife and baby son are inside. I left for home late last night to get a list of things my wife wanted. On the way back here, the power went off, and my car died in the middle of the street. I was miles from the hospital, so I had to walk. I am not that familiar with this part of town and made my way by talking to people who were mostly trying to make their way home.

"Taking a very long route, I eventually found my way here. It took me several hours to find this place. When I finally did, I found the doors locked, and a few people standing together saying they are glad they got out before the doors were closed for good. Everyone who chose to leave is gone. I'm here because I have nowhere else to be. My wife is likely scared and wondering what became of me. I need to be in there."

I turn on the cabin light of the truck, and recognition finds his face. "How is he doing?" I ask.

He replies, "He was breathing fine when I left. I can't believe I am standing out here with them inside. All for this bag of useless stuff."

We stare at each other in silence. There is nothing either of us can do.

I am completely helpless, knowing he is standing there because of me. I am stunned by the feeling that there is no action I can take that will help him get to his family. I am not used to feeling helpless. The feeling rattles me.

I am trying to think through the situation when he says, "You need to go, and I need to get back to work."

I have to decide to go with Grandpa or stay and help. "Do you think if I stay with you, I can be helpful?"

He shakes his head. "This is my place to be, not yours. Thank you, but it would be best for me if you go."

I try to hand him my bag when Grandpa says, "Hold on to your stuff."

He puts the truck in gear and drives forward with me in mid-question. He stops and puts the truck in reverse, backing up to the door. "I have a strap under your seat, do you mind?"

I open the door and remove my dog from the back of the truck, then pull out the emergency bag and set it in the truck's bed. I find the strap and hand one end to the father as I attach the other end to the tow bar of the truck.

The door is no match for the power of the truck. With a tug, no barrier to the inside of the hospital remains.

I stand in shock as the door is lying shattered on the ground. I find myself laughing as I roll the strap up and return it to the bag. The little one's father says his thanks and disappears into the darkness of the hospital.

I look in, but there is no way I am following him. I have no desire to explore the remnants of my old life.

I stand for a second and survey the scene. Grandpa pulls away from the carnage so that I can return my dog to the safety of the truck. When I climb in, all I can say is, "You tore the door off the hospital."

"I did." He smiles. "He needed to see his boy and his wife."

We stare at each other in silence, then we both begin to laugh hysterically.

I breathe deep and say, "That was one of the coolest things I have ever seen. It looked like a scene from a Clint Eastwood movie."

He turns to me and—doing his best Dirty Harry imitation—he says, "Well, punk, you have a choice to make. Are you coming or going?"

"Coming," I say without hesitation as I close the door of the truck. I need no time to mull over my choice. It is not nearly as hard as I imagined it would be. How impossible this choice would have been for me this morning, but the hospital is no longer my hospital. It is a shell of the place I loved. "That life is over. Thank you."

Grandpa looks at me and says, "Are you ready?"

I nod, and he begins to drive away. I am sad I never got to share my gratitude with the people I worked with for years. The few that I love and admire.

I look over my shoulder and say goodbye to yet another thing in my life. I wonder if anyone I know is still inside. There has to be. I say *thank you* in my mind as the truck begins to move.

I speculate if I wouldn't be more useful inside, then realize it doesn't matter. What was I going to be able to do? I have no energy left. I am exhausted. I examine my heart and know I have nothing more I want to give. Fate has spoken for those still inside; their lives will end here. Mine won't.

I sigh and say goodbye to a place I no longer love.

"Oh my God, thank you. That could not have been more perfect. Did you see his face when you tore that door off?"

He smiles and pats my leg, "You okay?"

I nod yes and hug him. He shakes his head, and we laugh again. We ride for a few blocks in silence punctuated by chuckles, neither of us wanting to speak. Us riding together is enough.

Out of habit, I lean over and turn the radio on.

He looks at me with a confused look. "Slow learner?"

I call him a smartass and explain, "Whenever I was with my dad, we would have the radio on and would usually be singing. Would you mind?"

He smiles and says, "What you got?"

"I know the perfect song." I start to sing, "I'll Take You There" as loud and clean as I can.

He howls with delight, "You got a lot of Mavis, darling." He joins in.

We sing harmony, me an alto, him a baritone. We make music that sounds so good it hurts. I am out of my mind with joy, "You can sing." I say.

"So can you, darlin'," he says as we ride. "Grapevine," "Respect," "Dock of the Bay," "Everyday People," "Dancing in the Street." We are like school kids driving and singing without a care in the world. We are delighting in each other's company. "Who knew the end of the world would be so fun?"

"We're not gone yet," he says.

"No, but we are getting close to my house; turn left at the next street." My heart gets heavy as we are getting close to saying goodbye. I ask if we can sing one last song.

He says, "What now?"

I breathe deep and start to cry.

Grandpa takes my hand, and I watch him try to keep his composure. I look him in the eyes and his dam breaks. The magnitude of everything hits us. He pulls over, and we share, without words, our loss, our loves, our last moments.

We are kindred spirits with no time to get to know each other, so we share intensely for the minutes we have.

CHAPTER THIRTY-FOUR

HE SLOWLY TURNS THE LAST CORNER. We are not ready to say goodbye as he pulls up in front of my house. We sit in the truck and wait, holding on to one more minute of our too-brief adventure.

I notice the bonfire burning and a few people paying attention to us. They stare like they see a ghost. I watch as he looks around.

He stops and stares at the people gathered around the fire and then to me. "Your people?"

"My clan," I say.

"Well, this is it," he says, extending his hand to me. I smile and shake my head. I hesitate knowing I can't stay, but not wanting to leave. "You sure know how to show a girl a good time. This is the second-best first date I have ever been on." I take his hand in both of mine.

"Second?" he asks.

"Second." I assure him.

He smiles, "I'll take that." We both laugh again. He thanks me for everything.

I thank him as I grip his hand more tightly. "I need to ask you for one more thing? You remind me of my dad. He was the finest man I have ever known. Can I get a hug?"

He gets out of the truck and opens his arms. I take a step forward and fall into his embrace. I savor feeling safe in his arms. I pull him tighter and hold on. I feel small in his embrace like I am twelve years old again.

He tells me I am an angel. I say he is one, too. I hold on tightly, feeling like I am not alone. I grasp him well longer than is usual, but I do not want it to end. He starts to step back, and I refuse to let go. We stand and embrace a little longer.

I finally loosen my grip. He waits, knowing I will change my mind and grip him even tighter.

"I love you," slips from my mouth. I lurch back, embarrassed.

He smiles and says, "I understand." As he turns, I steal one last hug, then slowly let him go. He smiles at me and walks back to open the tailgate to let my dog out.

I warn him to watch for broken glass. We both laugh and relive the moment the door skittered across the pavement.

I watch him grab my bike, and he puts it down in front of me. I step around it so I can give him one last hug, when he whispers,

"You are something else. I wish I had a chance to know you better. You sure you don't want to come home with me?"

I shake my head, *no.* "This is my space. I need to be here."

I tear up a bit as he slowly climbs back into his truck. He sits for a minute, looking at me. "Next time, you are going to have to show me that split window, but now I have to go."

"It will be ready soon. I'll come over and take you for a ride. I might even let you drive." I try to laugh but can't, as I have a frog in my throat. Somehow, I manage to say, "Kiss your grandbaby for me."

I lean through the window and kiss him on the cheek and grab his hand. I hold on. He looks at me. Through my tears, I gasp, "I don't want to say goodbye, but I know I have to."

He grips my hand a little tighter, "The invitation is open."

We stay in a place beyond words for a minute longer. Then I let go and shake my head *no.* We stare at each other; he sighs and mumbles, "Goodbye," as he starts to move.

I can't say goodbye. "I have had enough goodbyes." I let go of his hand and step away.

He says nothing as he pulls away.

I stand and watch as his truck disappears into the darkness. I stand for a minute longer, hoping to see him turn around, hoping he will take me home with him. Hoping he will keep me safe.

I have not been unsafe for a minute, but he made me feel secure, and now he is gone. The difference is stark. He is gone. The reality that I am alone rolls at me like a tsunami.

My dog stares at me. "What a day, my friend," I say as I pet her face. I linger on the street until all hope is gone.

Alone is hard, but I am grateful that I felt truly alive today. Alive is a magnificent gift, and I spent this day well. I pick up my bike, and together we head for home. The sun has set long ago. I'm tired and in need of a shower. I cross my fingers that the hot water still works.

I follow my dog. We are both happy to be home. I fumble my way through my dark house, feeling my way to the counter where I left candles, the lantern, and a flashlight. I take the candles. I strip off my nurse's scrubs with none of the fanfare I exercised when I put it on this morning.

I look at the pile on the floor and feel sad as I step over it on my way to the bathroom. I think, *see Mom, no more of my symbolic gestures.* I hear my dad laugh in my mind; he knows me too well. I stop, pick it up, and fold it neatly. "Another last," I sigh. I stare at it and say goodbye to all it means to me. Gestures.

I take a deep breath before turning on the facet. The water sputters, then out comes hot water. I rejoice. Gifts come in strange packages, and I am learning to recognize and celebrate them in whatever form they appear.

I had never once showered with only the flicker of a candle for light. I love it. It changes the whole experience for the better. I wish I had known; I would have done this regularly. A shower was mostly a morning "to do" item. It was a daily necessity, done quickly, because I was late and needed to run out the door.

Showering by candlelight seems to give me permission to slow down and be still. Stillness is a treasure. I am new at it and am learning the profound joy of silence and solitude. I have spent my life moving, rarely taking a moment to stop and enjoy what is around me. I was always chasing after something, looking for what to do next.

It took the last two days to teach me to truly savor my life. I sit in the stillness of my house and enjoy not having a to-do list. Now I have no choice. Before I make my way to bed, I decide to try a ritual taught to me by a patient of mine. I have never taken the time to do it until tonight. If not now—when?

She told me to sit on the edge of the bed and take a few minutes to review my day; to live it all again in my mind. I identify the gifts of the day and audibly give thanks for each of them. I am reliving each moment. This practice makes this day richer, and the lessons of the day are not so easily lost.

I sit on my bed with my dog, amazed by the day we have lived. A day she made possible for me.

I thank her, and she snuggles my face. I wonder what it is like inside the hospital tonight. Is it completely dark? Are my patients scared? Could I have helped? I ponder making the trip there tomorrow, then dismiss it as crazy. I picture my little warrior and his family together and laugh at recalling Grandpa's satisfied face as his truck ripped the hospital door off.

I think of him surrounded by his family and his new great-grandson. I think about all his family in one place, and wish mine was here. I remember my parents and being a parent. What would I be doing in this situation if my kids were little or sick? I feel a wave of melancholy coming, and I let it take me.

I wish I had tried this practice sooner. I don't have any more tomorrows.

My dog moves closer, and we can read each other's minds. "I love you, too," I tell her as I hold her. One memory leads to another.

I move to my favorite chair with a comforter sewn by women I worked with twenty years ago. I snuggle under it as I place the candle on the table. I sit and gently roll my foot, being soothed by the rocking, moving like I did with my children and grand-children. I am not ready to sleep quite yet. I am not prepared for this life to end.

I am not analyzing. I am letting my thoughts come. I let the pain and joy dance to the rhythm of the night. These hours could be my last, and I need to remember, to thank, to hug the people I love as best I can. I remember my parents tucking me in and feeling so loved. I miss feeling their kisses.

I smile as I recall my dad acting like Santa Claus every year of my early childhood. A spoon in a glass for bells and a *Ho Ho Ho* that shook the house, causing my siblings and me to race to the living room. I always just missed the sleigh disappearing over the house.

I remember my first puppy and how I loved her. Then my love for the dog with her head in my lap. I feel the echoes of all the life that has passed in this house. I hear the giggles of delight. The creaking of this chair as I waited up late into the night. The relief I felt when my kids finally were safe at home.

Memories are all that I have now. My whole life is in my

heart. I am cried out, and I am glad I am. I can now sit in the quiet, at peace with myself.

I think about my husband and our life together. I love the life I have lived. All of the Thanksgivings and Christmases. The heartbreaks and the triumphs. The dinners with my friends. I remember my father, husband, and son, watching whatever sport was on, listening to them roar as I sat with my mom and daughter enjoying a fall day, like today. I listen to my mom tell stories about her parents and my dad in their younger days— God, how I miss them. I have been so loved.

I have lived a great life. I sit still in my rocker, and I can only breathe deeply. I have nowhere to be and no expectations for a tomorrow that may or may not come. I let my heart continue to explore, to search for treasures I have forgotten. I rock in my chair for a little while longer. I sit quietly, letting memories come and go.

I remember the day my parents dropped me at college. They helped me put my dorm room together, both of them lingering, not wanting to go. I remember my anticipation growing as I wanted to join the party starting on my floor. I remember how long each hugged me before they said goodbye. I remember hugging each of my kids the same way.

I sing a line from a Judy Collins hit and wonder what side I am on now. Silly youth meets my equally ridiculous gray haired self.

I look around and see my husband's slippers. I go pick them up and set them on my lap. I put them on my hands, then onto my feet. I miss him so much. We have been together for longer than forever. My companion through this life is not here when I need him most.

In my mind, I walk through our meeting, dating, becoming engaged, and marrying. Our children. Our families. Our houses, jobs, and cars. The joy. The catastrophes. The love. The sharing. I remember too many goodbyes. I remember our last goodbye over a cup of coffee. Our morning coffee together.

Crap, I didn't get the camping gear out. I consider going now, but that is not going to happen.

I see the pictures of my children and relive the birth of each one. How are two people born into the same everything so different?

"My children," I sigh. Children I will never see again. I wish more than anything that they were here right now. I would give anything for one more word or hug, with each of them. My son joking if I had to pick one, it would surely be him. My daughter would laugh and play along, telling him how she had to convince her dad and me into keeping him. "Dad wanted to trade you for a basketball, but Mom wouldn't let him. She wanted a set of wrenches," she would say.

I miss hearing the excitement in all of their voices as they stopped what they were doing to chat on the phone. My dad's joyful hello when he heard my voice. I loved how he said hello to me every time I called. No one else ever greeted me on the phone the way he did. I sigh again and hug my blanket.

I pet my dog, who is now sitting in my lap. I feel her warmth on my legs. I remember the babies I have rocked in this chair, upon becoming a grandparent and rocking each of them here too. "The last loved one to be rocked in this chair is you," I say to her. Her tail wags, and I pet her.

I am surprised at the next face that crosses my mind. I see the face of the man that dropped me off a few minutes ago. He feels like family. He made me feel like part of his family, and I loved it. I wish I had years to get to know him better.

I have lived a lot of life. I am grateful for every second. I never knew a second was so valuable, and now I am holding on to each one.

My dog rubs against my hand. I pet her softly. "It is you and me now." She licks my hand wanting more attention. I am both happy and sad.

The candle flickers, burning low, and I use the flame of the last one to start a new one.

I think how life is like a candlelit path. The small amount of light on the trail is just bright enough to take the next step, but not enough to see beyond that.

I debate blowing out the candle and heading off to sleep, but decide to sit for a few more minutes. I think about the people that made my life my life. The friends that have passed through. The ones which have faded and those I have held on to. The hikes, the trips, the talks late into the night. The times they rescued me, and I rescued them. I wish I could gather each one for a glass of wine, a hug, and a thank-you. They fade as I fade.

We wander down the hallway to bed, and we both fall asleep.

DAY FIVE:

Today the lake is flat
the clouds heavy

My mirror?

The sun's light only bothering to
enhance the gray
to nuance the stillness

Not an echo on the water
Not a whisper in the air

I'm standing
like a tree
my feet damp
my legs as heavy as the mist

Am I reaching for an unfathomable star
or am I planted
roots holding me to this beloved place

I listen;
straining to hear which way the deer go
for a bird waking
for a leaf descending

With each inhale
A drop of dew dances across
the brim of my hat
It too unsure of the way to go

I think to step
but do not

Disturbing this sacred moment
even with a single step
seems blasphemy

Perfection hangs like a narrator
reminding me not to breathe

I am to be
to be stillness
to be in this place
to wait

CHAPTER THIRTY-FIVE

THE SUN IS FILLING MY BEDROOM. I am unsure about how to feel about what is likely Earth's last day. My mind swirls, some thoughts are too big to fit into a single moment. I have to break it down into smaller bites. I have to say it out loud to process the magnitude.

"Every single thing on Earth, and the Earth herself will likely be gone by the end of today." The words seem like nonsense, but I know they are not. Do I? Am I sure?

I sit, surprised to be alive. I have never thought about this before. I try to start my morning routine. I am restless because today, my mind is bouncing, trying to find a stable place to rest. "All gone...today."

I wonder if I'm crazy. The Earth ending? What the hell am

I thinking? The Earth is fine. She will always be fine. She has been here for 13 billion years, and today a toy built by man is going to destroy her?

No. Stop being foolish. In a day or two, everything will return to normal. The power will come back on. I will talk to my husband, and we will laugh about how hysterical we became. I will call my children and grandchildren. I will make plans with my friends.

Next year the news will give four minutes at the end of the broadcast to remember today. A news analyst will say, "Today is the first anniversary of the Great Global Blackout, what we learned and where are we now, but first a message from our sponsors." The ad will likely be from CERN, trying to restore its public image.

I smile and think a sponsor is a polite term for that relationship. I tell my mind to stop, as I don't have the energy or interest for the rest of that thought.

I am only sure that I am unsure of what to do next. My mind leaps back to walking into my husband's office and hitting play on the answering machine. I relive hearing the message that changed my world. "God, I hope you get this..." I think out loud.

I am going nowhere but in a circle. I can't stop playing and replaying that message in my head. The joy of hearing his voice, then the crush of the contents—hearing the man I love say good-bye. "God, I hope you get this..." Playing it over and over again. Knowing it is the last time I will hear his voice.

I remember the feeling when Grandpa told me the whole world watched my husband die. Millions of people were saying they are sorry, responding to the horror, but I suspect they also are thinking they are glad it is not them. My heart breaks again, knowing it was the man I had spent my life with dying before their eyes.

I wonder what he was doing. I am sure he was trying to save the world. I imagine him in a superhero suit, with a cape. I picture a room full of scientists working to stop what they had started.

My mind starts racing. Flashing from image to image of them trying to put Pandora back in her box. In the noisiness of my mind, I recall James Hillman saying, "It was only when science convinced us the Earth was dead that it could begin its autopsy in earnest." I wonder where that thought came from, and why now. They are making the whole thing disappear.

I am suddenly overcome. My jaw clenches and my hands turn to fists. "No," I shout, "No. No. No." Again, and again, I am too angry to do anything but shout.

I see the faces of the scientists I have met. They are sitting around a conference table with people from all over the world. The table is full of paper and electronics, all now useless given the certainty of what is happening a few feet away.

"You destroyed everything, and you tell me to pull out our camping gear. Fuck you and your need to know about bullshit like black holes and nano-particles. Look at what you have done!" I am breathing hard, trying to regain my composure. I inhale deeply and hope my emotional flair has passed when my mind explodes.

Fuck your gee-whiz science.

You were never satisfied with having everything. You were given billions of dollars a year so you could continue exploring with no responsibility for the consequences of your actions. You were treated like royalty. Your genius gave you a pass so that you never had to grow up. You were always racing to be first, and never having to look back at the mess you left in your wake.

All of you are always anxious to bring about an ever more prominent and more complex toy. Before you said enough, *your latest gee-whiz invention killed you and it's going to kill me, too. Your death was a slow-motion spectacle, broadcast for the world to see. Here I am, left all alone. Alone and facing my death with my dog and a gathering of strangers. All because you always wanted more; more money, more staff, more resources. You were constantly chasing more.*

I walk to his office so I can see a photo of him taken at a presentation of the Nobel Prize in physics. A gathering of those heralded for their exceptional minds. I look at the faces of the geniuses that brought about the end of the world. All of them were awkwardly smiling for the camera. My husband is standing next to the man holding the medal.

The man whose experiment will erase the planet.

I hold the picture as if it is dangerous and stare at it. I have looked into the eyes of every man in this picture. They are not evil. They followed a path where they were praised, recognized, and financed by our society to pursue. They are scientists, and this gave them special permission to run wild, never being held responsible for the unexpected consequences of every advancement they make. Each is spending their lives solving one problem, then the next, until they finally created a problem they couldn't.

I am babbling in circles. I take a deep breath, then another, and try to regain myself.

I go to set the picture down. I look at it closely. My feeling of despair slowly turns to disgust. Disgust for every one of them. Each smiling into the camera. They are entirely unaware of what their lives' work will become.

In anger, I pick the picture up and throw it. I hear it shatter when it hits. I look for a photo of my husband—just him. I'm forgetting what he looks like, what he sounds like, how it feels to touch him. I need to see his face.

As I look, I think about how people couldn't afford to go to the hospital to deliver a baby. Still, as a society, we can spend billions so they as a group can learn about things not one in a million people honestly give a shit about. One in a million? It's more like 100 million—the Priests of Progress always got their funding.

The more I reflect on his work, the angrier I get. *I love you, and you are now dead.* I lose control and am back on the roller coaster again. *There was never enough for you and your friends. You are always whining about needing more...of everything. Now you are taking everything. You told me that it was the wonder of the stars. Camping as a boy—that started the fire that drove you, pushing you to understand how it all came into being. I fell in love with you and your science. As a student, your dream was to understand the nature of the universe.*

Yours was to unlock the next layer of astonishment. Yours was to pull back the veil and show us, we mere mortals, the tapestry of the universe. I remember the glory of you explaining the strands of silk. You were revealing the unseen that made a walk in the forest, or sitting under a night sky with you a life-changing event.

I feel like a jilted lover. The anger rises as I remember what happened when the wonder faded, and the pursuit of funding took its place. The beauty of the dream died.

"Fuck you," I snarl. "Fuck you and your science. Fuck your need to know. Some fucking geniuses you all are. I am about to die because of your arrogance." Words stop as the flow is coming faster than I can speak. *I am going to stop. I am going to stop existing because of you. Everything is going to stop living because of you.*

I see the faces of thousands of my patients that lived lives because of technology. They knew joy, love, beauty, and peace because of science. I try to hold them in my mind and stay in this place, but I can't. All I hear is, "Get out the camping gear," and I explode again.

I stare at the picture of us together and try to remember the love. I can't bear to look at it. *Us, what is us? You and me sharing space and time, but us? Us?* If not you, I would have been "us" with a random other. I had a billion choices of people who could have taken your place. *"Us."* I throw his picture, and it smashes. *Us, what the fuck was us?*

My dog peeks around the corner, and I see her. "I am going to die. You are going to die. All of the people I love in my life are going to die." I look at her and I'm hit with knowing that she's my only loved one close enough to hug. This thought makes me snarl.

The more I ruminate about everything I love dying, the more enraged I become.

"I am trapped because of something as idiotic as a collider being in the hands of people who were so sure they knew everything. How arrogant you all were, every last one of you."

I recall asking about Murphy's Law, and how you scoffed at me. How sure you and your colleagues were nothing could go wrong. Not would but could, you left no room for the possibility that anything was beyond your control, beyond your stellar intellects. You treated me like a child, with your condescending smiles. Now I face the destruction of the Earth at your hands.

Two hundred years ago, religion's brightest minds debated the number of angels that can rest on the tip of a pin. Today, science's most intelligent minds discuss the existence of particles in the 13th dimension. The first time I had this thought, it made me smile.

I'm not smiling now.

I attended the dedication ceremony at CERN. I was being

assured by a group of PhDs: "Impossible. The collider was designed with a hundred fail-safes. It's impossible for it to malfunction catastrophically."

Standing where I'm standing, I guess you needed at least one more.

We are here for three reasons. Your fail-safes were designed and certified by people whose livelihoods depended on the project being built. The lowest bidder completed the construction. Lastly, politics and budget overruns forced the cutting of corners.

You geniuses pooh-poohed me when I pointed out that this was a recipe for disaster. You said it was unimaginable. I said Fukushima, Bhopal, plastics, pesticides, and antibiotics. I recalled years of interactions, years of being told by scientists that science can solve anything that goes wrong by applying more science. You, with absolute assurance, told me new scientific advances would always be designed to reverse the unforeseen effects of the latest technology gone wrong. I asked for an example of the model he was espousing. He went silent, then babbled gibberish about obvious advancements and inevitable strides forward. I was then dismissed for someone with an easier question.

When my husband showed me the announcement for the collider's construction, I said, "Science is building another temple for its priests. A place to practice your dark arts." He waxed on about research, and I remained quiet until I couldn't.

"It is your Saint Peter's Basilica. Science is your religion, and you are its evangelists. Science's pronouncement is it makes life better because it expands our understanding. I've heard this sentiment at dozens of your conferences. It is a tenant of your faith. You are not different from any devotee of any religion. You spout the core beliefs of your faith as fact. Your safe place when disaster appears is that it is too soon to tell and that more research is needed to be sure. You say science is about questions and that your method is the best way to explore."

Occasionally I would play the heretic.

"Science makes life more comfortable for a small group of people, period. Mostly first-world people, and your better life is defined by incremental increases in technological creature comforts. Science is deemed a miracle by the people selling the products your work makes possible, and then having those profits fund more research, new products, and private jets.

"There is not an indigenous culture ever that benefited from any of it, not one that ever sought to live the life your science offered. Your science destroyed their way of life, their land, their language. You killed them by the millions, all while you defined them as savages." He would smile and shake his head.

I admit I love and rely on the comforts as much as anyone. I hate to be cold, love strawberries in winter, adore being able to talk to my kids while sitting in my favorite chair, or driving my car. I enjoy being snug and entertained inside when it is ten below outside, equally grateful for being cool in summer.

Short-term comfort, however, has become the single measure of scientific success. When the longer-term truths becoming undeniable, science says *trust us*. The people receiving the benefits never examine the total cost of the exchange. The media ignores the lives and lands that are destroyed in this process, unless it is an application that is specifically designed to kill in an efficient and spectacular manner. Then it is proclaimed as an advancement for our protection.

My dog is tired of my rant and tries to stop me. I am tired of myself too, and ask her if she would like to take a walk. Then I look at all of the stuff in my house.

I pick a long-obsolete computer and think about what was lost to make it. What is lost is never weighed against the incremental comfort gained. What is the value of a pristine landscape, a pollution-free sky, drinkable water, unpoisoned food? This loss is never mentioned when the equation of benefit is presented. New was faster and had more memory. Progress has no way to account for the beauty that is lost or the chorus of frogs that once filled the night. Progress never retreats, it pivots and takes more.

Popes always give themselves the ability to stand above and assure everyone subject to their power that their God can solve any problem. Religion uses an all-knowing God to justify their beliefs.

Science uses ever-advancing technology in precisely the same way."

"Why do you reject progress?" they would ask, like the inquisitors of a bygone era.

I would respond, "Science is comfortable with the creation of nuclear waste so I can toast a piece of bread. Thanks, but no thanks."

At first, I felt it absurd that science would end the planet. Now, it is clear that this was the only way our most modern religion could end. Yours is a religion whose priests accept the creation of any toxic waste and killing anything deemed to be impeding advancement, as a necessary by-product. You are a cult that lives with the credo that no price is too high as long as it reveals the next great discovery. Given these parameters, this model is unsustainable for life as I know it. The failure to understand that what is unsustainable is unsustainable has me here, face-to-face with science's final move on the chessboard.

My fury waning, I am left broken. I always assumed that the Earth would remain, that she would shrug us off like the dinosaurs. I thought nature and life always won.

I laugh when I realize that the last remaining sign that the Earth ever existed will be a few deep space launches that will be sending information into the empty space where the Earth used to be. How ironic is it that a science project will be the only tangible proof that the planet science destroyed ever existed? Science irony is not as funny as God irony. How else could it have ended?

"Enough," my dog says. She lets me know I have better things to do. I pet her and thank her for knowing me so well. Let's go for a walk.

CHAPTER THIRTY-SIX

I DID NOT EXPECT TO START my day in such a foul mood. My dog is having none of it. I am standing on the tension of time and nonexistence, and have no idea what to do. I have lived on this tension my whole life, but today, I am fully aware of how tenuous my life has always been. My dog is growing impatient for our trip outside.

I open the back door for her and return upstairs to put on some clothes and prepare for our walk. The birds are singing like they do every other day. A squirrel runs across the power line and jumps onto my garage. The flowers are swaying in the breeze of a warm autumn day. I have tomatoes and peppers to harvest. My dog's tail is wagging, and she is bounding about like she has every other day. She asks me why I am not doing the same.

She tells me that nature treats life as impermanent. Life is an adventure that can end in a flash. I have always taken my life for granted, acting like I was assured a tomorrow as my birthright. I am a human being, after all. I live in a society that when life ends unexpectedly, it is an event that is cause for investigation. It becomes a story on the news, and political leaders assure that steps are being taken to make sure it never happens again. The very next day, it does.

I am a nurse and have seen firsthand that life is fragile. How is it I have believed mine is not?

I listen to the birds, feel the sun on my face, and pet my dog. I rejoice in my life. Standing outside reminds me that nature always wins. That safety is an illusion. Today every single human on the planet is forced to live without science and the technological advancements that have softened nature's rules. No one knows when, or if, the end will come.

This is no different than a week ago, but today it is palatable. The cloak of modern security has rapidly given way. In three days, nearly every system that made us as a species so arrogant about our place at the top of the food chain has failed.

I stop to watch my dog's tail wagging and can't help but be in a better mood. We are hungry. Today is going to be what today is going to be. I will make today my day I will live it. I have right now, and right now, I want coffee. I go to get what I will need from the camping gear.

My husband is a man of routine, and he always made sure his equipment was ready for a new adventure. I pull down the crates, open the first one, and rejoice. I find a water filtering unit, replacement filters, a manually-operated coffee grinder, and iodine tablets. I am happy because the water coming out of my tap is rapidly growing foul.

I get the next box and find what I am looking for: a camp stove, fuel, and an old-fashioned coffee pot. I move the boxes to my kitchen counter and take a cursory look at what is inside. I'm on a mission. I fill and start the camp stove and begin to filter water. I can't wait to have my first coffee in days.

"Get the camping gear" had pissed me off, but now I am so happy it is here. I hear the first *thunk* of the percolator and enjoy the smell. It makes my mouth water. As I wait, I begin to filter water into a five-gallon can. I dump the boxes to see what else they contain that will help me survive if the world doesn't get swallowed up as predicted.

The end. In the last two days, I have not thought about *the end*. What will my last breath be like? Do black holes make noise? I have no idea. I am not sure anyone does. I am sure I don't care to hear anyone's opinion.

Somewhere there is someone still opining that science is one second away from solving the problem; another sure it is the Illuminati that caused all this; yet another convinced that extra-terrestrial beings are running a test to see how humans respond. Any time now, they will be hitting a reset button and rewinding time so that I have to be at work on Tuesday.

Tuesday? I say "Tuesday," and the sound of it is odd in my ears. Nearly everything that has ever lived has never had any idea of what day of the week it is.

The concept of Tuesday exists to serve modern society. Time exists solely to make sure two people are standing in the same place to offer payment and accept the delivery of a good. It does other things, but if it did not do this first thing, it would not be a central component of our understanding of our society.

Time as a ruling force serves to reinforce my belief that nature always wins. Time is not nature, and the passage of time is not a measure of natural processes. The experts I am relying on are the birds.

Hundreds of birds are singing the same songs as any other day. I did not expect birds to teach me so much in my last few days, but they have reminded me that life goes on no matter how dire the circumstances seem. Birds continue to sing, as not one mechanical noise fills the air. The last mechanical sound I expect to hear is the percolator, and now it, too, has stopped.

I take the pot and a cup into the backyard to sit under a gigantic cottonwood tree that was here 200 years before my house. To call it *my* tree has always seemed ridiculous. I pour a cup and savor the smell. I think "the end."

The end? I remember cheesy Creature Feature movies at the drive-in. "The End?" was always the question asked during the final scene of these B-movies, and it makes me laugh.

The End? Was I surely going to cease to exist? I knew it would happen eventually, but I never thought about it happening today. *Today* and *dying* in the same sentence is an abstraction I can not get my head around.

I did not expect to be here this morning; to have one more today. Do I want one more day? My first thought is that in the night I wished the black hole would have taken me. I had a hope I would have been gone before I knew it. Sitting here, I ask if this is true. Last night I would have said I want to see one more morning. Now, if I am honest, I hoped I wouldn't have to face today. I am a fickle beast.

I take my first drink of coffee in days and feel its warmth as I settle into my space. I hold the cup like it is sacred and savor my second sip. The cup, the feel, the smell, the ritual, the peace, that is morning coffee; I love it.

I have no idea how many hours I have left. I stopped winding my grandmother's three-day clock and don't care to know the hour count.

Chapter Thirty-Seven

I AM HERE NOW, and until now, I have been busy doing things that I feel are important. Now *important* seems to have no meaning since there will be nothing left after today. I wonder how my children and grandchildren are doing, Grandpa and his family, the little warrior, my husband.

The thought is both natural and catches me by surprise. I can't reach out. I am helpless to do anything. I look around and realize I feel as alive as I ever have. I have no idea what to do next.

I sit and survey my backyard. My dog is wondering if coffee is as good as wine. I give her a taste. She looks at me with a startled look, then turns her bowl over, and we both laugh. The weather is warm and pleasant. I think about what I would do if this were any other day.

A dead blossom catches my eye, then another. I notice weeds. I stand and walk to my garage to get my gardening hat and clippers. I like my garden tidy, and we are both still here.

I open the garage door and see my Corvette. She is silver-blue, and last weekend I dropped a brand-new engine and transmission in her. It makes me sad I will never get to smoke her tires or go for a long drive in the country.

I dreamed my whole life about owning this car. I wish this catastrophe had waited sixty days. I could have driven her.

"Is, as is," I say to myself. A friend of mine used to say it to me when I would complain. "Is, as is," she would say. It was her way of letting me know that the reality of the situation is what it is. She would say, "You can work to fix it or forget it. Either way, please do it quietly." I would hug her.

If I were meant to drive my dream car, I would be sailing down a back road with a huge smile on my face. Alas, no—I guess I am supposed to dream. That is all I'll get to do.

I open the garage door and start her up. She purrs. The sound of her both delights and causes me agony. It is mostly together, and I realize I have never sat in the driver's seat. I open the door and look at her stripped-bare interior. I put a plastic step stool where the driver's seat will go. The seats are being reupholstered this week. In a month, I would have had a proper place to sit.

I climb in and take a seat on the stool.

Why does it surprise me when I begin to make the same sounds any ten-year-old would? I am making the sound of *vrooms* and tires squealing as I jerk on the steering wheel. I love working on cars because of my dad.

Thanks, Dad.

I have loved this project. I am sitting in what was always my and my dad's holy grail. It's so close to being a fulfillment of a promise I made to him. He had gotten a kick out of me building classics. Every day I wished he was here to help as I rebuilt this one. For most of my life, we shared the work on each other's latest projects.

Years ago, I helped him finish his last motorcycle. I wish I had bought it, but I had no idea it was going to be his last one. I was in denial. I assumed that aspect of my life would never change.

I look over to his seat in my garage.

When he was too old and frail to do the work anymore, he would sit in his chair in the garage, and we would reminisce about all the fun we had, the memories we shared. I would ask him to help me with a problem I was having. We would drink coffee with Irish whiskey. We listened to baseball. We talked nonsense and then shared secrets about our lives. I thought he would live forever.

After he died, I could feel him standing behind me as I worked, especially on this car. I can still hear his voice. Him teasing me when I drop a wrench, or hear a chuckle as a bolt skitters across the floor. He has helped me solve more than a few builder problems, and many of my life's problems, too. He is holding me now, telling me it is all okay.

I smile and thank him. I move over to the passenger space

and imagine him taking me for a drive, flying down a country road just the two of us as we had so many times in our lives. He and I are loving every second of it. *I love you, Dad.* I look over to see a man younger than I am today and check the rearview me to confirm I'm a young woman. I try to hold on to this moment. Then it is gone. Time is a bastard.

I get out of the car and close the door on this project forever. I spy a bolt and wrench it into place, and can hear my dad chuckle at me and my gestures. I imagine his hand on my back, teaching me what to do like he did when I was twelve. I set the wrench and the keys down on his chair, and wipe my tears as I return to my reason for coming to the garage.

I put on my straw hat, my gloves, grab my gardening tools, and return to my yard. From a distance, I fancy myself looking like my mom; she and I were twins. My mom taught me the ways of dirt and how to makes things grow. She was raised on a farm, and I learned to love the magic of seeds, soil, sun, and water from her.

I spend the next hour in the garden with her. I love playing in the dirt. My mom and I would share our stories, worries, joys, and dreams. We spent so many hours of our lives together with the soil, sweat, sun, and usually a glass of wine. She taps me and points at one of the last ripe tomatoes of this season waiting on the vine.

I go back into the garage for a salt shaker I keep there for this reason. I pull the warm, ripe tomato off the vine, salt it, and eat it. The seeds run down my chin. I melt. Eating a tomato this way has always frozen me to the ground, euphoric, as few things taste better.

Thanks, Mom. She wishes she could have a bite.

I smell a rose deeply and cut it to sit at my table, as I plan to read later. I liked to leave flowers on the plant. My mom preferred to cut them. The rose's amazing scent fills the air.

Happy—all this makes me happy. Maybe it isn't a Coca-Cola ad after all. After chasing the concept of happy my whole life, I find now that I live in it. Like a fish looking for water, it was everywhere, and that is why I couldn't see it. Maybe I have been chasing happiness. Perhaps I just need to let happy be, let me be, let everything be and enjoy being part of it all.

My mom rolls her eyes. *Get back to work*, she smiles and says to me. We laugh. I remember how soft her cheek was.

I wish my husband and kids were here, but they aren't. It has taken me years to embrace what is, to live without judgment of good or bad. So, I will live in this situation like I have tried to live my life. I will be as kind to myself as I can.

My mantra is: *the perfection of the universe is, whether I like it or not.* Every moment in life tests this theory. Given time and distance, I have never seen an occasion when these words did not make my life more understandable, my heart calmer, my day better.

Just then, my dog bounds out the door with her bowl in her mouth. I wonder what I have to feed her. The freezer has lost its cold, and a thawed piece of beef is my solution for her.

I bring the chop and put it in her bowl. I take another tomato.

I then return and pour both of us water from the jerry can. She looks up at me with an odd look. She has become accustomed to wine. I look at her and tell her she will have to wait; it's still morning.

I offer coffee. She is unamused.

With my cup in hand, I putter around my garden, thanking my flowers for sharing my space. I stop and look around. It is all so beautiful. I am delighted by the magnificence each has brought into my life.

I eat another tomato I find hiding in the vines, and then another. I look then hold what I know is —my last tomato.

I prune a hibiscus bush and decide whether I should pull the weeds or let them be happy for the few hours they have left. I choose to leave them.

I pull one last mallow. I drop it on a flagstone along with my gardening gloves and my knife. My mom laughs. I laugh. My parents take a seat by my chair. I change my mind, and to my dog's delight, I decide to open some wine.

I am growing tired of the thought of *one last one*. I will try to not live in *one last one* but in *content*. I look at my cleaned-up yard, and I then decide to sit on the grass and be quiet in one of my favorite spaces, under the tree.

"What does one do on a day like today?" I remember Grandma asking me yesterday.

A day like today? How many end-of-the-world events have you lived through?

I laugh to myself; what an odd week.

CHAPTER THIRTY-EIGHT

MY PARENT'S CHAIRS are empty as I bring wine out. I look up and notice the clouds. I get comfortable and decide to do what I did for hours as a kid, but haven't done in years. I lay back and watch the clouds.

When I was young, and the summer was in full swing, I would lay on the grass in the shade of a huge maple tree and watch the performance in the sky. The sun and the blue are the stage. The shimmer of the leaves and myself are the audience. We gave an ovation, in awe of the dancers in the sky. I forgot how glorious it is to watch clouds.

I have paid money for shows not nearly as good. The clouds are swirling and changing, using the sunlight as a prop. My dog settles next to me, and together we watch the clouds and play

Pictionary for our entertainment. Forming and dissolving, they put on a live visual performance that made me remember why I loved this as a kid. I see several familiar shapes, then the form of a man appears.

In the clouds, I see a figure of a man, and his shirt is open. The wind picks up. The form reminds me of another day a man just appeared. A smile finds its way to my lips. My imagination is stimulated as my heart shifts.

A long-ago memory fills my mind. I think it frivolous, then surrender. What the hell. The fire in my body grows hotter as I remember. I know it is not going to go away, and I don't try to fight.

I go inside and grab a man's shirt from the closet and the corkscrew I forgot. My dog is close at my heels and watches to make sure I pick up her crystal bowl. We walk across the yard, get comfortable, and open the wine. She is anxious. As I return to my chair, my dog stares intently at her bowl of water and then back at the bottle of wine. I place the bowl next to her and pour her a glass.

We return to the clouds and the trees; he is still in the sky as if waiting for me. I hold the shirt against my cheek and can't stop thinking about a man I loved once. I stop as I recall his face. He still makes me euphoric all these years later. He is forever young and beautiful. He has crossed my mind a hundred times since the few days we spent in Barbados.

He is why I love sex.

I noticed him before the bus stopped, and I took the seat

next to him on my way to the local market. We started to talk, I remember trying to listen to every word he said, but I did not hear a thing. I saw a beautiful man traveling. We travelers meeting in paradise for a few days—the magic of tropical breezes is legendarily real. We were young and fit and free. I see our reflection in the window of the bus. His white linen shirt and my white linen dress, we looked like a couple sitting side by side.

Without being obvious, I can see his arms, his legs, his chest. I can think of nothing but nipping each with my teeth. I feel like making him squirm. He looks at me like a wolf sizing up a sheep. If he plays his cards well, he might find I am no sheep. I sit in my chair, remembering that he made me feel alive. I was free. I was young. I was what my father used to call "undomesticatable." I was sitting on that bus, unsure if I was the hunter or the hunted.

He made me feel like I feel right now. Wild is wonderful.

I go for a sip and end up with a gulp of wine. I wipe my chin on my sleeve and recall sitting next to him on the bus. Feeling our energies, I try to think of something to say.

At home, we would have talked about baseball. So, I ask him about cricket, and we spend the next twenty minutes talking about a game I know nothing about and have never seen. He is charming and witty and smart, with bright eyes and a great body. I am relieved when we arrive at the market, as I had run out of things to say.

To my delight, when I stood, he did, too. I am thrilled at the coincidence, but markets draw people. I am enchanted and do not overanalyze the situation as would typically be my nature. *Vacation.*

I step off the bus, and he is following me. I offer him my hand, and he takes it.

The adventure begins.

We act as politely as we can manage as we wander the merchant's stalls. I plan to buy food for the next couple of days, enough to hold me until my friends call on me. I am enchanted by the sounds and colors of the market, the vendors calling us honeymooners. I touched his arm by accident, acting like I was going for the same mango as he was, and it sent a jolt of electricity through my body.

As we spend time together, the spark grows into a bonfire. What started as flirting, turned to a hand on my back, to light kisses, to sparks, then an inferno. I remember those days as clearly as if they happened yesterday.

Fate had brought us here, but we were hesitating. Fate being fate, decided we need a push. Thunder peals, and the market goes quiet. Then the clouds open, drenching us. We run for cover that doesn't exist. With each step, we are getting more soaked. I am noticing every detail of his body. I jerk his hand, spinning him toward me. We stop running. We stare at each other and without a word, decide to surrender and embrace the rain. Hand in hand, we walk through a market whose vendors are rushing to cover up their wares. We splash in the puddles and laugh as the warm rain washes over us. I find myself envious of a single drop of rain hanging off the tip of his nose.

I move his hand toward me, and he takes my waist. We stand in the rain, and he kisses me. The power of that kiss still melts me. He tries to take a step back, but I stop him. I kiss him back. I feel my toes curl as my hands reach under his shirt. My body quakes, the fire is now out of control. I don't try to fight it.

The rain softens. In our haste, we became lost and are looking for the way back to the taxi stand. Unsure where to go, lost in the storm, fate again intervenes with a rainbow. Not knowing where our yellow brick road will lead, we follow it. We couldn't have cared less where we are going to end up, as long as we are exploring together.

Our pot of gold is an available taxi. "A finer pot of gold no leprechaun ever found," I say in my attempt at an Irish brogue. He laughs with delight as I grab his hand and dive into the back of the cab. The door closes as our wet linen soon becomes an invitation.

He kisses me as I fumble through my purse for the card to my hotel. I find it and hand it to the driver. He smiles at us and says something neither one of us understands. The driver says something else, and then the car launches into traffic.

I feel self-conscious with my dress clinging to me, but my mind loses control as my focus turns to his rain-soaked shirt. The sight of him consumes me. I no longer care how tightly my dress is clinging to me. I growl as he kisses my neck.

The cab ride is taking forever. I try, with little success, not to attack him. It is like a scene from a romance novel, the starts and stops of the cab, the smells of spices coming through the open window, the tropical breeze, and my desire building with each turn. I watch for a second and realize our cabby is driving as if we have someplace to be. I love the islands.

In what seems like both a second and eternity, I see we are in front of my hotel. In my haste, I grab the fare and what I realize later to be a huge tip from my purse. I hand it to the driver with a distracted "thank you." He winks at me.

I am on a singular mission as I leap out of the cab, becoming more impatient with each passing moment. I watch as the object of my desire comes around the back of the taxi. The driver points to me and then to the back seat of the cab. I have one care in the world, and he is no longer in the cab.

My gorgeous man is coming to take me. My heart knows soon; he will devour me.

I turn as the cabby points again to the backseat. My life is now moving in slow and fast motion at the same time. I am lost in the wave of desire as I watch my lover grab my purse from the back of the cab with one hand and me with the other. I am sure my feet did not touch the ground as we head toward the hotel. The cabby shouts again, but we have one thing on our minds.

I take a sip of wine and smile, recalling the blur that the next few days became. I caress the shirt, running my fingers over it, remembering when it was touching his skin. I smile and close my eyes, the hair on my neck standing as the shirt takes me back to being young and reckless. I set my glass down and remember the feel of his hands on my hips as he kisses my ears.

It takes all my concentration to get my key into the door. I feel his hands caress my hips as his lips move to my neck. I finally get the key to turn, and we step into my room. I turn, breathing in the scent of his skin, I have no reason to remain in control.

In the next second, I send the buttons of his shirt flying across the room. I hear them skittering over the floor. He grabs me, and in what seems like one motion has my dress on the floor, and I am on my back.

I growl at him. His eyes widen, and he growls back. The bed creaks as the rest of our clothes scatter, and he lets out another small howl that has me pulling him into me. I lock into my memory how beautiful he is. He is muscle, and fire, and passion, all focused on me. I savor his smell as he makes each nerve in my body come alive. Every inch of me is longing for his touch. I feel wild, like an animal that has hunted and is now enjoying her prey. His taste, his touch, all of my senses are fighting for attention as ecstasy overwhelms me.

He lightly runs his tongue over my breast, and I feel the earthquake. I kiss him deeply, and we begin to move in unison. I listen to him breathe, to my moans, to my fingers digging into his back, and he responds to each. I can only kiss his arm as I am lost in the power of his body against mine. I feel his strength as he takes control of me, moving me to where he pleases and then taking me with an intensity I couldn't have imagined.

I roll on top of him. He snarls, grabbing my hips and moves beneath me until I find the perfect spot. I try to take control, but I am quickly consumed by the fury of his passion. He grabs a hand full of my hair and holds tight as I dig my fingers into his chest, then his hair, then his chest again. Him moving my body, him paying attention until I find my purest pleasure. I am lost in all-consuming rapture.

God, he is beautiful. I force myself to stop time long enough to drink in his naked body. *Growl.* I quickly fail as he moves slightly, and I am shattered by him bringing me to orgasm again and again. I moan, and am unable to catch my breath.

The rain has started again and is coming down in torrents, as lightning crashes right over the top of us. I am not sure if we are channeling the storm or the storm is channeling us, but neither one of us is letting up. We are both forces of nature, releasing fury. Building in energy as the lightning crashes overhead.

He lifts me and rolls me so that I am on my hands and knees. It is his turn to take control. I go from wolf to lamb. He can have whatever he wants. He seems to know my body better than I do. Each of his touches sends a current coursing through me. He brings me to a place where I can't speak. I groan loudly and turn my hips a bit. We are one. We are intertwined, exploring each other, pushing further, harder, wanting, and taking more. He is like a lion devouring his prey.

Completely exhausted, I am unsure if I have anything left to give. He takes more, and with my now-raspy voice, I mutter the word "uncle" and roll onto my back. He follows. We lay side by side, trying to catch our breath.

He envelops me, holding me close, kissing me. I feel safe. I remember thinking he shouldn't. A Cheshire cat smile crosses my face as I nip his chest. He moans loudly, his body flinching with pain. Fire burns in his eyes as he throws his head back, and

I watch as a wave of pleasure tosses him. We are primal, as he lifts me away from the headboard and back into the middle of the bed. He pins my arms above my head. I am unable to move as he kisses down me. He nips my shoulder, then my breasts, then my thigh.

Every inch of my body is jealous of the place he is kissing. I quiver, holding on, and wondering what he is going to do next. He leans back and lightly rubs his finger across me, and I tumble into another orgasm; he rubs a little harder, and I explode again.

I have no energy left, so I push against him and collapse into his embrace. I breathe in deeply and am lost to the universe. I crumple into a ball as he cuddles over me, making me feel cherished in his arms. He kisses me and holds me softly as I find my way back into my body.

Reveling in my ecstasy, he waits for me. I begin to find my breath when he steals it away with a kiss on my ear. A nibble on my neck. A handful of my hair as he kisses me. I'm returning to my body as we now seem to be mirroring the gentle rhythm of the ocean. He and I are savoring this calm between the storms.

Sweaty and exhausted, we lay knotted together. We kiss and talk as we slowly regain our strength. We feel the flame build again. He pulls me close, and I feel his desire to take me again. I kiss his neck to ignite him. He rolls on top of me. We are lost in each other again, the rain now a memory, as we can hear the thunder echoing in the distance. I wonder if it can hear us, too.

We are exploring our boundaries. I am fate's toy. He seems to be burning as hot as he was hours ago. I am holding on for dear life. He kisses me deeply, then my neck, then between my breasts, then a spot I didn't know would drive me wild. Is he some kind of sorcerer? As he kisses down my body, and I am instantly writhing in more pleasure than I had ever imagined, I grab a hand full of his hair, and he causes me to lose the last ounce of control I have left.

I am gripping the sheets like I am on a life raft in an ocean squall. I can no longer inhale, no longer exhale. I am suspended by ecstasy, hanging in the deliciousness of his embrace. My body writhes with his final touch. I can't take anymore and pull him away by his hair, leading him back up my body.

He breaks free. He waits for me to breathe, then I wait to take another, as my anticipation for what will come next grows at an exponential rate. I hear him breathe me in, I have lost myself completely and can do nothing but wait for him. For an eternity, I listen, then he softly kisses me. I collapse back onto the bed and high-five God as I pass.

He moves up me, then holds me tightly. I find my way back, filling my body, my lioness is now a kitten. I have no idea how long it took before I could think. He didn't speak; he held me and waited for my eyes to flicker open.

We are lying together, unable to move. I lay in his arms, lost in paradise. He kisses me, and I kiss him. We are all there is. We are still hungry for each other. For now, we are too spent to do more than lay together. We talk, kiss, breathe, and hold each other.

We stay in our Eden for as long as possible, then longer still.

Reality, in the form of hunger, sneaks into the room, and we finally have no choice but to move. I have to stop touching him for the first time in hours. I stand to go to the bathroom. I see him gazing at my naked body. I try to cover myself, feeling his eyes upon me. He tells me I am beautiful. For the first time in my life, in the reflection of his eyes, I feel beautiful.

As I return, he is standing. God, he is stunning. I stop and capture him, memorizing every nuance, until I notice he is doing the same thing with me. I become acutely aware of myself and shy away from his gaze. He moves to me and tenderly holds my face, looks into my eyes, kisses me and tells me I am the most beautiful woman he has ever seen. He stands back to admire me, and I grow even more aware of every inch of my body. He pulls me close and whispers, "You are stunning."

I try to get back in bed, but he stops me. He tells me he wants to look at me. He drinks me in, only his eyes are touching me, and I feel my self-consciousness melt away. I go to move, and I hear him inhale. I stop and kiss him. "God, you are beautiful," I tell him.

Time stops as I am at the center of his attention. I do not move as the purity of this moment has overtaken me. We are the only two people on Earth. I lean forward and touch his cheek. "I want to make sure you are real, that this is really happening, that…" He kisses me again, and we fall back into bed.

We hold each other. We are silent. We are sore. We are tired. We are starving. I remember the food I had bought from the market and jump out of bed to assemble the makings for a picnic. I look around the room, and remember that I forgot the bag in the back of the cab. We have no food, and, like Adam and Eve, are being forced out of paradise by hunger.

We laugh about our haste, but both of us know it was worth the loss of a perfect mango and some conch salad. I search for my clothes as he searches for his shorts. I watch him, and I ponder pouncing on him, but I succumb to my need for food. Only food or fire could have forced us out of room 1282.

I smile; 1282—this is a tiny one-story hotel, with an odd collection of numbers on the doors, hung in no particular order.

He searches everywhere looking for his shorts, as I pull a dry sundress out of my bag. The last unfound item is my sandal. We scurry around the room, looking until he finds it. He sits me on the bed. I think he is going to put my sandal on. Instead, he runs his tongue over my toes and lightly bites my insole.

My only thought is "Damn" as he slides my foot in the sandal. We move to the door when I comment that his clothes are all off-kilter. He turns me toward the mirror, and we burst out laughing. We take a minute to straighten each other until we are mostly together and as ready to face the world as we are going to be. My hair is wild, but I don't care. I run my fingers through his curls, and we head to the door.

As he moves away, I tug at his wet, button-less shirt, we are both exhausted and in bliss. We kiss and ready ourselves to face the world. We count to three and open our hotel door.

Hanging from the knob is my bag and a note that says, "You forgot this in my cab."

He takes the bag, and I take him back to bed. I tell him I was so glad he was going to the market.

He sheepishly smiles and says, "I wasn't going to the market, I was getting off at the next stop when you sat down. I had an appointment that was scheduled for hours ago." He mimes checking a watch that doesn't exist, on a wrist that makes me want to kiss it. I laugh and kiss him, "Really?" He smiles at me.

I pour the contents of my bag on the bed as we snuggle close to each other. We take the first bites and enjoy our picnic. We, like wolves, eat everything I bought. We are satisfied but not satiated. I take the last bite of mango, he licks the juice off my chin, and he kisses me better than the first time. I quiver. My lips tingle as if struck by lightning. He touches me. His energy runs from my jaw to my toes. We are finishing the last bites when I toss the wrappers from the bed, and we settle in for the night. Eventually, we sleep.

I pour, then drink my wine. I shift in my seat. A sore hip causes me to leave the perfection of my lover's arms, this body a far cry from the twenty-one-year-old version I was just in. I do not want to leave now any more than I did then. I take another drink and look at the life my husband and I built.

I try to understand when in life that young and fit and free gives way to living in a rut. I can set my watch to the predictability of my day. A hug, a peck, and the question, "What's for dinner?"

I shake this thought and return to Barbados. Back in bed. I was sound asleep when my eyes flicker open to kisses in the dark, I respond with fire. My body is sore, but it doesn't matter. Today if my husband woke me up at two a.m. I would wonder what was wrong, ask about the kids, go to the bathroom, check my phone, and try to get back to sleep.

My husband is a practical man. A man that, when we met, had an education, potential, and a bright future. We have done well with each other, but fire is hard to keep stoked for thirty years.

I am now passable for a woman "my age," and he is a "cute old man," as measured by my daughter's friends. In that white linen dress, I had stopped men in mid-stride.

Today I am invisible. I am hardly noticed by a clerk whose job it is to pay attention to me. When did I disappear?

My husband and I have come to a détente. We have boundaries that are much like baseball's unspoken rules. We know without saying what is acceptable and what will cause friction. As best we can, we stay inside our norms and have mostly stopped dreaming undomesticatable dreams.

I know undomesticatable isn't a word in Webster's Dictionary, but that never stopped my dad from using a number of words he dreamed up. I have a few holdouts that he used often enough so that they became part of my vocabulary as a kid. He would say, "Zebras, and wolves and you. You three can't be forced into anything. You never see a wolf in a circus. They are undomesticatable."

I loved—and still love—that image.

I look down at a shirt I first wore at least three lifetimes ago. It is a reminder of ecstasy so strong that, even now, it still makes me wiggle with delight. This shirt is proof that I was alive for at least one day in my life. I remember being so sore, my twenty-one-year-old body feeling like I imagined a tree feels after a hurricane. He is now well aware I am not a lamb.

I look at him with wild eyes. He stares back. We each are too tired to pounce.

We lay in each other's arms. We are holding on, knowing that the lives we have outside are quickly going to rend us apart. We are moving slowly, laughing at the damage we did to each other.

For the first time in days, I am aware that the clock is ticking. I soon will have friends calling my hotel room telling me when they will arrive to pick me up. Sailing was to be one last fling of freedom before returning home and starting my first real job. Little did I know that I was going to get two.

My lover has his path in life, and so do I. The force that brought us together is now ebbing. I dive on him one more time because great sex is its own reward. We ignore the phone ringing, then ringing again.

I return to my backyard. I am looking down at my legs as my mind fully arrives in the present. I take a sip of wine. I recall each of the tiny bruises he had left on my thigh. I smile about another left on my right underarm. I do love the memories from that weekend.

On their third try, I answer the hotel phone. The manager is confirming I am okay and tells me my friends are here. I ask him to come sailing. He asks me to stay with him. He kisses my ear and makes my body and brain have a standoff. We lay sweating on the bed and make promises about tomorrow. We exchange contact information and try our best to stop the clock from ticking. I never want to leave this space. My friends knock, and we reluctantly submit to this reality.

We shower, and as I dry him off, we ponder what to do next. He puts on his shorts and sits on our bed and watches as I pack my things.

We stand and stare at each other. We kiss hard. I hear the cab with my friends honking outside. I hold him as hard as I can and make a promise to call him when my sailing trip is over, knowing I have a ticket home out of Saint Vincent.

We finally open the door to the next day of our lives. He carries my bag down, and I hug him, nip his chest and think strongly about returning to our bed for at least one more night, maybe a lifetime. I remember closing my eyes; the flow of life has taken me out of that possibility stream.

I take a turquoise ring off my finger and give it to him. A touchstone, I tell him, "Until I see you again." He says he has nothing to give me. I smile and take the shirt off his back. With one last kiss, I say goodbye, but my feet don't move. I hug him tightly.I smile at him as I put this shirt on, run my fingers through his hair, and climb into the back of the cab.

I look up to see the cabby that had dropped us off, smiling at me and asking how was my weekend. "Wonderful," and I thank him for bringing my groceries to me. He smiles a broad smile and laughs from his belly. My friends start to ask me who my friend is and comment on my shirt.

I have carried this shirt as proof of the volcanic passion I am capable of. I pull it out when I need to reconnect with the younger me, the version that lived in unlimited possibility. I need the shirt today because I have no idea what to do, no one to do it with, and no tomorrow to do it in.

CHAPTER THIRTY-NINE

MY DAD USED TO SAY, "When it looks impossible, get up and move. You have been looking at the problem from the same angle for too long."

My dad never faced a black hole, but the principle is sound. I am free but also feeling the bounds of being trapped in a human body more sharply than at any time in my life. I am viscerally aware that I can't escape. The end of the world is coming, and I am going to be here when it happens.

I feel like a deer surrounded by a pack of wolves. I have nowhere to run. My heart should be racing. It isn't. My senses are heightened. I can smell the fear of the people in the park, and I hear the wind call my name. I howl in response. I am not a trapped animal. I am the freest I have ever been. Freedom is addicting. My old society could not have allowed it.

My old way of life is gone. As the bonds of society break completely, I feel the heartbeat of the Earth and imagine myself being able to hear nature the way the wolf and the zebra do. If we survive today, my future is going to be lived in a world that is wild. Technology is gone, and I am faced with living purely within nature's rules. My body is learning how to play; it is as if it always knew.

My mind is slower to shift. I have no choice but to yield to a primal way of life. I do not know nature's unspoken rules; my whole life, I have been sheltered from them. Mother Nature can be a ruthless teacher. If I am to survive, I'm going to have to learn quickly.

I stand up from my chair and brush a few bits of grass from my clothes.

"What do I do now?" I hold up the shirt and remember my man in Barbados. I look at the sky. He is gone. I hug my shirt and wonder what would have happened had I changed my flight. It was, and now is gone. I exhale and feel a twinge of the broken heart I had all those years ago.

My path led me here. Its been a hell of a run. I raise my glass and take a drink to them both.

All day I have been haunted by an ear-worm. "Sinnerman," Nina's song won't leave me alone. All day, it has never been far from my lips. I got nowhere to run. I got nowhere to stand, either. I sing it to myself for the courage. The fury of that song shakes me alive.

My dog has not moved. She is watching me. I lock eyes with her. Her eyes are growing feral. I am having trouble staying inside my skin. I need to move. I turn to her and suggest a walk. She is comfortable with her wine and yawns big. She tilts her head as if she is weighing her options. She scratches her ear and decides to be a good friend.

Reluctantly she gets up to join me. We drink one more drink and venture out to see what the park holds.

I get my shoes and her leash as we make our way toward the gate. She looks at me in a way I have never seen. I open the gate and lean down to put it on her leash when she grabs it and runs off. I call her back; she drops the leash and returns to my side. I walk to get the leash, and as I near it, she picks it up and carries it further away. I think to try to get to it again, but I know she won't let me.

She is not playing a game with me. She is refusing to wear it. She is alpha. I know there is nothing I can do about the way she is acting. We are living in a new normal. I can't blame her. I wouldn't let anyone put a leash on me. If someone tried, we would fight.

I am now following her to the park. She sees a small group of dogs and bolts. I whistle, and she ignores me. She has never done this before.

The park is full. I assumed it would be empty. I thought everyone would be doing what I have been doing or what I wish I could do. Spending their last hours with loved ones, getting one last of whatever last might be. I recognize many of my new clan. We gather because people need to not feel alone. We are all wondering what to do. We are gathered to face what is coming.

We are here to support and be supported. We are living in an unknown. We have seen the core of our safe and stable world giving way. I find I feel safer in numbers. The park is full of dogs without leashes, kids without rules, adults without a tomorrow. People's ever-thinning veneer of civility is giving way to our new reality. All of us are taking steps into freedom and fears, both to an extent we have never known.

The people I greet in the park are behaving inside established social norms, but I can feel a fierceness taking over. Like the dogs, my neighbors are beginning to act like a pack. I have thought wild and violent were synonymous, but at this point, it is clear that wild means cooperating in a way that was unimaginable at the best of times and impossible at worst.

We need each other if we are going to survive—not as a group, but as a talent pool. We need the best everyone has to offer if we are all going to thrive.

I can see the world I lived in a week ago was designed to isolate and individualize me. To force me to be a single flower trying to survive in a desert. I feel how it reduced me to be most comfortable as a cog in a bigger machine. I was taught to depend on systems and not community. Community became nearly impossible as screens became our environment.

I expect soon to face the violence and brutishness my old life of privilege had spared me. I take a drink of wine, and with this one act, I know my past life is not entirely gone. I am content in the group but can glimpse what is next.

We are all slowly submitting to a world without electricity, gas, and a future measured in years. We are being forced to accept a new reality. I know from my excursions with my husband this new life will be hard, wet, cold, and dark. It will also be free, beautiful, and an adventure.

Nature is now my teacher. I am trying my best to pay attention.

Industrial power insulated me from natural laws my whole life. I am now being forced into living like everything else on the planet lives. I have never had to submit to nature; I could always escape her. Escaping her was the sole reason my consumer's way of life existed.

I was going to have to learn how to compete for food. How to stay warm. How to live by my wits. I know that in a few days, I am going to have first-hand knowledge of what being wild means. Where are all the Priests of Progress now?

Three days. It has taken less than three days for the pillars of this "modern" society to crumble. It is because we believe the end is near that even the most basic of social norms are still in place. The new norm is forming, but I have no idea what it will look like after today.

The abundance of three days ago is going quickly, my neighbors are deciding if it is best to try to survive alone or to band together into a pack. It will not be long until the ability to bring violence or add value to the clan will become the currency of this reality.

My life is becoming a high-stakes poker game. How much of who I am and what I have do I hide—versus how much do I share? I am a woman with more gray hair than not. Clearly, violence is not going to work for me. I know to survive I will have to add value. What skills will be valuable to my clan when wild has taken over? I am a healer, a mechanic, and a musician. Will any of these be of value in a week, or a month, or a year?

All disclosures about myself must be done carefully. Who I am, my food and wine stocks, and the camping supplies in my house could be dangerous to me if people knew I have them. I know that taking by force will become commonplace very soon. I feel helpless when I imagine the world that is coming. I will not be able to stop anyone from taking what they want from me.

This life is unnerving, as many things society most valued last week are irrelevant today. My mind has not completely made the shift to the understanding that who I was yesterday is irrelevant.

I stand silent in the crowd. I am trying to be inconspicuous; invisible would be even better. I'm happy to be a shadow. I look for my dog; she is nowhere. She must be measuring her pack like I am measuring mine. We both are learning to listen with new ears. I see if I can catch her scent. I am surprised when this thought hits me. Scent?

I sit with it and it doesn't seem silly. I need to weigh my thoughts, to watch, and learn the ways of the wild. I look for her and think to call her name.

My attention shifts as a large man starts speaking. I listen carefully to the discussion and appraise the people around me.

They are hard to read because people under stress react unpredictably. I have never had to anticipate the reaction of a crowd that is 99% sure they will not see tomorrow. We are all, at varying rates, becoming feral.

I am playing poker, something else I learned while building my motorcycle so long ago. My dad taught me, "Poker is more about watching the other players at the table, than the luck of the cards in your hand." I am going to assume we all have about the same hand, so I watch my clan carefully, dividing them into categories.

I stop, I can't think of a single useful distinction. I have no idea who I will be, how can I evaluate anyone else? I will have to adapt. I will have to work on relationships and discover who to trust.

I listen as the concern about how to survive over the long term is replacing speculation about a black hole. They are talking about securing a supply of clean water and how we can ration the food in our homes to last the winter. We have questions and almost no answers.

I continue to study my clan. The one who takes most of my attention is the man who is speaking. He is accustomed to being armed and has served in the military. He is a force. He has trained in the art of violence and tactics. His biceps are bigger than my legs.

He is standing in the middle of the crowd, trying to get an idea of the skills and supplies of the people around him. "Who has served in the armed forces? Who is a doctor or a nurse?

Engineers? Construction?" The list goes on.

He then gets more personal: who is dependent on pharmaceutical or illegal drugs? Who has chronic illnesses that hinder them daily? He asks a long series of questions. He clearly has memorized a list generated by the military to assess a situation on the ground.

I am paying more attention to the people around me. I hear his question and am a little surprised how readily people are raising their hands when appropriate to answer him.

I am not. I am learning.

A woman next to me asks, "Do we stay in our home or commune in a few?" Heads turn toward her as she brings attention to herself. I put my face down and slowly move away. I do this because I feel attention is dangerous. I want to remain unnoticed and unmemorable.

The Admiral is accustomed to people performing at a high level when he lets his demands be known. I can feel him growing impatient with this group's inattentiveness, and he is not going to stand for it long.

He stops asking politely. He sharpens his tone and speaks like a man accustomed to giving orders. "We all have questions about the future and how we will function as a unit. Let's put first things first. Go to your homes and make an inventory of what you have to share. We need to know what resources we have as a team. I need to have a better understanding of our supplies by the end of the day. Go now."

I think it would be better to know what the expertise and

hobbies of each of the members of the group have refined. What skills we bring that will outlast our ready water and food supplies. At some point, we will need to go through all of the houses with a trained eye gathering what is valuable to support our skill sets. My ideas are not for today. For now, I will sit quietly. Watching and listening, trying to assess who is who.

I will proceed, behaving as if I know no one. I have no friends. I can trust no one. I will have to rely on my instincts. I will have to trust myself if I am going to survive. I need to learn from this new reality. For now, I will gather information and keep my mouth shut.

A man I have seen playing catch with his kids over the years suggests we have a big cookout with supplies that will not last another day. He says, "There is no point in wasting food. Most of our group has not even eaten together, it will be a good way to find out who we all are, and in the process have one last great meal. We need a farewell party."

The assembled group agrees and begins to disperse, heading home. I assume they'll do an inventory and gather what they want to share, but who knows.

CHAPTER FORTY

I SCAN THE PARK FOR MY DOG and see her with a large pack. I whistle for her. She looks up at me but doesn't move. I call her, and she stares at me. She has never acted like this before.

"Come here!" I call. Her tail wags, and she takes a few steps toward me, then stops. "Please come here," I cry, a little more desperately than I intended.

She bounces with indecision toward me, then stops. She then turns her back to me and returns to the pack. I stare at her. "Please?" I implore her quietly. Only loud enough for me to hear.

I see her head jerk toward me, but her feet stay firm. I turn and walk toward my house, hoping to hear her paws on the ground. Silence. I am feeling emptier with each step. More and more alone. The pain is becoming unbearable.

I turn to look for her, and all the dogs are gone. My trusted friend has left me. I am alone.

I turn back toward home and force my feet to keep moving. I can be sentimental later. I know some of my new tribe is watching. I do not want the judgment of being weak so I force my feet to move. Each step is a mile as I walk further from my dog and closer to my empty home. I strain to hear her paws on the ground.

I finally make it home and whistle. I wait. There is not a sound. I try again and sit on my porch, hoping for her. She doesn't come. I whistle one last time and stand alone for what seems hours. I finally force myself to enter my house and close the door behind me.

I collapse. I am alone, completely alone.

I have me to rely upon, and I feel so small against this reality. My bravado about my instincts has faded to nothing. My world, my house, my voice, is quiet.

I misjudged my dog; how can I trust myself? I feel for the edge of my despair and can't find it. I go deeper and deeper into the emptiness that surrounds me. It engulfs me, and I feel hopeless and broken. There is no one I trust, no one I can reach out to for help. My last love from my old life is gone.

A wave of emptiness hits me, and it feels like my heart being ripped from my chest. I spread my arms and let it hit. In three days, I have lost my children, my husband, my friends, and my life. My dog is last. I can't take anymore.

I am buffeted by a wave of grief and loss more intense than before because it is so complete. I have nothing left but quiet. I let the agony of her leaving overwhelm me. Then the tsunami of the full extent of my isolation hits without mercy.

I try to cling to the hope my dog will return, but I can't hold it for long. She was the last bit of my old life, my family, my love. I tried so hard to hold on to my persona of being strong and unflappable, but the weight of my losses breaks me.

I cry out for my husband and am met with silence. I call out for each of my children, knowing this effort is futile. I don't care. I have nothing and am willing to try anything. I listen to the stillness I once so wanted, but now would give anything for the sound of any loved one's voice.

I need to hear my husband's footsteps coming to help, but my world is absolutely still. Not even the birds are chirping. I sob uncontrollably, feeling the depth of my heartbreak. I try to find anything to hold on to, something to grab to slow my fall. I search my soul in vain for something in my life that will comfort me. Is there any remnant I have missed?

I recall all of the people that have been through the door of my house. The people I love. The gift of a fuller life because I have known each of them. "Where are all of you now?"

My pleas are for my ears only. I whistle for a dog that has left me.

I feel my situation is disgraceful. I am ashamed that I am alone. I have no tears left to cry, no strength left to fight back, no hope to build anything. How did I end up here?

My mind broadsides me as I am unaccustomed to shame. It brings a ruthless judgment of myself. It makes me feel like a failure. I try to stop and get ahold of myself, but I can't. I am going crazy. In my insanity, I savor the anguish of it. Then call myself a fool for doing so. I am hungry for anything that focuses my attention, given the amount of turmoil I've suffered. Three days ago, I was camping at home. Today I am…what the hell am I?

My mind shatters. I have lost everything. What is the point of suffering a few hours more?

My life is over, and I contemplate if I should take my end into my own hands. I have learned all too well the weakest points of the human body and know I have the tools and know-how to end my life quickly. I have the expertise to use the pills in my bathroom effectively.

I stand and start to make my way to the bathroom. Will my sanctuary be my final resting place? A thought only yesterday unthinkable now seems a perfectly logical and reasonable choice.

I'm shattered into unrepairable pieces. I try to push the darkness away, to find any reason for hope, but the gloom intensifies. All the loss of the last few days has destroyed me. I am out of my mind. I thought I was facing my reality like a champion. It took my dog leaving for me to finally turn and face myself.

Not my husband or kids, my dog. What kind of monster am I?

I try to give myself the grace I would give and have given everyone I have met on the worst day of their lives. I seize this grace with all my might, but my well is dry. I am a failure. I am alone. Silence is usually safety. Now it is a cage in which I'm trapped. My mind is reeling faster and faster.

Alone pulls me ever deeper into my despair. "Even my dog left me," I cry. The weight of her abandonment forces me deeper into myself, further than I want to go. My heart betrays me by showing me her face when she was a puppy, and my body hiccups. I remember her asleep on my chest. I recall the days we spent together. The love I thought we shared. My heart can't find anything to hold on to.

I sit with myself in this space. "There," I think. There it is, I test to see if this is the bottom or is there deeper depth to my despair. "Go do it," my mind says to me. "Make this pain stop."

As I make it to the bathroom doorway, I stop to look at a photo. On the wall in the hallway is a picture of my father and me. He is hugging me, and I am looking at him in the way my daughter looks at my husband.

Looked at my husband.

We were both so young then. My life was full and ahead of me.

I never dreamed I would live a moment like this. I open the medicine cabinet and pull down several medicine bottles. Reading the labels and choosing each carefully. *Dad, I will see you soon.*

I look back at the picture and remember. My father was the first of my parents to pass away. His death taught me not to resist the pain of great loss, but to let it pull me down as far as it can. Grief is relentless; it must be suffered head-on, and wide open. I found facing it fully made my dad's loss more bearable. It is not working. All I feel is misery.

I have not hit bottom. I wait to see what else surfaces.

I stare at the pill bottles in front of me, and I know I have deeper to go. I look in the mirror and see a destitute and broken old woman. I am frightened that this brutish world will ravage me. I am not ready to face being weak. I have never been weak. Today I am not enough. Tomorrow I will be even less.

Now I am frail and facing a savage reality that I am sure I cannot contend with alone. I stop and breathe. I feel my bones under my skin. I count the beats of my heart. I am aware of my tear ducts being dry. I then remind myself that my dog stared at me and turned her back. I go limp. My brain is silent. Not a sound fills the air around me. The silence in my head is even more frightening. I can't form a thought.

I sit as still as I can be. I am waiting for the next thought to push through. I don't know what rational means anymore. What is sane on my bathroom floor?

"You are not going to be enough in this new world. Look at you. You're pathetic" escapes from my mouth.

Is that it? Is that the bottom? I do not resist as my brain says, "You will die alone. Where is your perfection now?"

I grasp for relief. I feel myself sinking deeper. I push back, but feel like I am drowning. I feel my life ebbing away. I can't see a way that is better than the brown bottles on the counter. They will end my pain.

I try to move for the first bottle, but I can't. In my mind,

I stand up and say to myself, *start from here to find the way back*. How can I possibly find my way back to the person I was yesterday? Yesterday was forever ago.

I have no idea who I am. I can sit in the dark, or I can move— my life has come down to this.

I try to move again, but I am unsteady. I cannot stay in this dark place. I am feeling beaten, lost, broken, and alone. I am open to anything that will make it darker or lighter.

I search for a way, anyway. It hurts too much to stay here.

Fight or flight? I want to run, but I have done that before. With my mom's death, I went in circles over and over again. I sit still and announce to the universe that I am here.

I snarl to creation, to myself, to anything that is listening, "Here I am. It is your turn because it is here that I make my stand." I rise to my feet. Willing my body to take one step. I breathe shallowly, as a complete breath is impossible. I blink, then hold my eyes open. I feel the echoes of my loss slamming against me. I collapse. I feel beaten.

I know from losing my mom and dad that the way out of this cave is to crawl until I can walk. Then, when strong enough to walk, I will move one step at a time. I'm not sure that I will know if I am moving forward, because forward has no meaning. I decide to move even if my path is a circle. Each time around, I will try to make the circle bigger. I don't care; I am moving.

I have learned not to shy away from the darkness, but to try to find a flicker of light inside myself. To let go of despondence and look for gratitude. The darkest nights are the moments in my life that have helped me to see who I am most clearly. This space is pitch black. Everyone I love in the world is gone.

I am contemplating suicide, to end this misery my way. I am alone. No one will hurt. No one will care. If I am going to die alone anyway, why not on my terms?

I see my son's face, then my daughter's. This is not fair. I raised a family, was married to a man I love. I have many good friends. I tell myself that I did everything I was supposed to do. My grandchildren's faces flash before my eyes. I shouldn't be sitting alone in an empty house. On my final day. My very last day.

I am so tired of last; fuck last. I yell, "Just fucking end this. I have had enough."

My neighbors are not alone; why am I? I am not supposed to die alone. I am supposed to die with my children and their children around me. I am supposed to die as the center of everyone's attention; the source of grief for my family. My loss is supposed to be felt by each of my loved ones.

I want my death to be felt. I feel selfish, but I don't care. I want my death to be felt by my daughter while driving to work. The ebbs and flow of loss I had known when my parents died, she is supposed to feel my being gone.

The pain of my passing is supposed to consume my son, keeping him awake until the wee hours of the night as he tries to find me with his heart.

My husband is supposed to hold my hand and cry on my lap. Friends are supposed to bring food and mourn my loss.

I don't want to share my death. I want my death to be like

my birth, with all the attention on me. I hate that I feel this way, but I do. I hate that everyone has someone but me. I hate that I am sitting on my bathroom floor. I hate that my dog has deserted me.

I gave love. I gave care. I made sure my family lived well. It was my sweat and hard work that paved the way for the life they all enjoyed. Why do I now sit in the dark, alone, feeling my life was pointless? I have no one to share with or lean on, no one when I need my loved ones the most. I have no one to provide hope or a different perspective. Someone to say. "You did a great job," and "I love you!" Someone to hug me, a hand to hold, to kiss goodbye. I am all alone and hate it.

I scan my horizon for a north star, a way for me to follow. I will have to be my guide. I hear the voice of a dear friend who, when visiting, would often tell me if she is ever reincarnated, she will choose to be my dog. She would point to my dog and say to her, "You are the luckiest hound in the world—would you look at how she loves and takes care of you? I have never been taken care of like that, not ever."

I am confused, but embrace this. I have nothing else. It is the first bit of light to find my dungeon. Darkness ebbs back. Where is she? Where is my friend now with her cheery words? Where is man's best friend? My ungrateful dog, running with a new pack, leaving me to fend for myself? I fed her and cleaned up her poop. How the hell does that work?

I mumble to myself, "The little bitch."

Did I give to get, or did I give out of love? I breathe in deeply, and I feel the ebb and flow of my despair. It ebbed. I catch one deep breath. I settle into the chaos of my thoughts and try using my heart to find a space where this reality and the desires of my mind can coexist.

I am tearing my sense of self apart, struggling between my dream and this reality. I want to yell at something, anything I can make responsible for my situation. I stay still, knowing that it is in the hardest times that I have found myself.

"Where is the perfection?" I hear my mom ask. How can she ask me that? I have no life left to live. I have nothing, no one, and no time. I hear her impatience with me. She reminds me that adversity is one of the well-worn paths I have traveled to discover a place where I can be at peace. Pain is very focusing, one of the sure ways that have always led me to who I am. Anguish allows for no other distractions. It focuses my attention and desire. It makes me ask myself the hardest questions. Face the most difficult truths. What is my mom asking me?

Alone, I have only myself to consider, only myself to count on, only myself. Am I enough? I will find out who I am in this space because I am my mirror. Is this why I am here? I look up and see my reflection in the medicine cabinet. I see the wrinkles. Wrinkles are weakness, but then I remind myself that they are a sign of strength. I have always been enough. Why will I not be now? I have earned my wrinkles.

I lock eyes with myself. You don't have time, energy, or reserves to wallow in self-pity or to be angry with what is. You have preached is, as is and perfection for years. You have talked endlessly about living in the moment.

It is time to test my rhetoric. I think I have found my truth and try to push off the bottom of my darkness.

I try to move but don't. I am surprised, and collapse back onto the floor, searching for anything, anything that can steady me. I breathe and sigh, feeling for why I am stuck. I look in the mirror again. "You still have breath."

I smile. I sit and wait to see how my heart unfolds. My eyes stare back at me. "You will, right now, find out if your life has been true or a lie."

I turn to my husband in my mind. He says he saw it, the black hole. He predicted the collapse of the grid and my need for camping gear. I stop and thank him for this act of love for me. I sit with his memory and find joy in it. I am relieved that my loss of him hurts so much. He loves me. He took his last breath, trying to save me.

I look up at the pills on the counter, when a single bird sings. The closeness of the sound startles me, and I feel a bit of my sorrow release. I don't know why, but it does. Then it sings again, and I feel a bit better.

My focus changes to listening. A bird gives me hope.

I look at the pills. I want to live the life I dreamed about—life on my terms. I hear my mom again: "Didn't you? You lived the life you wanted, and now you want the death you imagined. Too bad. You get to go out how you go out. Last time I checked, nobody gets a choice, and neither do you."

Her words fade. I stare at me in the mirror. I reach out to

the things in my life I love. I wish I had another word. I wish I had a word for what I feel for my husband and another for my children. I ponder a word for the love of my friends that is different than the one I have for ice cream.

I remember my children's voices and wince at their effort to get ahold of me. The sound of relief and joy when we heard each other's voices. The love we felt and gave as we all tried to share our hearts at the same time.

Love, I am loved.

More birds sing. Did they just start, or was I unable to hear them? I let go of a bit more pain and leap for the truth that right now, I am cherished. As I cherish them, I know they cherish me. A single beam of light has found me. The magnitude of my isolation has revealed the depth of my love. Not just for my family, but my love for myself.

I let go and begin to float slowly back to the surface. *Alone* is not going to serve me. I don't know what will happen next, but I know this is my life, my path, my choices.

I put the pills back in the cupboard. I notice the beauty in the darkness.

CHAPTER FORTY-ONE

LIFE IS AN UNKNOWN. Tomorrow has always been a mystery. Today is no different than every other day of my whole life. "I am here," I shout at the universe. I stand and look at my disheveled face in the mirror. I am here. I have survived it all to this point. I am going to live this day to the fullest.

"You are here!" I say to my reflection in the mirror. I notice I am becoming comfortable with the unknown. It is unfair. It is brutal. It is as it is. That is all it is, all it has ever been. It is my life, and I love it. I have seen thousands of people who went to work and ended up in the emergency room. Life is an unknown, and it is beautiful.

I am in the same place I have always been. My life could have ended in any of the seconds I have lived, but it didn't. I look into the mirror again and stare at my eyes. "Today is no different than a year ago." I point at myself, "You are in the same place as your little patient was a couple of days ago. It is time to face what is, and to move without having to know where."

I thank my little patient for the lesson of being a warrior. It is time for me to stand strong, time for me to go nose to nose with whatever comes next. I realize that my fists are balled, and I'm aware of how tightly my jaw is clenched.

I continue to stare into my eyes. I watch the fire return. I have the eyes of a wild beast. I have unlimited choices. I have always had unlimited choices. I need to act like it. I will make a choice, then another, and another. I realize to make a choice is not difficult. I know in each moment I will have an infinite set of options available to me.

It doesn't matter how much time I have left. This is my life.

For now, I choose to face whatever is next, standing sure in myself and paying attention to what needs my hand to care for it. To do what I was put on Earth to do.

I blow my nose, take a washcloth to my face, and brush my hair. I go to my closet and get a *Go Big or Go Home* hoodie I bought the day I first started to learn how to snowboard. I turn back to the mirror. "If this is it, then this is it. I will go out on my terms."

I strike a Superman pose in the mirror. I feel my feet move underneath me, my heart beat, my hand brush my cheek. I hear my grandparents, my dad, my mom, my husband, my kids, my friends, and my dog rejoice.

"Go find out why you are in this time and this place," I tell myself in the mirror. "Go do what you have challenged yourself to do for years. Go find your best self in the time you have left." I begin to leave my bathroom. Then I turn back to the mirror.

"I love you," I say to me. "I love you, too," I say back.

I am a woman of substance, a woman with scars to prove the tenacity of my fight, a woman with pain to show my love, a woman with a thousand touchstones in this house that each confirms I am a force. I have nothing more to prove, and I am exactly who I am supposed to be, precisely where I am supposed to be. I know I sound like an *Afterschool Special* or a Tony Robbins fanatic, but I don't care. I will put aside my story and face what I know is coming. I am sure of what to do next, and I am ready to do it. Enjoy, share, love, be loved.

I start looking for the most exquisite foods I have in my house. I gather them and put each item into a basket to bring to my new tribe. If today is my last day, I am going out sharing the best I have to give. Fearlessly giving love as I have my whole life.

I begin to put together what I will carry to the park. I gather items from all over my house. I have lots to share. I soon see my basket is not enough. I will need my gardening wagon to move all I have to bring.

I set down what is in my arms and open the door.

My dog is looking up at me, trying to act put out that I had left her outside for so long. She quickly breaks as her tail is frantically wagging, and she nearly knocks me over as she pushes herself against my legs. It seems I am the only one who thinks she abandoned me. We hug each other with limitless joy. I sit and hold her. We stop and look at each other in the eyes and say, "Thank you."

I tell her I am grateful for her love. *I am complete with or without you. I am enough.*

My dog looks at me, and I say, "We may be plenty, but I would rather be plenty together. God, I am glad you are here."

She kisses my face and asks me what I am doing.

I hug her and tell her I wish I had one more embrace with the people I love. I wish, but I don't. I have her. I have now. I have things to gather to share.

We head to my garage to get my son's childhood wagon. I have used it in my garden for over thirty years.

Together we scour the house gathering food, a photo album, my guitar, and a case of world-class wine. I grab a dozen wine glasses and wash her crystal bowl. I search and find a corkscrew my parents used at Woodstock; the same one I took with me to college.

I remember one more thing—I retrieve my stash of Dieter's Chocolate.

I am ready.

I stack my favorite backyard chair on the wagon. I am going to be comfortable. Then I neatly pack all the other items I chose on my chair. I use some tie-downs to make it secure. Feeling visible, I begin to make my way back to the park. People notice us as we make our way into the crowd. I smile, thinking I resemble the truck on *The Beverly Hillbillies*. I am starting to see faces that are becoming familiar to me.

Some ask if they can help. I let them.

I scan the park. I see a couple that looks a lot like my grandparents. I do a double-take and think to introduce myself, but I am on a mission to get to the center of the crowd. If this new life is poker, then I choose to have aces.

Card players with aces don't hide. They have to stand out to play their hand. I see the gentleman that had asked for an inventory. I walk to him and start to unpack my wagon. I start putting my contribution on a picnic table. Last off the wagon is my chair, and with a little help from the Admiral, it is removed, and I sit down.

I do a quick inventory and decide the best thing to do is to pull out a bottle of my finest. It is time to get to know my tribe. I hold up the bottle and the corkscrew to my new friend. "Do you mind doing the honors?" I ask.

He turns the bottle in his hand and smiles. "My pleasure."

His grin continues as I hold up three empty glasses. He fills the glasses as I take two from him. I ask him to help me bring the food I brought for the feast to the woman who is managing food preparation.

She looks at what I offer, takes a drink of the wine, and says, "Where have you been hiding?"

I smile and say, "Hiding."

She raises her glass and smiles. "I get that. You okay?"

I nod *yes*. "You?" I ask. She shrugs, takes another drink, and returns to cooking.

I return to the table. I set my glass down and begin to open my favorite noshables.

Still holding the bottle in one hand and his glass in the other, the Admiral asks me if I am Bedouin.

"Gypsy," I say as I eat an olive I made while in Spain. I wipe my hands and lean down to remove my guitar from the case. "This party needs music."

I look into his eyes and see wildness in them, too. His glare looks like a hawk. Dark and assured. I can almost hear his screech to complement my howl.

I settle into my chair to play. I can feel my body tighten. I always feel this way before I start the first song. I am enjoying my clan around me. We are unwinding in a way that is untamed, and are coming together like a pack of wolves. I am delighted that wild feels so good.

Everyone is alive. I feel like what a wolf on the hunt must feel. I can hear my dog's heart beating and can understand why she had to run earlier. I take a deep inhale of my wine and let it fill my nose. I growl low with pleasure.

The Admiral hears and looks over at me. I see I have his attention, so I say, "I will steal from Allen Watts, tell me what you love because I have no interest or time to care about what you do?"

"I love that I get to drink this bottle of wine," he says. We sit facing each other, wine in hand, my dog sitting in front of me, staring at the bottle. I notice that she is looking for her bowl.

I reach into the wagon, place her crystal bowl on the ground, and pour her some. He watches with a puzzled look on his face.

I say, "The last few days have not been typical."

He raises his glass and says, "Mine either."

We laugh. I toss him a piece of chocolate.

"You asked for an inventory. I am a nurse. I have camping stoves with gas, water purifying devices with filters, a ton of canned food, and a set of tools that I know how to use. Do you want a more extensive list?"

"No, that question is a quick way to get information on what is available and finding out what is important to the person making the list." He puts his nose into his glass and inhales deeply, then moans a bit. "What I love?" he says. "This wine."

"Try that," I say pointing at the chocolate.

He bites into it and looks up, "Dieter's?"

I nod. We sit quietly, enjoying a perfect fall day and nibbling chocolate. He starts to ask me a question when I stop him and ask him to answer my question first.

"My loves? My wife, my kids, my dogs, my work, this wine, maybe you, and watching the sunrise with a cup of coffee on the deck of my cabin. Best time is when everyone is still asleep, and the water is like glass. My dogs are usually too excited in the morning for it to be as peaceful as I would like. Maybe I need to be quieter as I try to sneak out," he says.

"What work?" I ask.

"I thought you didn't care?" he quips.

"You listed it as a love, so now I care."

"I spent fifteen years as a SEAL team commander. I have

worked in special operations for most of my career. I am sitting here because I have no idea what to do, other than to wait and see what happens. If we are still here tomorrow, I will put a number of you to work, but for now, I will savor this wine and enjoy the day."

"Point out your wife and kids?" I ask.

He shakes his head, and fights back the tears. "My wife, kids, and dogs are visiting her sister. They are gone." He holds back his emotions long enough to say, "You?" He is breathing deeply, chest heaving.

I wait quietly until composure finds his face; until I can form a sentence myself. "My husband is at CERN." I stop and wait for his reaction. He stops mid-sip and looks directly at me, then gestures with his free hand. "And?"

"He left a message on my home phone, saying that this is inevitable. He has seen the black hole as it formed and it is growing." I point to a woman cooking salmon on a grill, "She is part of the physics staff at the university, and she thinks so, too."

He nods, "That is what I heard, too." He asks, "Who is your husband?"

I say his name and the Admiral gulps. I look into his eyes and nod.

The Admiral takes a deep breath. "Damn, you are full of surprises." He drains his glass and grabs the bottle. "I will have more of this." He fills his glass and smiles broadly. He takes a drink, and says, "I am now sure that I love you."

My dog looks up and then down at her bowl. I pour the last of the bottle for her.

He moans, "No."

I shrug and point to the other bottles on the table. He pulls each out of the box and reviews them one at a time. "I'm sticking close to you tonight."

"Typical man, you love me only for my full-bodied reds."

He laughs and says. "Your reds are spectacular, and I have no trouble using you so that I can enjoy them." We clink glasses. He smiles. "I have world-class whiskey and a couple of other treats if you prove to be worthy of them."

I reach to take back his wine. We both chuckle. "I am worthy, get off your ass, and go get them."

He turns to my guitar case and looks at me.

"Go ahead," I say.

He opens the case and lifts out my D-28. He looks it over and then strums it. "Nice," he says as he tunes it.

"It's about time," the women at the grill jokes.

"May I?" he asks.

I smile. "Yes."

He begins to play, and "Blackbird" starts to come out of my guitar.

"Perfect." I nod. I hum and wait for him to reach the chorus. When he does, I begin to sing. He fills in with his harmony. We sound great.

"Fine wine, Dieters, and a great voice," he says as he shows off with a flourish on my guitar. "You didn't have any of this on your inventory. You left out the best stuff."

I gently slap his knee and say, "You haven't seen anything yet," and we continue singing. We finish the song, and I get ready to sing something else.

He instead excuses himself and takes my wagon. I act surprised. He smiles. "It will be worth it."

I give him my *I doubt it* look, but he doesn't look back. I notice others leaving. I hope they are going to bring treasures to share and not leaving to get away from my voice.

As I pick up my guitar and think about another song, I scan the crowd for the couple that reminded me of my grandparents. I don't see them. I sit and think about what to play next while listening to people talk about what they love and what they regret; spouses and children, art and books, place and past, parents, and grandparents. People are sharing photo albums, memories, and hugs.

In five minutes, what started as me and a guitar is now twenty people with a variety of instruments. I play "Fire and Rain" as the band gets ready; I sing it from my heart.

I love this song. It reminds me of my dearest friend in the world. A friend with whom I shared some of the finest days of my life. God, how I love that woman. I wish she were here right now. I sing through the chorus, thanking her for the hours of love we shared.

The song ends, and I begin to think about a suitable song for my new band. Twenty musicians readying to make music, it is a cacophony. I am a little sad that so many players lived on my block, and I never knew—or was curious enough to ask.

"I wish I had known you all played. We could have made music for years. That said, I am so glad we are all here. Let's have some fun." I wait as everyone is getting ready.

Having returned, the Admiral asks, "Ready to play an Earth-shattering show?" I groan at the pun. He starts handing me items as he unloads the wagon. The last thing he hands me is a dusty bottle.

I start to pour tastes of whiskey for the people around me. I hand him his as he takes his seat with his guitar in hand. I lift the glass, and we all take a strong pull. He waits for me to react. I lick my lips and finish all that is in my glass. "Stunning!"

He smiles and tips his hat. He then looks around at the assembled musicians, "Are all these yours?"

"Yes, my garage band," I reply. "I hope you can keep up." I raise my voice, "Is everybody ready?" They nod. I watch as my band settles in and is ready to play.

"Let's see what you guys can do. Who knows 'Three Little Birds'?" Nearly all of the hands raise.

"Three Little Birds" is a great song. For today, it seems to be ideal. I count *one* and *two*, and we start playing. People begin to gather around, and soon, the whole park fills with music. Worries fade as we sing together.

People are softly bouncing to Marley's rhythm. The day is crisp, and the smell of food is filling the air. For a group of people that have never played together, we are doing fine. Music is like chocolate; it may not help, but it never hurts.

It wasn't long before the gathering becomes a party. It feels like a spontaneous college blowout the Friday afternoon before finals week. People who need to let loose. This is so much fun. We all sing as a few people begin to dance.

We play a couple more warm-up songs to get the mood right when one of the horn players starts the opening riff to a song that makes everyone laugh. Soon we come to the chorus, and the whole crowd sings like the big game is ending. They are all waving goodbye, their hands in the air.

I see a young man bobbing by that brings me back to being young with my husband. Us dancing in Grant Park, blues legends on stage pushing the crowd to sing the chorus for "Sweet Home Chicago" for over five minutes.

He stops, and we lock eyes. I am shocked by how much he looks like my husband as a young man. He winks at me, then disappears into the crowd.

After about a dozen songs, I grab my guitar buddy by the hand, and I have him open two bottles of my favorite Barolo. "Let's go get food." He follows, and so does my dog. The music continues.

We find a seat at a table. It is a feast fit for a king. I refill the cook's glass, leaving her the open bottle, and thank her for her efforts.

"You sound great; this is a blast," she says. She takes a drink and smiles at me and says, "Oh my God."

I say, "My favorite wine on Earth. Well, one of them."

I pick and choose to fill my plate. This could be my last meal, and my stomach is only so big. I set my dog's wine down and make her a plate of food.

The three of us eat together at a community table and two of the three of us savor each bite. One eats like a dog.

The food is delicious. The cooks in our tribe are skilled, and this makes me delighted. It is not a talent I have. I am engulfed in the joy of how delectable everything tastes. I am surrounded by the sounds, the flavors, the energy, the music, and the outstanding company. Perfection.

My eight seconds on the back of the bull are going to be just fine.

I survey the crowd and see every human emotion on display. The waves of grief have left me alone for a bit. I am letting loose like I haven't since I was twenty-two, unrestricted and uninhibited. I envy my dog's tail. If I had one, I would be wearing it out.

"Margaritaville" ends, and I hear the opening chords to "Brown-Eyed Girl." I put my hand out, "Shall we dance?" He stands. "This was my husband's song for me and I…"

He smiles, takes my hand, and we dance slowly. He holds me tight, but not quite tightly enough. I pull him closer and put my head on his chest. I feel the urge to nip him, but I think better of it. I decide to lose myself in his arms instead.

I make believe he is my love. I think he does the same with me. I let my heart go back to a time when the future was real, when I had tomorrow, and the man in my arms was my beloved.

I see the young man I saw earlier. He is sitting and staring at me for a few seconds longer than is polite. My partner turns me so that I can no longer see him.

The hair on my arms stands up. I scan the crowd to find him again as my partner turns me back to where I saw him. He is gone.

I feel the Admiral pull me closer. I feel him against me; being held feels wonderful.

The song ends, and I ask if they will play it again. He looks at me. I nod. "I'm not ready to be done," I say as I feel his tears on my cheek. I hold him tightly. He whispers his love's name as we dance.

When the song ends, we hug as the crowd sings the last, "la te da."

I miss my *La Te Da.*

"Thank you," we say in unison. I hug him again, and when he moves to separate. I grasp him tighter, "Not yet," I whisper. We stand, and I wait for the universe to inhale. It finally does.

I step back and dry my tears. We stare at each other in silence, red-eyed, and sniffling.

"Ready to play some more?" I grab his hand as we dance through the crowd back to our chairs. We sit as others go for food. I wish Grandpa were here. I wish and then hope my little warrior is in a gathering with music, too.

My tribe has now mostly settled around the musicians, and I take the liberty having a guitar provides. I stand up and say, "We are a tribe now. You are my clan." I smile, meeting the grins of the unfamiliar faces. I say to them what I said earlier. "I will paraphrase Allen Watts, tell me what you love because I have no interest in what you used to do."

I point at a man in the crowd, and he says a name. I point to the woman next to him, and she holds up her baby for all to see. Around and around the circle we go, sharing what we love. It is a celebration of each of our lives.

We go for quite a time. It is joyous and heartbreaking as I stand and listen to my tribe. We wipe our tears and cheer with delight until the crowd is ready to dance again.

I hug my friend, decide between whiskey and wine, and drink both. Then I reach for my guitar. I am ready to play. I lean back and howl, my clan joins in, and we all laugh, immersed in our growing freedom.

We are growing wild and loving it.

I start playing, "Here Comes the Sun." In what feels like a group hug, everyone joins in. Nothing is holding them down; nothing is holding them back. I love playing songs people know by heart, the crowd singing and dancing without their selves getting in the way. Remembering something that song evokes in them, they are all swaying to the rhythm.

We finish when someone behind me starts the next one. With him taking the lead on the song, I look at a crowd that is all a little wasted. We are having the time of our lives. We play louder and sing with joy.

We are having a blast.

Everything slows when my dog stands up and tugs at my leg.

I know instantly what is happening.

I look up to see my parents and grandparents. They are younger than I am. Then I see my husband. He is with our first dog. I see my sisters and a cat I had when I was a kid. My mom says to me, "It is time to go. Follow us."

I sit for a second, trying to take in this moment fully. I stand and look at the park. I take a big drink of my wine. I reach for the pecan and caramel turtle sitting in front of me. I break it, eat half give someone—I'm not sure who—the other bite.

It is noiseless and moving oddly slow. I am perfectly calm as I notice the horizon is disappearing. I see my tree go, then my house.

I lean forward and kiss my new friend deeply on the mouth. "No regrets."

He doesn't hesitate as he kisses me back. With the last seconds I have left, I step around my chair, and strum my guitar hard, then set it down. I love that guitar.

He stands up to face me with a confused look on his face. I turn him around to see the black hole coming at us. We share a last drink, as I feel my dad's hands and look into my children's faces as it moves nearer.

Some of the people around me start to run, but I stand fixed. Feet planted and eyes forward, I have no fear. My eight seconds are up.

I wait as it moves ever closer. I take someone's hand as the Admiral takes mine.

Time stands still.

My dad's face is the last thing I see before I jump.

I miss many of the lives
I have lived this time around

Although a life appears to be all one event
I find I have lived many small lifetimes.

My memories are the recollections of a self
distinctly different than my current self.

Living days remarkably different
than the day I am living today.

Life is more a Eurail summer
riding tracks to many stations.

Staying for what seems a long time
but in retrospect each only lasted a moment.

Myself the only common element
at every one.

Sometimes I wish I could go back and visit
Me
Then

I like to think myself more awake
than the last time I arrived on this particular platform.

Last time here I was lost
doing my best to make it through.
In my wake are mostly things I have broken.

I would love to wander around like a tourist
not worried about the milestones
visiting something simple
because that I am there would be plenty.

I would drink a beer at my favorite places
and visit the Chinese dives I loved best at each stop.

The one with "Good Foob" painted on the window,
the one I shared with my dad,
the one I can walk to.

I would get off the train
and stand
and watch as I came by.

Seeing me with friends I remember
and those long forgotten.

I wouldn't sit to talk to me
because
I know neither of us would listen.

The best I could hope for
would be to let each station open my heart
so I could be kinder to myself when I got home.

ABOUT THE AUTHOR

STEVE SCHROEDER had been a budget analyst for 20 years when the numbers game lost its magic for him. After a close encounter with a mystical muse, he left his day job to become a novelist and transform his muse into his heroine. Steve is also a poet and creator of "Mosaic," a weekly poetry newsletter that followers say is a welcome and inspiring relief to a stressful day. He now finds joy in combining his love of poetry and prose with science fiction. Steve also thrives on Ikebana flower arranging, tending his garden, and the taunting of a guitar he can't play.

PLEASE LEAVE A REVIEW

I hope you enjoyed reading *Vanish Like a Dream*.
If you are so inclined, please review it on
Amazon and Good Reads. Thank you.

INVITE STEVE TO YOUR BOOK CLUB

It would be my pleasure to share time with your book club, whether on an internet chat app or in person, to discuss, *Vanish Like a Dream.*
Contact him at undomesticatable@gmail.com